FINAL KILL

MATTHEW HATTERSLEY

VINCI
BOOKS

Vinci Books

vinci-books.com

Published by Vinci Books Ltd in 2025

1

MIX
Paper | Supporting
responsible forestry
FSC
www.fsc.org   FSC® C018072

Printed and bound in Great Britain by Clays Ltd, Elcograf S.p.A.

Also by Matthew Hattersley

Acid Vanilla

Final Kill

Seven Bullets

The Hunt

Sister Death

Exit Wounds

Never Say Die

I am a Killer

Bad Blood

Fallen Angels

Annihilation Pest Control Series

White Heat

John Beckett Series

Darkness On The Edge Of Town

When The Kingdom Comes

A World Of Sun And Violence

A Bullet For The Past

For AJH x

Chapter One

Darkness. Confusion.

Then a familiar taste in the back of her throat.

Iron.

Blood.

Damn.

She fought herself awake, realising immediately she was on her knees with her hands tied behind her back. It wasn't the best situation to find oneself in on waking.

Peering through the shadowy veil covering her face, all she could make out were vague shapes and distorted silhouettes. She did, however, notice her left eye was swollen shut. Which was when she remembered the rifle butt.

Oh shitting hell...

The general.

"Hey, Ratty," she called out, fully conscious now and straining at the thick hessian sack covering her face. "Are you there?"

"Right beside you, kiddo. You hurt?"

"Not too bad," she told him. "Where are we?"

"Underground. Some kind of cell."

She struggled at her constraints. "I guess I went off script again."

"You sure did. I mean, you might have pulled it off. If you had eleven arms."

Images of the attack flashed across her mind. There'd been seven of them – mercenaries. She'd killed four of them before the others had overpowered her. Not bad going considering she'd been armed with only a pocketknife.

She flinched, remembering something else. "I want to speak to Ramos," she called out into the room.

"Save it, bitch," a man's voice came back. "The general is on his way."

The general – General Luis Carvalho Ramos, to give him his full title – was a local politician and part-time gunrunner, whose approach had become too erratic and violent even for the corrupt officials here in Fortaleza. Considering the city was widely known as the murder capital of Brazil, that was saying something.

She shifted her awareness back to the room, slowly lifting her hands to her belt. The air was cool but stagnant, and she had a sense they were underground. With great care and the slightest of movements, she slid the push dagger from out of the concealed sheath in her belt. Whoever had tied her up had missed it. But everyone did.

Concentrating on moving only her wrists, she sawed at the thick rope. Like always, her senses were heightened, but her hearing was even more so - over compensating for her lack of sight. She heard grunts from outside the room. Heavy booted footsteps, coming her way.

A moment later the door crashed open and a voice boomed, "So, these are the pigs sent to kill me?"

The same voice as before answered him. "Yes sir. I've

had run-ins with this organisation in the past whilst working detail for Al Shaitan in Sudan. They're assassins but call themselves Elite Eradication Specialists."

"Well, not elite enough, huh?"

"No, sir."

"Let me see them."

She flinched as the heavy sack was ripped from her head. She blinked her eyes into focus as Ramos loomed down at her. He was an old man, much older than his picture in her file, and with a disgusting, thin moustache that twitched as he spoke.

"Seems you aren't as good as they say, bitch." He grabbed her by the throat, forcing her to peer at him. "You might have killed four of my men, but the buck stops here. Who sent you?"

She smiled, exposing a set of blood-stained teeth. "I'm going to kill you," she whispered.

Ramos laughed and leaned closer, his foul breath in her face. "No. I don't think that's going to happen." Straightening, he moved over to the back wall to join the remaining mercenaries. There was four of them now, including the general. All armed.

She sucked in loo long deep breaths, all the while sawing at the bindings around her wrist. She was almost through the first rope. Thirty seconds more and she'd be free. If she lived that long.

Ramos walked over and removed the bag from her partner. "What the fuck are you supposed to be?" he asked, curling his lip at the large, muscular man with camouflage-green hair and silver rings running down the curve of each ear.

"Go to hell," Davros Ratpack snarled back. Although not so easy with a bust lip. "Just get this over with."

"Oh no, amigo, I like to savour these moments," Ramos sneered. He pointed a stubby finger her way. "She screwed you both, this one, huh? Crazy bitch. You know, I've half a mind to let one of you go – so you can tell the world that the great General Ramos cannot be killed." He sighed, theatrically. "But I don't think I will."

She watched the soldiers as they bristled with readiness. No doubt they were all highly trained, with years of combat experience under their belts, but they were also overweight and pushing fifty. Two of them carried Walther MP submachine guns, and the other a Kalashnikov assault rifle - an AK-something-or-other, it was hard to tell with the light in her face. Ramos himself carried a Colt pistol, or perhaps an IBEL, the Brazilian-made equivalent. Either way it added up to a lot of firepower.

She kept going with the push dagger, fine-tuning her play as she gauged the situation. From this angle the soldier with the assault rifle would have to step back to take a shot. He'd be third. Ramos – who had now holstered his pistol and was lighting a fat cigar – fourth. She glanced at the soldiers holding the subs – one aimed at her, one at Davros – they'd be first and second. She bowed her head as one of the ropes fell away.

One to go.

Ramos blew a large plume of cigar smoke into the room and smirked. "So, tell me, who wants to die first? You? Or you?" He waved the cigar between her and Davros, bathing jubilantly in their apparent fear.

"Why not both at once?" she replied, readying herself, almost through the last rope.

"Not a bad idea."

He blew another large cloud into the room and turned

to his men, about to give the order. But before any words could leave his mouth, she was on her feet.

Springing forward, she moved between the muzzles of the two Walthers, slashing with the push dagger across the throats of both soldiers. Blood spurted from the open wounds as she spun and flung the dagger at the soldier with the rifle, embedding the sharpened steel between his eyes. As he groaned and fell to the floor, she grabbed one of the Walthers, turning it on the solider carrying it before finishing off his friend. As the two men buckled against each other she aimed at Ramos – now frantically trying to release his gun from its holster. He jerked erratically in a macabre dance for a few seconds, before she released the trigger and the great General Luis Carvalho Ramos dropped to the floor with a thud.

She pulled in a deep breath as she surveyed the scene. Not bad going. All of them dead in under three seconds.

She walked over to her partner, a smirk forming. "What? You didn't doubt me, did you?"

"Oh no. Not for a second," he said. "You crazy mare."

"You love me really." She untied him and helped him to his feet. "Anyway, let's get the hell out of here and back to dear old Blighty. I'll meet you outside. Don't be long."

Before he had a chance to reply, she slung one of the Walthers over her shoulder, shoved Ramos' still smoking cigar in her mouth, and casually sashayed out of the room.

Job done.

Time for a celebratory drink.

Chapter Two

The moon hung low over the rooftops of Pimlico, silhouetting the long-dead chimneys of the large town houses in this part of London. Despite the recent rainfall, a sinister mist lingered in the air, giving the wide, empty streets an almost Victorian feel – as if Holmes and Watson might suddenly appear under one of the many lamp posts that studded the pavements. To further add to this anachronistic atmosphere, a 1963 S-Type Jaguar in racing green was parked on the corner of St George's Square. Sitting inside, a man and woman watched the first-floor apartment of the building opposite, waiting for their night's work to begin.

The woman (codename: Acid Vanilla) rested her forehead against the window and sighed. It was a long, drawn-out kind of sigh. The kind of sigh that would normally elicit query from a companion – perhaps asking after the sigher's wellbeing – but not today. Not in this setting. Next to her, the man (codename: Banjo Shawshank) teased at his impressive moustache in the rear-view mirror.

"All I'm saying is, these days it's hard to know what women want." He twisted the ends of the moustache as he spoke, more than aware of the cliché. "To be honest, I don't think they know themselves. That's the problem."

Acid Vanilla didn't reply. Banjo had been talking incessantly for the last hour and she was getting antsy. The job should have been completed by now. Boxed off. She should be at home. She watched out the window as a woman in a Burberry overcoat waited for her dog to defecate at the foot of a tall tree. The woman looked to be a real piece of work. Nose in the air. Snooty. The dog just as much. On the tree, a sign read, *Bag It & Bin It*. A tenner said that wouldn't happen.

"Take this graphic designer chick I was seeing a few weeks back," Banjo continued. "One minute she's all over me like Weinstein on a starlet. Pull my hair. Spank me. Then the next morning she gets needy because I won't go for a walk up to Primrose Hill. I got out of there sharpish, I can tell you. Talk about mixed messages. You see what I mean? Hey, Acid. You listening to me?"

Acid shifted her focus to two droplets of rainwater on the other side of the glass and watched as they zig-zagged to the bottom of the pane where one engulfed the other to form a larger droplet. Then they disappeared into the foam abyss between the window and the doorframe.

"Yeah, mixed messages," she murmured. "Awful. You should write a blog post about it."

"Oh. My. God. Have you heard yourself? No one writes blogs these days. Jesus."

Over by the tree, the dog finished its business and the woman led it away, leaving a steaming pile of turds in their wake. Acid smirked to herself. She was good at reading other people. Always had been. It was just herself she had problems with.

She scanned the street. "Where the bloody hell is he? You sure this is the correct address?"

Banjo leaned over her and eyeballed the building. "Yep, Raaz confirmed it. Says he gets home between half eight and ten. So anytime now."

A familiar prickle of annoyance tickled Acid's nerve. Technology's encroachment on the industry always bothered her whenever she considered it. She pined for the good old days when fieldwork was visceral and exciting. It was more dangerous too, but she liked that. You had to think on your feet, keep your wits about you. Scrapes happened, sure, but how you got out of them sharpened you, prepared you for the next job. These days it was all too safe, too regimented. Off-site tech-wizards like Raaz Terabyte analysed every eventuality, saw problems before they happened. Acid wasn't a Luddite; she understood the importance of technology. But this wasn't the life she'd signed up for.

She clicked open the polished walnut glove box and pulled out a photo. The guy looking back at her wasn't a looker. In fact, he might have had the most average-looking face Acid had ever seen. His hair was average-length, mousy, parted to one side. Under that were a pair of average eyes, an average nose, lips, ears. John Brown. Even his name was average.

Still, John Brown's actions recently were anything but average. He had a list of crimes a page long: fraud, embezzlement, blackmail, mistreatment of illegal workers. But the main reason for Acid and Banjo being here tonight was that he'd royally screwed over his business partner and was now systematically destroying his reputation too. Not to mention stealing a client list worth well over eight figures.

Understandably, none of this had gone down too well with the business partner – a no-nonsense Scot called Brian Rand - and he wanted revenge. In fact, he wanted it in the most bloody and painful way possible. So he'd done his research, asked around in his secret gentlemen's clubs, spoke to people with knowledge of the sort of services he was after – nefarious businessmen, Russian oligarchs. One name cropped up time and time again. The best in the business for what Rand required.

Annihilation Pest Control.

Which was how Acid Vanilla and Banjo Shawshank came to be outside John Brown's apartment building on this cold September evening.

Acid glanced at Banjo. "Are you ready to move? Soon as we get eyes on him?"

"Relax, babe. I have done this before."

"Well focus, please. And quit the cute talk, okay?"

Acid shoved the photo back in the glove box and removed her trusty Glock 19 along with a suppressor and push dagger. Banjo watched her with a stupid grin on his face.

She arched a perfectly groomed eyebrow. "What now?"

"I can't believe you're still using that hunk of metal."

"It's not let me down yet."

She screwed the suppressor onto the end of the gun as Banjo pulled out his own pistol, a Colt M1911, and held it in the light coming from the streetlamp.

"Now this – this is a real man's weapon." He peered down the length of the barrel.

"A real man?" Acid said. "Hmm. Wonder where we can find one, this time of night."

It took him a second to register. "Get lost. You know you want me."

"Sure I do."

Banjo was starting up again, bemoaning the lack of decent masculine role models in modern literature, when Acid shushed him down.

"I think that's him. There, with the briefcase."

A man had emerged from the small grassy area on the opposite side of the street. They watched as he scurried down the side of a black Mercedes SUV. Then he scurried up the short flight of steps that led to the building and frantically pushed his key into the lock. A security light came on, highlighting his dumpy potato face.

"That's him." Acid zipped her leather jacket. "Give it five, then we'll move. You ready?"

"I'm always ready." Banjo winked at her. "Ready for you anytime."

Acid fingered the trigger of the Glock, imagining how good it would feel to put a bullet through her colleague's cheek. Caesar wouldn't be happy, but it'd be worth it. She looked at her watch. Maybe later.

"Come on, lover boy." She slapped Banjo on his skinny-jeaned thigh. "Time to go to work."

Chapter Three

John Brown closed the door of his grand first-floor apartment and locked it behind him. It felt good to be home after the day he'd had. He'd met with solicitors, board members, investors. Plus a lengthy Skype call with the CEO of Executive Armour, the personal security firm he'd hired to provide him round-the-clock protection. Just until the dust settled. One couldn't be too careful.

He went through into his large master bedroom and undressed. The plan now was a hot shower, order some take-out from the Thai Garden, and then bed ready for tomorrow. That was when Brown would put the final piece of his plan into play - framing Rand for insider trading and getting the swine sent down for good. That'd teach him, and that bitch Vanessa.

He twisted the dial on the shower unit and stepped inside the cubicle, enjoying the sensation of the hot water on his skin. He was exhausted, but all the planning, stress and illicit meetings these last few months had been worth it. Closing his eyes he shoved his face under the water, imagining the powerful jets washing away all his troubles. Until he heard a strange noise.

"Hello?" John switched off the shower and lifted his ear. "Who's there?"

He reached for a towel and wrapped it around himself. It was music he could hear, but with the door closed all he could make out was the rise and fall of the bass. He felt it more than heard it. He eased open the bathroom door and stepped into the bedroom, where the unmistakable voice of Chris Rea was echoing down the corridor, singing his classic *The Road to Hell.*

"Who's there?" John Brown shouted, wishing his voice didn't sound so shaky. "Whoever you are, please leave."

Executive Armour had controls in place for situations like this. They'd taken great pride in telling him about the panic button app they'd developed, that could be triggered by the volume buttons on his phone. Only, up to now, John had been rather flippant about his situation and had not yet installed the app. Also, his phone was in the kitchen.

"I have people on their way," he called out. "Security people. You should leave!"

There was no reply. He was half-way to the lounge now. The door was ajar. He craned his neck, trying to see into the room without moving any closer. He realised now it was *The Road to Hell Part Two* he could hear, the single version. He'd been a huge Chris Rea fan since his teenage years and had seen him play live eight times. Though right now he wished he was listening to anything else. Wished he had his phone on him. Wished he'd installed that damn app.

"Take what you want and leave me alone," he shouted through the door. "I don't want any trouble."

John Brown wasn't sure what he was expecting to see when he poked his head nervously around the corner of his front room. But it certainly wasn't the strange-looking pair who were sitting on his brand-new Darlings of Chelsea couch. On seeing John, the male half of the duo stood and pointed a large handgun at his face. "Johnny Boy. There you are."

The man was in his late twenties, and made-up in that old-fashioned style typical of the East End art crowd. Not that John Brown ventured east much these days. Not if he could help it.

The man gestured behind him at the stereo. "You don't mind me putting Chris on, do you? It is somewhat of a classic."

"W-what do you want?" Brown spluttered. "W-who are you?"

The man didn't answer. Brown turned his attention to the woman. She had a mysterious expression on her face. Amusement, maybe.

"W-what's going on?"

"Calm down, sweetie," she said, examining her nails. "Getting worked up won't help you."

She was well-spoken and her voice was husky. It gave her an air of nobility, he thought. Though the gun sticking out of her jacket negated that impression just as quick. She was older than the man, early thirties perhaps, but he'd had always found women harder to age. She had thick black hair, cut with a fringe, and good cheekbones that framed a fire-red pout. But it was her eyes that got him. They were wild, intense. And as he looked closer... Were they different colours?

John smiled meekly at her, hoping to reason with her feminine compassion. But he'd picked the wrong girl. She just rolled her eyes as if she'd rather be anywhere else. Well that made two of them.

"I have money," he tried. "You can have whatever you want. My Rolex. Anything. Just don't hurt me."

"Oh Johnny," the woman purred, getting to her feet. "We aren't interested in your money. Or your trinkets."

"Then what do you want?"

"Isn't it obvious?" she whispered. "We're here to kill you."

Chapter Four

Acid Vanilla was exhausted. But you could also add bored and tetchy and frustrated to that list. She'd been subjected to Banjo's ridiculous monologue for the last two hours, and now it was Chris Bloody Rea grating at her nerves – not to mention this pathetic little man.

"Sit down. There's a good boy." She pointed to the chair in front of her, a vintage Van Der Rohe in cream leather. She had two matching ones in black in her apartment. John hesitated, then did as he was told. "Do you know what we're doing here?" she asked him.

He shook his head. "You want to steal from me?"

"If only it were that simple." She removed her phone from the inside pocket of her jacket and shoved it in his face. "Say cheese."

The phone flashed and John screwed his face up. "What was that?"

"Facial recognition."

"What? Why?"

"Insurance. Certainty. This gets pinged back to our girl

at HQ who runs it through a special database. It ensures we've got the right man. Don't worry. It'll all be over soon." Acid looked over at Banjo who was perusing the large bookshelf along the back wall. He pulled out a thick, leather-bound book and began flicking through it. "Are you having fun over there?"

"I think this is a first edition Kipling," he mumbled, not looking up.

"Take it. It's yours," John Brown whimpered. "I mean it. Have all my first editions. They're worth a small fortune."

He flinched as Acid moved around the chair, blocking his path to the front door. She looked at her phone.

Connecting...

"We got a positive ID yet?" Banjo asked.

Acid shook her head. This was why it was so much easier before the likes of Raaz got involved. Back then you could put a bullet in the mark, maybe two to make sure, and be on your way in under a minute.

Although, whilst it was certainly more straight-forward, mistakes did happen. Like when Barabbas Stamp gunned down a roomful of nuns, not realising there was another convent in the next town, where the actual Russian agents were hiding. Gaffes like that made the whole industry look bad.

"Get a move on," Acid whispered at her phone.

She looked at Brown, who was now bent over and sobbing into his towel. She had a strong urge to put a bullet in his skull right then, but she held her ground. Annihilation Pest Control had strict guidelines, and when a plan was made, you stuck to it. No deviation. The way Caesar had explained it, "People getting creative leads to people getting killed." Then, realising what he'd said, "The *wrong* people getting killed."

The narrative they had to create for tonight's job was 'break-in gone wrong, death by blunt object'. The easiest option would be something in the apartment, further enforcing that this was an amateur job. Acid slid a slender finger along the mantelpiece towards a heavy marble vase at the far end.

"What do you think, Banjo?" she asked. But he'd disappeared through an open door opposite the bookcase. "What's through there?" she asked Brown.

"A spare bedroom," he replied. "But look, whatever you're being paid, I'll double it."

Banjo reappeared, holding an overcoat against himself. "Double it? You sure about that, squire?"

"Yes. Absolutely. I can pay. I will pay. What would it be, five? Ten?"

"Pfft. Double would be two hundred."

"Thousand? Bugger off. Is this Brian?" He tutted, more angry than scared. "Of course it's bloody Brian. Jesus. He's paying you one hundred thousand to have me killed?"

Banjo draped the coat over the back of the couch. "The firm gets fifty. We get twenty-five each."

Brown hurried over to an old bureau in the far corner. "Fine. I'll pay it. Two hundred grand. Each, if that'll do it. But don't kill me. Please." He was shouting now.

"Should have thought about that before you screwed your partner over," Acid told him. The phone screen hadn't changed.

Connecting…

"Bloody hell. Ring Raaz, will you, Banjo? Find out what's going on." But Banjo had placed his gun on the coffee table and was sitting on the Van Der Rohe with a strange look on his face. You could almost see the cogs turning. Acid scowled at him. "No. Don't be bloody ridiculous."

"Yeah but think about it. Two hundred K. Each."

"Yeah but think about it. What would Caesar do?"

"We could sort something out."

Acid was about to tell him the only thing getting sorted would be his insides. Into bowls then fed to Caesar's dogs. But she didn't get a chance.

"John?" a voice boomed through the front door. "I heard shouting. Is everything okay?"

They glanced at each other. Acid pointed a finger at both men. "Stop," she whispered. "Nobody speak."

There was a loud bang on the door. Brown jumped. Then came another shout. "John, I can hear music. Are you there?"

Acid narrowed her eyes at Banjo. More banging on the door.

"All right, come here." She pulled out the Glock and stuck it in John's back. "Now, we're going to walk over to the door, and you're going to answer it, okay? Tell him you're fine. Tell him you were in the bath, singing along to a record. That's what he heard." She jabbed the muzzle of the pistol into his kidneys. "Don't do anything stupid."

Bundling Brown over to the door, she concealed herself against the wall to his right and indicated for him to go.

"Ah, there you are, old boy," a voice said, as John Brown eased the door open. "I was worried. It's not like you to be a noisy sod."

"No, it's… been a weird day. I was… having a bath. Singing along to a record. To wind down."

"Oh, I see…"

"Yes. Nothing the matter here."

His face went stern, concerted. It was as if he was trying to project a message with his eyes. Acid raised the Glock and made sure he'd see it in his peripheral vision.

Don't be an idiot.

"Well, that's good to hear, and… Oh crikey, is that a gun on your coffee table?"

Shit.

Acid swung the door open and dragged the guy inside. She pushed him into John and slammed the door shut. "Who are you? Quickly."

The man went cross-eyed at the gun in his face. "M-Michael Carrington. I live across the hall." He was a small, gnome-like man with a white goatee beard.

"Sit down, both of you." Acid gestured at the couch with the gun.

The men did as she instructed, almost tripping over one another as they went. Acid stayed by the door and tried to centre herself. It didn't help she'd not slept for the last few days or that the bats in her head were back. She'd get this job out of the way and ask Caesar for a holiday. She needed one.

"What's going on?" Carrington whimpered. "What do you want?"

"They're here to kill me. But we're coming to an arrangement - aren't we?" Brown twisted around to look at Banjo. "I can transfer the money over right now."

"I don't understand. Who are these people?" Carrington asked, eyes darting fearfully between Acid and Banjo.

"They've been sent by Brian," Brown replied. "To bump me off. They're hit men."

Banjo coughed. "Erm, professional killers, thank you very much."

"What's the difference?"

"About half a mill a year, for starters," Banjo replied. He walked over and sat on the end of the couch, facing the two men. "You see, hit men, they're low down on the scale. They do other jobs as well as killing people, as part of a broader criminal organisation. Your Mafias, for instance, your Triads, they work on retainers usually. Real grafters. Whereas professional killers – assassins – we work on a per job basis and killing people is all we do. And we do it very well."

Acid checked her phone. Nothing. She sat and tried to stay calm.

Banjo kept going. "We're more efficient. Have a better skillset. A hit man does a job and people know it was a hit. It's all about sending a message. One gang member hitting another. People who hire us don't want any attention. We do our job and it's never traced back to the client. We do our job really well, it's not even classed as a homicide, it's a suicide, an unfortunate twist of fate." He played with his moustache. "Remember that government scientist who died of a heart attack whilst walking in the woods? That was us. Or the African despot whose jeep turned over last year and he broke his neck? That was us. Or what about that disgraced financier who did a swan dive off the twentieth floor of the Shard last week?" He pointed to his chest and winked. "But you'll never know it. No one will. And that is why we make on one job what most hit men make in a whole year." The way he said *hit men*, he might as well have said *paedophiles*.

"What that also means, is we can't be bought," Acid cut in. "Means we don't make deals. Right, Banjo? Because that would be bad for the brand."

Banjo blew out his cheeks and checked his fingernails. "Yeah, I suppose. Sorry, gents." He walked over to the fireplace and lifted the marble vase, the one Acid had her eye on. "We're going for a break-in vibe for this one. So as far as your concerned, struggling is good. Go for your lives. Struggling is what we want." He tossed the vase in the air and caught it by the base, giving him a better grip. "It won't be long now that we get the all-clear."

Carrington made a noise like someone had stood on a cat and made a dash for the door. Not easy in slippers. He'd got all the way there and was tugging frantically at the handle when Banjo drew his pistol and blasted his brains up the wall.

"Jesus Christ," Brown cried as a dark, wet patch seeped into the couch where he sat.

Acid looked away in disgust, her gaze falling on Carrington's lifeless body. This wasn't going well. At all. She walked over to the window and rebooted her phone in the hope this might sort out the connectivity issue. Though getting Brown to look into her camera without screwing his face up all red and teary was now somewhat trickier.

While she was trying for a decent shot, Banjo dragged Carrington's body away from the door so they could open it. Then he went to work ransacking the place, pulling books from shelves, emptying drawers, creating a real scene - a break-in gone wrong.

"I beg of you," Brown sobbed. "Tell Brian I'll do whatever he wants if he calls this off. I'll leave the company. Anything. Please. I don't want to die…" He dragged the last word out into a staccato wail, giving it at least six syllables.

Acid closed her eyes. She'd rather be anywhere else right now.

"What if I gave you the money then left the country?" Brown said, getting to his feet. "You could pretend Carrington was me. I'll be gone, never to return. Everyone's happy. Brian gets the business. You get two hundred grand each and—"

Acid jumped as a large bang rattled her hearing and Brown flew onto the couch. Banjo had shot him, right between the eyes.

"What the hell?"

"He was pissing me off."

"Yeah? Remind me not to piss you off." She looked down at Brown's body. Her head was pounding. "Right, well, this is a real bloody mess. You best ring Ethel and Doris."

She hated having to involve them, but at times this like Ethel and Doris Sinister - AKA the Sinister Sisters - were the only option. With a combined age of well over a hundred and fifty, Caesar's clean-up team were still the best in the business. They could remove blood from any surface, could dissolve an adult corpse in under twenty minutes.

Banjo sauntered into the bedroom to make the call as Acid's phone beeped. It was the facial recognition software confirming a matc. They had their man.

"I've got a positive ID on Brown," she called through. "Take what you want and let's get out of here. I need a drink. And before you say anything, that's not an invitation."

Acid picked up the marble vase for a closer look. It was a nice piece, better without the addition of brains. But they'd messed up tonight. Caesar would be calling her in to explain herself. Again.

She shuddered. Best not to think about it right now. She moved over to the front door as Banjo returned with a holdall full of books and the overcoat.

"Is that all you're taking?"

"They're all first editions. Worth a bomb. Anyway, the sisters are on their way. They can help themselves. There are plenty of watches and cufflinks the bedroom but not to my taste."

"Fine." Acid opened the door of the apartment and did a quick scan of the corridor. It was clear. She padded along the landing and headed down the stairs, beckoning Banjo to follow her.

Job done. Time for that drink. And to work out how she was going to explain this disaster to the boss.

Chapter Five

Banjo dropped Acid off on the corner of Old Brompton and Queen's Gate, telling her he'd see her later.

"Not if I kill you first," she replied.

He liked that one, laughing to himself as he drove away. Acid waited until the car had disappeared down the road and then checked her phone. Maybe a night cap wasn't the best idea. The problem was, these days she never stopped at one, and the last thing she needed was to wake up tomorrow feeling like shit. Times like this, out on the edge, she felt invincible. But coupled with depleted nutrient levels and no sleep, there was always a risk the chaos would consume her, make her do something she'd regret.

Though when your whole life was a regret, it was hard to know what that might be.

The clock on her phone made it half past the witching hour. She considered more sensible options. But lying in bed staring at the ceiling seemed like a terrible prospect right now. Like always, the bats would get their way.

Acid turned into the next street and ducked down the

alley half-way along. She was heading for The Bitter Marxist, a late-night drinking den she often frequented after jobs. It was small, dingey and never seemed to close. The drinking establishment of choice for the city's miscreants. People there knew to leave one another alone and not ask too many questions. Perfect for her needs.

On the pavement outside, a young man hunkered down in a grubby sleeping bag. His sunken, watery eyes looked right through Acid as she neared, and his gaunt, cadaverous cheeks shone white in the moonlight. The decay and degradation of city life -you saw it more and more every year that went by. Though, it could be a cognitive bias on her part, Acid reasoned. Her focus had been skewed lately.

She made her way down the rickety Victorian stairwell and, as she opened the door the deep rhythm of heavy rock music hit her in the chest. It was Motörhead's Ace Of Spades. An absolute classic. It felt like home and, as always, the bar was reassuringly dark - the red paper lanterns dotted around the ceiling giving off a warm glow but no real light. There were three small tables along the side wall, with the bar taking up two-thirds of the floor space. At the far end of the counter, two foreign-looking men were sitting on high stools engaged in animated chat. Next to them, an old guy with an eye patch nursed a bottle of something dark.

"What can I get you, darling?" The barman leaned over as Acid took her place on the stool nearest the door. "Cocktail maybe?"

Acid didn't recognise this one. But the smile on his face said he fancied his chances. He was good-looking, with beautiful dark brown skin and a deep smile. Acid toyed with the idea of returning his advances but decided against it.

She needed rest, and more than anything she needed to keep herself in check.

"Chivas Regal. Double. Two chunks of ice," she told him.

"Coming right up."

"And a Mojito."

Winking at her now. "Great choice."

Acid Vanilla rarely drank Mojitos, they were too sweet for her palate, but she figured the preparation would keep him busy. While the barman took his frustration out on a bunch of mint, Acid sipped at her whisky, willing the stress of the last hour to leave her system. It wasn't easy. If anything it was getting harder.

"Excuse me, are you waiting for someone?"

Acid looked up into the face of a middle-aged man sporting a large grey beard and a lusty expression. His long hair was pulled into a bun on the top of his head in a style not intended for his advancing age bracket. He wore a black shirt with the sleeves rolled up to reveal tanned forearms that were covered with tattoos, and far too many bracelets.

Acid remained poker-faced. "I'm just having a quiet drink."

"But how awful. An attractive girl like you drinking alone." He held out his hand. "Simon."

She sipped her drink, ignored the handshake.

"What are you drinking? Whisky? Can I buy you another?"

"No thanks. I'm good."

Simon pressed his hand to his chest in a show of mock surprise. Clearly he was unused to rebuttals. Or wanted her to think as much. "Not a big talker, hey?"

Acid turned on her stool. "You don't want to talk to me. I'm bad news."

"Is that so?" He flashed his eyebrows.

"Sure is. I'm a total bloody maniac."

He laughed. "Me too. Me too."

"No. You don't understand," she said. "I mean it. I have a condition." She waited for his reaction. Nothing. "It's like bipolar, but not as severe, easier to control – most of the times." She took another sip of her drink. "Other times all I want to do is dig a hole, climb in and never come out."

Acid had wanted to hug Dr Kingston when he'd first given her the diagnosis. Cyclothymic Disorder, to give it its full name. Not that a label made her feel any better, but at least she understood what was going on inside her now. Dr Kingston had gone on to explain how Cyclothymia patients usually experienced mild forms of both mania and depression – referred to as lowercase m and lowercase d on the spectrum - but went on to say that Acid was special. She was a lowercase d but an uppercase M, meaning she was more manic than depressed. And, in the right circumstances, that manic energy almost felt like a superpower. Her thinking was grander, more creative, she took greater risks, needed less sleep, felt invincible. A side-effect of her condition, however, was a fluttering pressure on her nervous system – what Acid called 'the bats'. Usually, she could harness that pressure – it helped her do what she did - but then there were times like now, when she found herself in a nihilistic slump, oversharing with strangers.

"Well, you ask me, we're all a little crazy," Simon slurred, ogling her some more. "All the best people are. Bukowski said that."

Acid sipped her drink. "I think you'll find that was the Mad Hatter, sweetie."

"Whatever." He waved his hand drunkenly. "Tell me, what do you do for work?"

"Me? Oh, I'm a hired killer." She leaned in, whispering, "A deadly assassin."

"Well you certainly look deadly." Simon laughed, mistaking her comment for flirtation once more and eyeballing Acid with a growing lust. "Have you killed anyone today?"

Acid stared at herself in the mirror behind the bar. "Two people actually. Though one was an accident, truth be told." She widened her eyes. "Probably going to get a spanking for that."

She swilled her drink around the glass. Dr Kingston had suggested she try a new course of medication that would dampen her mood swings but she was adamant - no pills. She was the best at what she did, and those manic feelings of invincibility were a big part of why.

"Never been a fan of the old rye myself." Simon gestured at her glass, almost empty now. "Wine for me. Lovely glass of Shiraz. Do you like wine…? Shit, I'm sorry, I didn't catch your name."

"That's because I didn't offer it." She made eye contact with the barman and pulled a 'save me' face before turning to Simon. "But yes, I like wine. Though I'd say it's more of a social drink and, as I already told you, I'm here for a quiet one. On my own."

Simon swerved the comment. "Oh my god. I've just noticed your eyes," he cooed. "They're amazing. Like David Bowie's."

Acid looked away. "How do you mean?"

"You know, one brown, one blue. Very striking. Bowie's were the same you know."

"Actually, they weren't," she replied. "Bowie had two blue eyes. Only, one got damaged in a fight, leaving him with an enlarged pupil. It looked like they were different colours, that's what people think, but they weren't."

Simon stared at her, open-mouthed. "But yours are different colours."

"Yes. How observant of you. But it's not caused by trauma, I was born like this. So, not like David Bowie."

"Fair enough. You're not a fan?"

Acid sighed. "Yes. I'm a big fan. But that wasn't what we were talking about."

He paused a moment. Then, laughing, "Oh, you're a feisty one, aren't you? Let me buy you another drink." He placed his hand on her knee. Acid tensed. She felt for the push dagger in her belt and imagined sliding the cold steel through Simon's ribcage, straight into his heart. He'd never see it coming. With the music this loud, no one would hear him yell. She'd be out of here and into the night before he hit the floor.

She closed her eyes.

No.

That was the bats talking and she had to stay in control. No matter how satisfying it would be.

"What do you do, Simon?" she asked, shifting her leg away from his sweaty hand.

"I do loads of shit. Bit of this, bit of that. Mainly I'm a photographer. Some would say I'm deadly too - with a camera." He leaned closer. His breath stung Acid's eyes. "I'd love to shoot you some time. You've got such an amazing look. In fact, my studio isn't far from here."

"Maybe another time," Acid told him. "I wouldn't be much fun tonight."

"Here we are. Classic Mojito for the lady." The barman placed the drink down in front of her.

Simon sat back. "Now that's more like it. I think I might join you in one of those."

"Here, have this one." She slid the drink over to him. "I'd say it's more your style."

"Don't mind if I do." His hand was back on her leg, sliding up the inside of her thigh. It was a bold move, but one he would regret.

"Move that. Now," she hissed.

"Ah, come on. We'd be great together. Couple of deadly assassins like us." His hand reached Acid's groin, pushing at the seam of her jeans.

That was it.

She jumped to her feet and grabbed Simon by the wrist, twisting his arm behind his back and slamming his face onto the bar. "I said, move it." She pushed his face down onto the polished surface, mashing his smug features into the wood. "Was that hard to understand?"

"Fuck you," he mumbled, squirming to get free.

Acid pushed down harder "I'm going to use the bathroom and then I'm going home. Alone. I suggest you keep your mouth shut and keep your hands to yourself in future. Understand?" She shoved his arm further up his back. "Yes?"

Simon whimpered in agreement. Acid noticed the cute barman watching the exchange. He winked at her conspiringly but that was all. She released Simon and marched to the bathroom, the door hitting the wall with a thud as she yanked it open. A single cubicle stood in one corner and, opposite the door, a large graffiti-covered mirror hung over a small sink unit. She walked over and gripped the white porcelain, holding on for dear life.

Her heart was racing. This wasn't like her.

She peered at her reflection, pulling at the thin skin

beneath her eyes and opening her mouth as wide as it'd go. It did little good. She adjusted her fringe, then headed for the cubicle. The fact she sat directly on the cold toilet seat without first laying out a carefully constructed halo of toilet paper told her all she needed to know about her current state of mind.

Usually when the needle of her sanity went so far into the red, it wasn't an issue. She saw it coming and would take herself away for a few weeks - a log cabin in the mountains, a deserted beach somewhere. That way her system could reset itself before she did anything stupid. Only, this time the chaos had sneaked up on her.

She was fastening her belt when the bathroom door opened and loud music drifted in from the bar. She paused and held her breath. A woman would have knocked on the cubicle to see if it was in use, she would have made some sort of noise, at least. But Acid already knew it wasn't a woman out there. She gave it a beat, cracked her knuckles and opened the cubicle door.

"Dumb bitch." Simon was standing in front of the cubicle, his face bright red. "You'll pay for that."

"Oh dear. Did someone hurt your feelings?"

Before she had a chance to move, he lunged forward and got his hands around her neck, pushing her back and smashing her head against the wall.

Shit.

Her eyes bulged as he pressed his fingers into her windpipe. He was trying to kill her. But that was good. The pain helped. Not that she liked pain in some kinky way, she wasn't a sadist, but it focused her, got her head back in the game. It was enough.

A sharp knee to the groin followed by a push kick sent Simon flying out of the cubicle. He stumbled, banging into the corner of a hand dryer as Acid made for the door. But he righted himself in time and came at her with a flurry of punches. One of them caught her in the temple rattling her brain for second, and then he was behind her, dragging her into the centre of the room with an arm around her neck.

Come on, Acid. Keep it together.

The guy was stronger than he looked. She kicked out at the sink hoping to knock him off balance, but she couldn't get purchase. He pulled her away and tightened the sleeper hold, putting more pressure on her windpipe. Reaching down with his other hand, he began unbuckling her belt.

"Not so fucking deadly now, are you?" he rasped in her ear.

A black fog seeped across Acid's vision. She met Simon's eyes in the mirror as he shoved his hand into her knickers. The bastard was laughing.

Despite the angle, she managed to raise her right foot and scrape her boot heel down the front of his calf. He yelled out and his grip slackened, enabling her to access the push dagger in her belt. She pulled it out and stabbed the blade deep into his thigh muscle. A part of her – the bats – had been yelling for the femoral artery. But she'd spared him. She wasn't sure why.

With a yell he let go. Twisting away, she grabbed him by the hair and dragged him forward, smashing his face into the hard edge of the sink unit. His nose exploded on impact, the cartilage turning to mush. She released her grip and he slumped onto his knees, upright but barely conscious. His right eye was swollen shut and his nose was no longer what you could call a nose. Yanking the push dagger from his leg, she held it to his throat as the bats screamed in her head.

Finish him.

Kill him.

Simon stared at her with his one good eye. "You're fucking dead," he sneered. "I know people. Scary people."

Acid looked away. She was embarrassed to realise there were tears in her eyes. "Why is it pricks like you think they can take what they want without comeback?" She gripped his shoulder to stop herself from shaking.

Simon sneered. "Screw you."

"No." Acid grabbed his man-bun in her fist and sliced it off with a slash of the knife. "Screw you."

She stuffed the hair into his bleeding mouth and shoved him to the tiled floor. He was gone, out for the count. She wiped her eyes with the back of her hand before crouching beside him and going through his pockets. Flipping open the tan leather wallet found in his jeans, she counted out a hundred in twenties and tens. She stuffed the notes in her back pocket and the wallet in her jacket. Then she adjusted her fringe in the mirror, applied some lipstick, and returned to the bar.

"Was that dude bothering you?" the barman asked her as she passed by on her way to the door.

Acid hit him with her sweetest smile. "I can take care of myself, sweetie," she purred. "Though I noticed the floor was wet back there. You wouldn't want anyone to slip and hurt themselves." She pulled out a twenty and slung it on the bar top before skipping up the stairwell.

The homeless man was still there as she got to the top of the stairs.

"Here you go, mate," She pulled out the remaining notes and handed them over. "Buy yourself some food."

The man looked fearful for a second, then reached out with his bony fingers. "Thanks," he wheezed. "I will do."

Acid shrugged. "Or, you know, spend it on drugs and booze - whatever gets you through the night."

The man sat up. It looked like it hurt him to do so. "You're a good one," he told her.

"Not so sure about that. But you take care."

Her heart was beating fast as she hailed a cab and gave the driver her address. She could have handled Simon better, she thought, as the car pulled away. But she hadn't killed him. She hadn't lost complete control.

There might be another issue, however. Simon had said he knew people. Scary people. It was probably bullshit, but she had to be careful. After tonight she'd be in Caesar's bad books, and the boss hated his operatives drawing attention to themselves. She sat back on the cold leather seat and considered her options. Simon did look the type who might know dodgy people, and if he was in The Bitter Marxist he must have some sort of underground connection.

But screw it.

If someone was coming for her, let them come. She'd handle them or die trying. And right now, either of those options was fine by her.

Chapter Six

In a large, windowless office in Canary Wharf, Team Purple's late shift was coming to an end. It had been a long, eventless night, and this was no more evident than in the blank-faced stares of every member as they waited for the last few minutes to tick by and they could re-emerge into the real world.

The four-till-twelve shift was always the hardest. You started work when most people were signing off for the day and had to walk past them as they skipped to the pub or met friends on street corners. It was even worse in the winter months, having to venture out into the cold and dark, with only the prospect of a gruelling eight-hour shift to look forward to.

The small digital clock on Spook Horowitz's monitor screen showed 11.49 p.m. Almost there. She clicked out of her current feed and began the logging process. She was somewhat premature perhaps, but she'd risk it. Jacqueline Madeley – the user she'd been assigned to this evening – had been reading in bed for the last hour. A total dud.

Spook sat back in her seat and glanced around the room at her colleagues. She immediately wishing she hadn't as she locked eyes with Kelvin Walker over in the corner. He waved.

Damn it.

Spook snapped her attention back to the screen but it was too late. Kevin was getting to his feet; he was heading her way. She tensed, readying her stock response, the one she gave Kelvin every time he asked her out for a drink.

Thanks, but I've got plans.

Except she never did have plans. And tonight more than ever, falling asleep in front of her Xbox seemed a particularly grim prospect.

Spook removed her thick-framed glasses and tucked her black bob behind her ears, making out as though she hadn't noticed Kevin. She breathed on the lenses of her glasses and was rubbing them on the bottom of her flannel shirt when he got to her desk.

"Hey there, Spook," Kelvin mumbled into the floor, like he always did when he was around her. "The shifts almost over. Do you fancy going for a drink? Or…whatever?"

Spook looked at the clock on her screen. 11.55 p.m. "Yeah," she said. "Why not."

It was clear Kelvin was not expecting this. "Wow, okay. Great." His eyes widened as he considered what to say next. "Arsenio's is open till three. We could go there."

"Cool." Spook put her glasses back on and they stared at each other a few seconds.

"Hey, is that an Overwatch shirt?" Kelvin asked, pointing at Spook's chest, at the large Overwatch logo emblazoned there. White on black.

"Sure is." She held up her fist self-consciously. "Team D.Va all the way."

"Awesome. Junkrat for me. But check it." Kelvin lifted his white button-down to reveal the same t-shirt. He laughed. "What about that? It must be fate."

"Yeah." Spook smiled. "Must be."

Not that Spook believed in fate. She was a woman of science, and a computer genius to boot - ever since she'd sat behind her father's Apple LC 500 aged six and wrote her first piece of code. At age ten she'd set developed a state-of-the-art record database for her school, her skills baffling even her IT teacher. Aged thirteen, she'd hacked into the White House's mainframe undetected - just for a look around. In terms of hacking, Spook was strictly white hat. Any hacking she did was a way to test herself and her abilities, rather than for any immoral gains.

"Well, that's great news," Kelvin whispered, backing away as their team leader, Terry, appeared at the far side of the room. "I need a few drinks after that shift."

"Me too." Spook watched him shuffle back to his desk and sank back in her chair. Was this all she had to look forward to these days - an awkward drink with Kelvin-freak-ing-Walker? She might not believe in fate or destiny or any other cosmic force, but surely, after all she'd been through these last few years, the universe owed her a break?

It had been no surprise to anyone when Spook had achieved a perfect 1600 in her SATs and enrolled at the prestigious Massachusetts Institute of Technology to study Computer Science & Information Systems. After that, an illustrious career in tech seemed to be foregone conclusion. The plan was that she'd move to Silicon Valley after college, work at a start-up for a few years, maybe launch her own. Then, once she'd established herself in the industry, it would only be a short while before a COO role was on the cards with CEO a few years later.

So exactly how Spook Horowitz came to be in London, with nothing to look forward to except a few beers with Kelvin, was a long and rather tragic story. One that involved both her parents dying within a year of each other, and an incredibly messy break-up with her boyfriend of six years. Spook had turned to prescription painkillers and Valium to help with the grief. But all they'd done was make everything ten times worse. So with her mental and emotional health in tatters, she'd taken the only reasonable option left - she'd run away. More specifically, she'd booked a one-way ticket to London. Her plan was to see the sights then travel around Europe for a few months before returning to the States to see how things looked with fresh eyes.

But after a month staying in a small Airbnb in Hackney, she realised she liked the British way of life. The tech world in the US was intense, cut-throat, and it wasn't much different in the UK, but the talk in the media here was about gender pay gaps and there was a sense that change was coming. Plus, no one knew her in London. She could be anyone she wanted to be.

Before her visa expired, Spook found herself a place to live and got a new job: working for Cerberix Inc. at their brand-new London office. The job was a godsend for someone like Spook. A dream ticket. Despite being a relative newcomer in the tech world, Cerberix was already a major player and readying itself to take on Apple over the next five years. This alone would have seemed like a preposterous goal if it wasn't for its charismatic CEO, Ethan Clarkson, who was fast becoming the new poster boy for forward-thinking innovation.

Spook had initially interviewed for a coder position. It was what she knew, what she was good at. But on her first day, a man had taken her and six other specially selected candidates to a sealed office and told them they were to be employed in a newly created role as *Covert Data-Gatherers and AI Facilitators*. 'Covert' because it was a project Cerberix didn't want the public knowing about. And as Spook quickly found out, it was a project they didn't want the authorities or the police or the media knowing about either.

Her role was simple. She was to monitor the webcams and inbuilt microphones of any laptop that ran Hadez - Cerberix's ground-breaking new operating system. As this included the majority of the online world at this point, it was set to be an enormous project, especially as webcams could still be accessed when the computer was in sleep mode. That was the beauty of Clarkson's invention. The initial contract was for one year, and at the same time as monitoring people's data, the Watchers, as they called themselves, were building a global AI interface. This would take over the monitoring once the Watchers' role in the project was complete.

It was all highly illegal of course. But that was one reason Spook had been selected. She was a blue-sky thinker, a maverick. She understood, they told her, that whilst one might construe this work as a touch reprehensible, it was for the greater good. By watching users, Cerberix could provide a unique, tailored experience, able to cater for people's true needs. No guesswork.

"We'll even save the world while we're doing it," the handsome, all-American Ethan Clarkson expounded in a video message played for the Watchers on their first day. He went on to explain how the new technology would catch terrorists, quash fake news, and stop high school shootings before they happened. It was good what they were doing. The world would catch up soon enough.

"You ready to go?"

Kelvin appeared by her side. He was wearing a black hoodie that said *Show Me The Beer* across the front. Spook shuddered, wondering if it would destroy him if she backed out of the drink. Wondering if she cared either way. She swung her rucksack onto her back, too weary to do anything but go along with the plan.

"Yeah, I'm ready," she told him.

Chapter Seven

Kelvin was a nice guy. But, boy, was he dull. And too nerdy even for Spook. The realisation of this had begun to dawn on her after beer number three when Kelvin had asked her what Harry Potter house she was in. She'd told him the truth: she wasn't a fan. Which killed that conversation dead. But then Kelvin had doubled down, clumsily asking about her ethnicity (half-Malaysian – her mom.) Now on beer number five, he'd just hit the jackpot in the game of *Questions Spook Hated To Be Asked.*

"Is Spook your real name?"

"Yeah. It is. My folks were hippies. Thought it was apt." Kelvin looked confused. "You know, Horowitz. Horror-witz. Spook. Horror."

"Oh. Right. Yeah. Man, you must hate them for that."

Spook was poker-faced. "They're both dead."

"Oh, I'm sorry."

"Yeah. My dad two years ago. My mom last year. Both cancer."

Kelvin looked like he was about to throw up. They sat

and drank for a few minutes while the silence grew heavier. Kelvin tried again, asking about her childhood, what the MIT was like, benign stuff, dull. But then the conversation drifted to past relationships, which Spook took as her cue to leave.

"I didn't mean to pry," Kelvin said, as she pulled her coat on. "Let me buy you another drink."

"It's fine," she lied. "But it's nearly two, and I was only going to have a couple of drinks. Besides, you've bought every round."

He giggled. "I guess I'm a typical Gryffindor. You know, chivalrous."

Spook grabbed her rucksack and got the hell out of there. She was drunk enough to opt for an Uber home rather than the night bus, and by the time she got home an hour later the drink had hit her hard. Five bottles of American Pale Ale on an empty stomach was never a good idea. Maybe that was Kelvin's plan, Spook thought, as she slung her rucksack off her shoulder and unzipped it, pulling out her trusty laptop. The sensible move now, of course, would be to drink as much water as she could stomach and go to bed. Tomorrow was her day off. She could sleep in late, try and swerve the hangover. But no, here she was, making herself comfy and easing her laptop open. She logged in and immediately a notification slid in from the right at the top of her screen, informing her of a new article from Entrepreneur Magazine. She read the head-line, almost sicking-up in her mouth as she did.

Eugene Goldman becomes Applications Architect at Apecom Industries.

Spook screwed her nose up. "You have got to be kidding me."

Goldman had been her classmate at MIT – a pugnacious, rich kid from upstate New York who thought he was God's gift to tech. He'd also been a real shit to Spook for the whole three years, culminating in him calling Spook and her mother slitty-eyed immigrants. So a real nice guy.

Spook clicked on the article, getting angrier and more resentful with every word she read. Turned out Eugene had taken the position after leaving his business partner in the lurch and bankrupting their start-up. That figured. Goldman was one of those impenetrable Alpha-personality types. With the sort of confidence that only comes from being super privileged and wholly unscrupulous.

She slammed her laptop closed and marched into the kitchen. A full bottle of red wine stood on the side. She poured herself a large glass and drank it one go. Then she poured out another and went back to her laptop. She'd had an idea. After logging onto the Watcher portal, she found her old classmate within seconds. There was only one Eugene Goldman in San Francisco. But if there'd been hundreds, Spook would have found him. She was good at her job.

She clicked on the profile and entered her pin-code, granting herself access to the microphone and camera of Eugene's MacBook. The screen went white for a second, then the webcam feed appeared on her screen.

"Oh, man. Gross."

Spook looked away in horror at the image already burning itself into her eyes. Eugene with both feet on his desk and a deodorant canister shoved where deodorant canisters were not intended to be shoved. She quickly clicked off the feed and took another gulp of wine. It wasn't the first time Spook had witnessed sordid displays on her computer screen, of course (you watch people using the internet all day, you see a lot of self-love) but she'd never seen anyone do it like that before.

She was about to go to bed when she had another idea. What was Ethan Clarkson doing right now? What did the big boss get up to behind closed doors? Spook typed his name and date of birth into the search feed:

Ethan Clarkson.

Almaden Valley, San Jose.

DOB: 21 July 1978.

Founder/Chief Executive Officer: Cerberix Inc.

Accessibility available: London, California, Berlin.

Spook clicked on the London link and regretted it instantly, met with a blue screen and a screeching noise that was damn uncomfortable on the ears even through her laptop speakers. She clicked off the feed, angry with herself. Why didn't she think of that? Obviously the man who invented the Watcher project would have scramblers on his own system. Spook once more considered the possibility of bed, but she was too on edge to fall asleep. The sight of Eugene was still there when she closed her eyes, and her bitterness at his unwarranted success still tightened her chest.

She turned back to the screen. The Watcher database showed linked profiles for each subject at the bottom of the screen. Colleagues, family members, university friends. It was to help the AI with name and place recognition when analysing audio tags. As Spook scanned Ethan Clarkson's profile, one name stood out:

Sinclair Whitman.

Atherton, Palo Alto.

DOB: 19 November 1959.

Chief Financial Officer: Cerberix Inc.

Accessibility available: California, Paris, London.

Spook had met Whitman at the secret launch event for the Watcher project. He was a tall, willowy man with a thick head of white hair and an air of callous arrogance. An unlikeable man. Spook clicked on the California link to reveal the image of a beautiful beach-front apartment. Early evening there, just after seven. On the wall facing the webcam, above an ornate fireplace, hung what looked to be an original Pollack. But no sign of Whitman.

Spook clicked on the Paris feed next and was presented with another lavishly decorated room. Clean lines, expensive fabrics, incredibly modern. But empty. She finished the wine. There was always the London feed. Third time lucky. Spook clicked on the link, expecting to see more of the same. So when she was met with the image of a very pale and very naked Sinclair Whitman, she almost spat wine all over her laptop. She watched, open-mouthed, as he knelt over a low coffee table and greedily snorted a large line of white powder from a mirrored tray.

"Someone's a dark horse," Spook whispered, as Whitman vacuumed up the last of the cocaine, exposing his bony ass to the webcam. Without missing a beat, she clicked on the ScreenCam app and clicked record. It was foolish, Spook knew that. But she also knew of the kudos she'd receive from her colleagues when she played them the recording. She'd prove to them all she wasn't the shy, prissy little mouse they thought her to be.

And it got better. A woman entered the scene. She was small and shapely, with blonde hair and a pretty face. She was also at least half Whitman's age. Spook gasped as she slowly sashayed into the centre of the room and made a show of undoing the belt on her trench coat. How clichéd, Spook thought, as the woman slipped the coat off her shoulders and let it slide to the floor. Underneath, she was as naked as Whitman. Albeit less pale and a lot less wrinkly.

Spook's hand trembled on the tracking pad of her laptop. She shouldn't be watching this. She certainly shouldn't be recording it. Even if Whitman wasn't her CFO, there were rules. Watchers weren't allowed to digitally record anything in their work. Yet Spook was transfixed as the two bodies entwined. Kissing, stroking, exploring each other. Whitman guided the girl over to the couch and lay back as she got on top of him. More kissing, then Whitman placed a bony hand on the girl's head and forced it down onto his groin. Spook turned her face away but kept on watching out the corner of her eye, as if this somehow might make the scene more palatable. It didn't. It was like one of those awful videos she'd happen across by accident on 4chan or Reddit. *The Faces of Death.* But much worse.

On screen the drama grew. Whitman was back on his feet, standing in the middle of the room with his back to the camera. He gesticulated wildly at the woman, her shaking her head in response and shouting, making weird faces. They were too far from the microphone, so Spook couldn't make out what was being said, but the flailing arms and glared expressions said it all. Whitman was enraged about something, balling her out and raising a tight fist in the air. He grabbed her by the wrist and pulled her to him before spitting in her face. Then he slammed his fist into the side of her head.

"Woah." Spook was unable to take her eyes off the screen. Whitman was a good foot taller than the girl and seemed deceptively strong. She struggled, trying to pull her hand away, but he kept hold, striking her with another fist, to the nose this time. And another. Then Whitman let go of her and she fell to the floor.

Spook hoped that would be the end. The poor girl's nose was bleeding profusely and a deep cut had closed her right eye. But if anything it spurred Whitman on. His face was red with fury as he kicked her repeatedly in the chest and stomach. Then he leapt on her. Put his big hands around her throat.

"Oh shit." Spook wanted to look away but couldn't.

Whitman was strangling her.

He was actually strangling her.

Spook sat there, powerless and frightened, as Sinclair Whitman, billionaire co-founder of Cerberix Inc., squeezed the life out of the poor woman. She struggled under him as best she could, but she didn't stand a chance. She kicked around for half a minute or so, then her right leg shuddered. Then she was still.

Spook stared open-mouthed at the screen. Her heart was pounding. She hadn't taken a breath the whole time. She clicked *Stop* on the screen recording software, watching as the video rendered down and was saved onto her desktop. Then she closed her laptop, climbed off the couch, and threw up an entire bottle of red wine into the kitchen sink.

Chapter Eight

The apartment was cold as Acid Vanilla locked the front door and went through to the bedroom. She took off her leather jacket and flung it on the bed, retrieving Simon's wallet from the inside pocket and checking the name on the cards. Simon Cooper. She chucked the wallet at the wicker waste bin in the corner, already overflowing with cotton wool balls and lipstick-blotted tissues. She looked around and blew out her cheeks. The room was a real mess. The bed hadn't been made in weeks, and piles of clothes and bits of underwear covered every inch of the carpet. Even Acid's prized vintage dressing table was awash with make-up and various bits of weaponry, magazine clips, bullets. She flirted briefly with the idea of tidying up, but it was getting late and, frankly, she couldn't face it.

Back through to the lounge, she headed straight for the drinks cabinet, hoping another Chivas would help settle her nerves. She sloshed some into a heavy-bottomed glass and took a long drink. Times like this she missed having a TV, something to distract her. She thought about firing up the stereo, some Velvet Underground perhaps, but she settled for the dull hum of the traffic.

She moved to the couch and pulled her MacBook onto her lap, logging into the new dark web search program Raaz had created. Better than Google, apparently – for people in her line of work. In a few clicks you got ID confirmation, addresses, recent whereabouts. She typed *Simon Cooper* into the search box, followed by *London* and *Photographer*, and a profile flashed on screen complete with photo. Simon Cooper. He was a photographer, like he'd said. But for *Best Home* magazine. Not the cutting-edge figure he'd made out. The profile also said he was divorced and lived with his mother in Bethnal Green. Typical. He was full of shit. Didn't know anyone. Not a threat in the slightest. Acid closed the laptop and lay back on the couch. She felt tired for once. Maybe she would get some sleep.

Then the intercom buzzed.

"Bugger."

She sat upright, her eyes wide and mind racing as to who it could be at this time of night. The best option was a delivery boy, buzzing the wrong flat, but something told her that was wishful thinking. The intercom went again.

"All right, keep your knickers on."

She walked over and swiped at the screen, bringing up the camera feed and the face of Banjo Shawshank, distorted somewhat in the fisheye lens. He looked worried. He went for the buzzer a third time.

"All right, calm down." She pressed the talk-button. "Second floor. Number nine." She buzzed him in and unlocked the front door before returning to the couch.

Two minutes later Banjo was pacing in front of her.

"What do you think it means?" he asked. "Are we going to get eradicated?"

Acid gave it a beat. Caesar calling them in for a meeting the day after a job wasn't unheard of, but it was rare.

"No, we aren't going to get eradicated, dummy. If he wanted us dead, he wouldn't do it at HQ, would he? And he sure as hell wouldn't be giving us prior warning." She sipped her drink. "He'll want a rundown of what happened, that's all. Ethel and Doris will have been stirring the pot. You know what they're like."

Banjo was wired. "It was a real shitshow, wasn't it? Thinking about it. I can see why he'd be pissed off."

Acid twisted her mouth to one side. She'd seen worse. Been at worse. Caused worse.

Banjo went on. "He wants to see us first thing. 9 a.m. I was wondering if I could crash here for a couple of hours. Otherwise I'll only be getting home before I have to set off again."

Acid gave him a look. "Fine. You're here now. But don't be getting any ideas." Banjo stopped pacing. The hint of a smile appeared. Acid held up her hand. "Not a chance, sunshine."

"But think about it for a second. We're both good-looking, healthy. Both a tad frazzled. I know I'd benefit from the release. No strings attached, of course."

"Aww, no then, sorry. I only like it with strings attached."

Banjo relaxed. "You're terrible. You know that, don't you?"

"Stop flirting, the answer's no."

"Well, what about a drink then? Settle my nerves."

Acid sighed. Sleep had been wishful thinking. "What do you want? I've got whisky, vodka, gin."

Banjo thought. "You got Amaretto? If so, I'll have a Godfather. If not, make it a whisky. Large."

Acid didn't have Amaretto. She fixed them both a large Chivas Regal and sat, gesturing for Banjo to do the same before he wore out her Kashmir silk rug. They both drank in silence a few minutes, maybe realising at the same time that they'd never had a proper conversation.

"So, how did you get into this game?" Banjo asked, putting his drink down.

"Come on, you know you don't ask those sorts of question."

Talking about your past was against the rules. That and knowing anyone's real name. Not killing the mark's neighbour was probably in there somewhere too.

"I'm only curious. We might both be in the Thames estuary by lunchtime tomorrow. What will it hurt?"

Acid paused. "It's a long story."

"Well, we've got time. Tell me, who was your first?"

"First kill?"

"No, first crush. Yes, first kill."

Acid considered the question. She hadn't talked about this in so long. She didn't know if she could do it. Banjo was staring at her, waiting.

"All right," she told him. "It was a guy my mum knew."

"No shit. Like a boyfriend?"

"Not exactly," she said, not looking at Banjo but into her drink. "You see, it was only me and my mum, growing up. She was a dancer. Did some acting here and there. Until she fell down some stairs one night and that was her career over. After that, money was hard. We moved around a lot. Then Mum got into turning tricks, to help put food on the table. A couple of regular callers at first. But word got around. She was a good-looking woman."

"I bet she was."

Acid ignored him, took another long drink.

"There was this one guy who'd visit her. A real vicious bastard. By this point I was fifteen, so I knew what was going on. Could tell when she was hiding bruises. One night I got back from a friend's house to find her bloody and naked and this guy stood over her, holding a wine bottle… that he'd been…" She drained her glass. She could see it like it was yesterday. Could feel the anger bubbling in her stomach. "The police said I stabbed him seventy-two times in total. Almost decapitated him."

She paused. The atmosphere in the room had changed. A stillness had descended. Banjo sat upright. Hanging on her every word. "Seventy-two times," he whispered. "Shit."

Acid ran a finger around the rim of her glass. "I was still sitting on the kitchen floor when they turned up. Didn't resist. It went in my favour though, in the long run. The severity of the attack meant they put me in a secure unit rather than jail. A home for psychologically dangerous children. Some bullshit. The type of place does more harm than good. But it prepared me well. You learn how to look after yourself pretty quick. That's where Caesar found me. He got me out of there. Took me under his wing. Trained me up. Been working for him ever since. Sixteen years now."

She went to get another drink, one for Banjo too.

"Your mum still around?"

Acid paused. The bottle hovered over the top of her glass. "No. She's dead." She poured the drinks and returned to the couch.

"Some story." Banjo whistled, accepting the glass.

"It is what it is. It's so long ago now it's like it happened to someone else. And you know what? It did. The person I was back then doesn't exist anymore." She stood. Her turn to pace. Nervous energy bristled down her spine.

"You okay?"

She stretched her arms in front of her. "Yeah, fine. I need a holiday, that's all. Gets to you, this job, after a while."

Banjo turned his mouth down. "I love it. All the power. It's like we get to play God every single day. Gets me hard."

Acid kept on pacing. "Don't you think it's suffocating, all that power?" she asked. "Don't you want to find some space inside of all that? Remind yourself you do have a soul?"

Banjo smirked as he drank. "Nah, I don't have one. I like the power."

Acid wasn't listening. She was on a roll. The bats spurred her on. The drink just as much. "Recently I've felt out of sorts. It happens now and again and I get over it, you know. I make peace with what I do. But lately there's been this recurring sense of something sinister stalking me." She walked over to the window and looked down onto the swirling blackness of the river. "Forget it. I'm talking absolute crap. I know I am. I'm overtired, that's all. Like I say, I need a holiday."

"I don't know, babe, sounds to me like you might need more than a holiday."

"God. Will you give it a rest?"

"No, I mean, it sounds to me like of the game. Looking for redemption, maybe."

Acid turned from the window and gave him a stern look. "Don't talk shit," she said. "This is who I am. I'm the best in the bloody business. Everyone knows it. Of course I don't want out."

Banjo held his hands up. "Fair enough. Sorry I spoke."

"Even if I did, Caesar would never allow it." She

finished her drink and went to the cabinet to pour another. "I need a few weeks away. That's all."

She sat on the edge of the couch. Neither of them spoke for what seemed like forever.

"A naughty girl's home, hey?" Banjo said at last. "Bet that was hot. I figured it'd have to be something like that with you. You're too much of a rebel to be ex-military."

Acid laughed. "I'll take that as a compliment. That what you are?"

"God no. Look at me. I'm far too lithe and fabulous for all that."

"So what's your story?"

"Nothing much to tell." He threw his matchstick legs onto the couch and put his hands behind his head.

"Come on, I've told. Spill."

He closed his eyes. "It's simple, babe. I'm a total bloody psychopath."

"Oh, is that right?"

"How do you think I got to be such a charming fucker? All part of the brand, isn't it?"

Acid got to her feet. "Well, on that note, I'm going to try to get a few hours. Best we're rested before meeting Caesar. I see you've made yourself comfortable. I'll be through here." She turned to look at him. "Again, not an invitation."

Banjo grinned at her. "I might go through till morning, work out what to tell him."

"Well, no more booze if you're driving. I mean it. There's coffee through there if you want it. But try and relax, okay? We tell Caesar the truth, he'll be fine. Shit happens."

"I hope you're right."

"Hey. I'm always right."

She went to the bedroom and closed the door behind her, listening for the click.

He'll be fine.

Now if she could only convince herself of that, she might get some of that elusive sleep she'd been talking about.

Chapter Nine

Spook Horowitz had already resigned herself to the fact sleep wasn't going to happen. Not tonight. Not when she still had so many unanswered questions spinning around her brain. She poured herself another drink – coffee this time, a safer option – and went back to her laptop, refreshed her emails. Still nothing.

"Come on, Kelvin."

Once she'd cleaned herself up, Spook's first thought had been to call the police, tell them what she'd seen. But Cerberix had made the Watchers sign some hefty NDAs when taking on their new role, and whilst she knew murder trumped breaking a contract, Spook was a computer genius, not a lawyer. She wasn't certain how it worked. She did not want to get sent back to the States. Or worse.

The wise move then would have been to delete the recording. Forget what she'd seen. But this was someone's life and that didn't seem right. So instead Spook had transferred the file onto a thumb-drive – for safe keeping until she figured out what to do – and gone to bed. She was exhausted and could do nothing to help that poor girl now. Except then a terrible thought had hit her, one she needed an answer to right away. Which is why she was now mainlining coffee and refreshing her inbox every five minutes in the hope Kelvin would see her message and reply.

The clock said 5.30 a.m. Spook thought back to yesterday and Kelvin droning on about some new fitness regime that involved an early morning run. That meant he'd hopefully be awake soon. She refreshed her screen again. Her right leg shuddered like a jackhammer. Too much coffee. Or maybe she was in shock and didn't realise it. She stood and walked around her kitchen, looked out the small window above the sink as the new day's sun rose over London Fields. She thought about going for a walk. A way to distract her from this nightmare. Or a shower might do it.

She was on her way to the bathroom when she was drawn back to her laptop. One last time. She hit refresh and let out a soft yelp. There it was. Kelvin's reply.

Hey Spook. Good to hear from you. Sorry but I'm not sure what you're asking. Want to jump on a quick video call so we can talk?

Spook sighed. Not what she was hoping for, but if this is what it took. She typed back, *Sure, I'm logging on now,* and hit send. A few seconds later she heard the familiar beep-beep-beep of an incoming video call: *Kelvin Walker is attempting connection.*

Yeah. Not for the first time, Spook thought.

She settled herself in front of the screen and accepted the call as Kelvin flickered into focus.

"Good morning, Spook. I wasn't expecting to hear from you so soon after last night."

He was red-faced and sweaty, wearing one of those elastic headbands that held his glasses in place.

"Thanks for getting back to me." She was conscious of her tone, trying to sound calm. "Something occurred to me last night. It's nothing. But I thought you might know the answer."

She could tell Kelvin loved that she needed his help. "You said in your email something about recording your screen?"

"That's right. As I say, no biggie. I was curious, that's all. When we're watching subjects, what's the policy if we were to like... I don't know... accidentally record the screen, for instance? I mean it happens, right?"

Kelvin whistled. "Yes, it happens, but Cerberix don't like it. No siree. Didn't you hear about that guy in Team Yellow? The black guy with the blue hair? Used to walk around like he owned the place?" Spook hadn't. This wasn't doing anything for her anxiety. Kelvin went on. "The way I heard it, he'd been collecting data on this guy who was a friend of a friend. Only he was having an affair and Blue saw it all, recorded him in the act. Idea was to blackmail him. That is, until the bosses found out and he was slung out on his arse."

Kelvin took a large drink of something that resembled pond scum. He gulped it down noisily and smacked his lips.

"How did they find out what he'd done?" she asked. "The bosses."

"Not sure. I guess it gets flagged if anyone hits record. Easy enough to set up. I'd be surprised if they didn't have something like that in place."

Spook's eyes drifted to the thumb-drive next to her coffee mug. "How do you think it works?" she asked, her voice straining. "Would it be someone actually monitoring our activity? Or more automated?"

Kelvin sat back. "What's going on, Spook? What did you do?"

"Nothing. Just curious."

Kelvin didn't look convinced. "I can't imagine there's any real-time monitoring going on. The logs get checked once a week maybe, and if any recording has been flagged it's dealt with then."

"Okay, cool, yeah," Spook replied. Her mind was racing. "Thanks. And these logs, where do you think they'd be stored?"

Kelvin tilted his head. "What did you record, Spook? Wasn't me, was it?"

Spook ignored him. "Thanks so much for that, Kelvin. You've been a massive help."

Before he could reply, she closed the laptop. All at once she felt in need of a shower. Then she had some thinking to do. Thinking and planning. She might even say a prayer. Spook hadn't been to church since she left home, wasn't religious. But right now she needed all the help she could get.

Once showered, Spook dressed and went back into the kitchen. Out of the small window that looked onto London Fields she could see the sun was already up. A new day had begun. She took a bottle of coconut water from the fridge and drank half of it in one go. Then she went through into the lounge and flicked on the TV. There it was in black and white, at the bottom of the screen, today's leading item:

Woman's body found in London home of Sinclair Whitman, Chief Finance Officer of Cerberix Inc.

Spook sat, not quite believing what she was reading. She switched channels. The reports differed as she went through the networks, but the main thread was the same for all.

They said Sinclair wasn't in London at the time of the murder. Said his private chef had been arrested.

Spook turned up the volume on a female reporter standing outside Whitman's Mayfair apartment. She was telling the anchor how the police had arrested a thirty-year-old Hispanic male this morning.

Shit.

They were covering it up.

Spook thought back to her conversation with Kelvin. The recording. Being flagged. The Watcher logs.

Shit.

She needed coffee. She went through to the kitchen and switched on the kettle, seeing the tell-tale thumb-drive on the kitchen table, mocking her. She had an idea to shove it into the waste disposal unit and have done with it. But she couldn't bring herself. Instead she stared at it impotently as the kettle boiled. However, if Kelvin was correct and the logs were only checked once a week then she still had a chance. She already knew the Watcher logs were air-gapped somewhere, meaning she couldn't hack her way in. But if she could get in front of them she could hard-wire it and delete the evidence. It would be risky, of course. But the alternative was much worse. She had to try, she had no choice. She tipped a heaped spoonful of coffee into a mug and added boiling water. Then she went back into the lounge to make a phone call.

Chapter Ten

It took Spook three hours to get across London, but the travelling time allowed her to calm herself and get her analyst head on. Luckily, Michael had answered her call and was more than happy to answer Spook's questions, once she'd assured him they were purely for research purposes. A screenplay she was working on.

Spook had met Michael in her induction week at Cerberix. He'd started in the cybersecurity team at the same time and, although not directly involved in the Watcher project, he was part of the inner circle. They'd got on well. They liked the same films, the same games. Spook had been upset to discover Michael was gay, but they still met for drinks on occasion.

Michael informed Spook that there were twelve servers on the sixth floor of Cerberix's main building in Canary Wharf. Each server was situated in its own air-conditioned room, and number three was the one Spook was interested in. This was the air-gapped storage unit that was only accessible via a limited intranet link and dealt specifically with the formatted user logs from the Watcher project. The logging agent carried the data here at the end of each session, where it was stored for forty-eight hours before being analysed and then deleted. Spook couldn't help but squirm with joy when Michael told her that. She'd be able to delete her session log before anyone saw it.

Her heart was racing as she approached the main reception desk and smiled sweetly at the woman on the other side.

"Hey, how you doing?" Spook asked.

The woman looked her up and down. "I'm fine, thank you. Can I help?"

"I certainly hope so – Carol," Spook said, clocking her name badge. "Not a biggie. I just need to get to six to check on one of the servers."

Carol fiddled with her mouse. "Do you have clearance?"

"Uh-huh." Spook rummaged in her rucksack and flashed her ID badge. "I'm from the Watcher project. My supervisor asked me to investigate as we've been experiencing awful latency issues on the server." Spook held the woman's gaze.

"I've not been informed of any visitors today," she said.

"Hmm, that is odd. But you can ring John Rimmer if you want clarification. He's my supervisor. I mean, it's the weekend and he'll be at home with his kids today, but if you want to bother him, go ahead."

Rimmer wasn't Spook's supervisor, but he was the most feared supervisor on the Watcher project and well-known for being a real prick to subordinates. Carol looked to be thinking about it, then handed Spook a clipboard with a sheet of A4 paper attached.

"Okay. Sign in, will you? Name, department, time."

Spook did as she was told, putting her name down as

Karen Walker. Then she thanked Carol and called the elevator. Only as the door shut and she was safe in the confines of the metal box did she allow herself to breathe again. That was close.

Once on the sixth floor, she hurried along the windowless corridor and found server room three. You needed a passcode to open the door, but Michael had already let this slip on the phone. Spook keyed it in and slid inside as an intense chill from a large air-conditioner unit hit her in the face. It woke her, at least, focused her attention. She moved over to the far corner of the room and pulled her laptop from her rucksack followed by a handful of USB cables, an Ethernet cable and a rollover cable too. She wasn't sure what she would need, so she'd brought everything. After examining the main storage unit, she plugged her laptop into the central control panel and fired it up.

Accessing the system wasn't easy. There were more passcodes to get through, an expertly set up firewall, but nothing Spook couldn't handle. She checked her phone. It was 3 p.m. With any luck she'd have this done and be home by 7 p.m. at the latest. Job done. In the clear. Enjoying her day off.

She got through the backdoor of the system in about fifteen minutes. Folders and sub-folders filled her screen, all with long serial numbers. They were stored in team and then date order and Spook found her log file easily enough.

"What the hell?"

Every day Spook had worked over the last five days had its own folder – with sub-folders inside each main directory that contained search data, trending tags, analysis captures and service records. Only there was a folder missing. The one that corresponded with yesterday's activity. The one that would have been flagged as soon as she hit record. As soon as Sinclair Whitman began strangling that poor woman.

Someone had deleted the folder.

A shiver ran down Spook's neck. They knew what she'd done. More importantly, they knew what she'd seen. And if they were prepared to frame an innocent man for murder, what would they do to her?

Chapter Eleven

"That's our story, yeah? We tell Caesar the guy went for the gun," Banjo shouted across at Acid. Shouting, because he had both windows down on the vintage S-Type and was going well over the speed limit. Shouting, because Bob Dylan was turned all the way up on the stereo. "We tell him the neighbour was trying to be a hero and we had no choice. I mean, it's the truth. Sort of."

Acid Vanilla closed her eyes behind her sunglasses. "In my experience, the more you plan out what to say, the easier it is to trip yourself up. We've done nothing wrong. That's the only energy you need go in there with."

Banjo cleared his throat. "I wish I had your confidence."

"Who says I'm confident?"

"Well, it's easy to be when you're the boss's favourite, I guess."

"Who says I'm his favourite?"

Banjo looked at her. "Come off it, everyone knows you can do no wrong in Caesar's eyes. What's that about, anyway? You guys had a thing?"

Acid pulled down her shades and stared at him. She waited for him to catch her look. To see she wasn't messing around. "Absolutely bloody not. And don't ever say anything like that to me again. You hear me, Banjo? I'm good at my job. That's all. Now shut up about it. We carried out the hit. Got the right mark. That's all that matters."

She returned to looking out the window, at the imposing structure of Battersea Power Station, now more of a shell than a building. Rumour was they were turning the shell into high-end apartments. That'd be about right, Acid thought. Soon enough the whole of London would be high-end apartment blocks. That and Tesco Metros, maybe the odd Subway restaurant. The people born here were being priced out of their own city. Like Acid and her mum had been all those years ago. It's what happened. Progress, they called it. She looked at the clock above the rear-view mirror.

"Is that the right time?"

Banjo looked, then at his Rolex. "Yep, we're going to be late." He stepped on the gas.

Chapter Twelve

Beowulf Caesar was not a happy man. Two days ago he'd been in sunny Monaco, meeting with an Omani oil baron and completing plans to rid him of a troublesome rival. They'd drunk well, eaten well, the whole trip spent in luxury. Now he was back in miserable rainy England, having to deal with idiotic operatives who should know better.

"Bloody buggering piss."

He stood in the large bay window that looked out over the vast grounds of Kennington Place. It was a nice day outside – sunny for the time of year – but Caesar rarely left HQ in the daytime these days. He hadn't done since they'd moved operations here a year earlier. A move he'd been regretting lately. Kennington Place was a magnificent country house that Caesar had acquired a few years back that stood in the beautiful surrounds of Royal Tunbridge Wells. It was grand, extravagant, and most importantly set the right tone for visiting clients. But Caesar missed

London. Missed the fine dining, the expensive boutiques. Missed the beautiful boys of Soho, too.

There was a knock on the door. Caesar walked back behind his desk and composed himself. He was a large man in both height and girth. Especially since he'd taken a more sedentary, executive role in the organisation. But he liked to think the extra weight only made him more intimidating.

He placed his cane on the desk. "Enter."

The door opened and Acid Vanilla strode in with her head high and her chest out. "Morning, boss. You wanted to see us?"

Banjo Shawshank followed on behind, dragging his Cuban heels on the antique crimson carpet. Caesar didn't look at either of them but gestured for them to sit in the two chairs facing his desk. They did as instructed, watching quietly as Caesar went through a well-played-out show of tortured contemplation. He liked to make his operatives sweat. He moved over to his large, leather-topped desk and placed both hands down, leaning over to speak to them.

"Tell me, chaps. How do you think it went last night? And before you say anything, I've already spoken to Doris this morning. So choose your words very fucking carefully."

Acid opened her mouth but Banjo beat her to it. "Yeah. About that. What happened was, there was this neighbour... Bloody nuisance he was." He spoke fast, jittery. "We were all set. Waiting for the facial ID software to give us a match, and he bangs on the door, screaming the place down. We had to let him in. Didn't we, Acid?"

Caesar considered Acid Vanilla as she folded her arms and huffed. She would have had this handled in a quick minute, but Banjo was digging a hole for them both. He saw her eyes drift to his cane, taking in the ornate Chinese carvings down the sides. Caesar had had it commissioned from a weapons expert in Bangkok a few years earlier. Acid had been the one sent to collect it. So she knew it wasn't simply a cane. A sharp blade was concealed at one end and a Taser at the other.

"We've got them both sitting there, freaking out, and we didn't know what to do," Banjo went on. "Then out of nowhere the neighbour screams, tries to get my gun off me. I don't know what happened but my gun went off, shot him in the face."

Caesar paused a moment, then got to his feet and prowled around the room, coming up behind his two operatives. "Banjo, stand for me, will you?"

Banjo swallowed loudly, showing his hand. He stood up.

"How long have you been working here now, Banjo?" Caesar asked.

"Two-two years."

"Two-two years? What, is that four?"

Another loud swallow. "No. Two years, boss."

"Hmm. Not that long. But you enjoy working for me? For my organisation?"

"Sure do. This is the elite. The only place to work if you're a hired kil—" He stopped himself in time. Luckily for him. Caesar wasn't fond of that term, he thought it gauche, too on the nose. Banjo coughed. "If you're a pest controller, I mean. An eradication expert."

"Tell me again, Mr Shawshank, what happened last night?"

"I-I've told you. We ran into a small issue. But we got the job done. The mark was eradicated. It would have gone like clockwork if the facial recognition system hadn't crashed."

Caesar gave a forced cough. "Oh, so it's not your fault.

It's my fault. It's Raaz's fault. Shall we get her in here, see what she has to say for herself?"

"No, I didn't mean that. I was only trying to point out: last night was a series of mishaps that happened beyond our control. No one's to blame."

"You are to blame!" Caesar yelled. "This is on you. And it's on her. So please tell me again: who is to blame?"

"But I... If it was..."

Before Banjo had a chance to formulate the right words, Caesar lunged forward and jabbed the Taser into his neck. The skinny fool vibrated in mid-air for a few seconds then fell, banging his head on the back of the chair and knocking himself unconscious.

Caesar looked at Acid. "Silly me. Wrong end."

"Sorry about him, Caesar," she said, sitting upright. "He's cocky. But he'll learn."

Caesar returned to his chair and placed the cane on the desk, pointed straight at her. "Maybe he will. But I'm already tired of talking about this."

He looked out the window and ran his hand over his bald head, drumming his stubby fingers against the layer of fatty muscle where his cranium met his neck.

"You've been getting sloppy, my dear." He glared at her. She went to speak but he waved her down. "I'm not just talking about last night. I've noticed a distinct lack of focus in you recently."

Acid looked at her hands. "I need a holiday. Get my head together. I was planning on speaking to you about it. Even before last night. Before you called us in. It's not an excuse."

Caesar chewed at the inside of his cheek. "You're not losing your edge, are you?"

"Come on, Caesar. Do you honestly believe that?"

"I don't want to. But here you are telling me you need a holiday. *Need?* Like some pathetic civilian who's been working too hard on the spreadsheets. Oh boo-fucking-hoo."

"It's not like that," she told him. "We all need rest now and again. Even you. I make it sixty-one jobs I've done so far this year. That's fifteen more than any other operative. Give me a few weeks off and, I swear, I'll be my old self again. I'll work right through to the new year. Deal?"

"Deal?" Caesar growled. "Do you think you're in a position to make deals presently?"

Acid held up her hands. "Bad choice of words. But I'll be a much more efficient employee once I've had a few weeks of rest and recuperation."

Caesar glanced again to the window. "Fine, take two weeks. Do what you have to do."

"Seriously?"

"Yes. Now piss off before I change my mind." He waved her away. "Keep me informed of your whereabouts and don't tell anyone I'm giving you time off. We don't want the world thinking I've gone soft, do we?" He pointed at Banjo, who was coming around. "Take that with you."

"Do I have to?"

"If you don't want me to turn him into a new rug, yes. Get him out of my sight."

Acid stepped over to Banjo who was now laughing to himself. She grabbed him under the armpits. "Time to go home, Sleeping Beauty," she said. "I've got a holiday to book."

Chapter Thirteen

Spook sensed something was off the second she stepped into her building. A strange energy hung in the air and it tickled her intuition, made her uneasy. As a scholar of maths and science, for her not to simply dismiss this as magical, superstitious thinking, it had to mean something, didn't it? She crept up the stairwell, walking backwards to sooner get eyes on the door of her apartment. As she got half-way up, she stopped dead. Her stomach dropped into her butt. The door of her apartment was wide open, the lock hanging loose from its splintered housing.

Spook's next thought was to get the hell out. Go to the police. Show them the recording. But she'd seen enough movies where people who blabbed to the police ended up dead. She couldn't trust the authorities to protect her. Not yet. If Cerberix were sending people to break into her flat and framing innocent people for murder, it wasn't a massive leap that they could bribe a corrupt cop to silence her.

As far as Spook was aware, she had the only existing

copies of the recording. One on the thumb-drive, and one saved on her laptop. Both of which were in the rucksack on her back. That meant she had some leverage. Protection. For now. The second she handed the recording over to the police she could forget about it.

She got to the top of the stairs and padded along the corridor to peer into the front room. Every drawer was open, tipped out onto the floor. Comic books and papers littered the carpet. They'd even slashed her couch. But there was no sign of any intruder. Whoever had been here had already left.

Spook shut the door and stood with her back against it. She half-expected someone to leap out at her. But nothing happened. She went into the lounge and inspected the damage.

"Ah, man."

They'd smashed her Manga figurines. Snapped her Xbox discs. She couldn't help feeling that was unnecessary. The poor couch, too. She sat on the arm and tried to gather her thoughts. She couldn't go back to work, not after this. But she couldn't stay in her apartment either. Not if they were looking for her.

She walked through into her bedroom. Her idea now was to pack a bag, get on the first train out of London. Brighton, maybe, or Cornwall. She'd book herself into a little guest house on the seafront. It was off season, but that was a bonus. Once she found somewhere safe, she'd do the right thing. Tell the world the truth about what happened to that poor woman.

With renewed energy, Spook pulled her suitcase from under the bed. That was it. She'd hide out. Find somewhere where no one would look. Then set up some cast-iron encryption and send the recording to the police. The FBI too. Plus the media. They couldn't hurt her if they were in prison. They couldn't hurt her if the entire world knew what they'd done.

But as Spook slid open her wardrobe door, all thoughts of seaside guest houses and doing the right thing went out the window. A masked man leapt out at her. Spook screamed as he forced her onto the bed and jumped on her. He was big. Almost twice her size. His hands gripped her throat.

"Where is it?" he asked. He had a gruff London accent and spit flew from his mouth as he spoke. "Tell me where it is and I'll let you live."

Spook pushed her pelvis up, trying to wriggle free. But he was too heavy for her. "Okay... I'll give it... to you," she said "Please... don't kill me..."

The man stared down at her. The mask was black wool with holes cut for the eyes and mouth. His lips were pale and unkind. His eyes bloodshot, filled with hate.

"Get up." He released his grip on her. "But don't try anything clever or you're dead. Understood?"

Spook sat up and gasped air back into her lungs. She looked at the man. "Understood."

"Where is it? Show me."

Spook slid off the bed. Her analyst mind was working overtime as she assessed the situation. She knew the second she handed over the recording she was dead. But if she didn't give it him, the result was the same. What she needed was that elusive third option. She walked into the front room with the guy close behind. Her rucksack was on the couch. She tried not to look at it.

"So?"

She turned to look at him. He'd drawn a knife.

"I put it on a thumb-drive," she stammered, thinking on her feet. "It's in the kitchen."

The man gestured with the knife for Spook to move. She walked slowly, playing for time. In the kitchen she headed to the three drawers underneath the microwave, searching her peripheral vision for anything that might help: the coffee machine, one of three kitchen knives in a block by the fridge, a metal corkscrew.

"I mean it. I'll kill you," the man growled behind her. His knife toyed with Spook's lower back, jabbing into her kidney. He grabbed the corkscrew as they passed. "Don't get any ideas."

"I wasn't. I swear. All I want is for this to be over."

"It will be. Soon enough."

The way he said it, he might as well have done an evil laugh afterwards. That settled it. Spook had to do something quick or she was dead. She knelt down and made like she was pulling on the bottom drawer.

"It's in this one," she said, twisting round to look at the man, showing him the earnestness in her eyes. "I put it here for safe keeping, but it's stuck." She went back to the drawer, tensing her arms and shaking without pulling. "I think something's jamming it from inside."

She went at it again, giving it the full routine but still unable to get the drawer open. The man hopped from foot to foot and mumbled for her to get a move on.

"I'm sorry," Spook whimpered. "I can't get it open."

The masked man shoved her out the way. "Let me try."

The second he knelt down Spook jumped to her feet and grabbed a knife from the block. She stabbed down hard, aiming for the man's neck but only managing to embed it a little way into his shoulder. It was good enough. He yelled out in pain.

"Fucking bitch."

Spook made a dash for the lounge and grabbed her rucksack. But she wasn't quick enough. The man was already on his feet and blocking her only exit. He had her, and he knew it. He pulled off the mask, revealing himself to be in his mid-forties with droopy features and heavy stubble. Spook's stomach turned over. Him removing the mask was bad news. People like him didn't show their faces if they were expecting to leave witnesses.

"You're fucking dead." He sprang forward and got an arm around her neck. She struggled to free herself but he was too strong. The sharp bone of his wrist pushed against her throat. She tried to scream but no sound came out. It couldn't end like this. She was starting to pass out and she knew if that happened she wasn't waking up again. She had to try something. She managed to lift her legs onto the arm of the couch and got purchase with her feet. Then, as her head spun and her vision faded, she pushed off with all the strength she had left.

The force sent them both flying backwards into the door. The man hit it hard and Spook heard a strange squelching sound. Moments later he released his grip and Spook dropped to the floor, clasping her neck and fighting for air.

"Leave me alone," she cried, snot pouring from her nose. "Please leave me alone."

The man stood in front of the door with a strange expression on his face. As though he'd seen a ghost. Spook got to her feet and cautiously moved nearer. Ready to move if he did. But it was soon clear his moving days were over. The metal coat hook that hung off the door was embedded deep into the back of his skull. Blood was already gushing from the wound.

Spook let out a small yelp that was part relief, part surprise, part... *What the hell do I do now?*

She ran back into the bedroom and stuffed clothes into her suitcase. Then she grabbed her passport and credit card, picked up her rucksack and, leaving the dead assailant hanging from the hook, got the hell out of there.

Chapter Fourteen

The leaves were turning a rich amber and falling from the trees as Ethan Clarkson and Sinclair Whitman strolled through the impressive grounds of Ethan's country retreat. A humble affair was how he often described it, but the reality was over four thousand square feet not including servant quarters, sitting in its own vineyard along the Sonoma Valley.

"How are you holding up?" Ethan asked, once they were far enough away from the house. "Have you slept since you got back?" He shoved his hands deep into the pockets of his Stefano Ricci cashmere gilet. It was cold, even for this time of year, but they were outside for a reason. Away from the help. Away from microphones and webcams.

"I slept like a baby," Sinclair replied. "Straight after take-off and the whole way back. And yes, before you ask, I made sure I got out and got seen. Went to my poker night, went to my club. It's all good, Ethan, don't worry. There's at least three people who'll swear they were with me that night."

"Well, I do worry," Ethan said. "You know I could care less what you get up to in your private life. But when it affects Cerberix..." He trailed off, noticing a rise in his voice. He took a deep breath. A reminder to himself to stay calm. "All I'm saying is, this is a new world we live in. One that we've helped to create. Eyes are everywhere. You can't carry on like you used to."

Sinclair stopped. "Are you scolding me, Ethan?"

"No, I'm not scolding you. But I need you to be more careful."

They set off walking again, Sinclair with his head raised and arms held behind his back. "No one knows I was even in London. I took my private jet. There and back. No records exist of me even being there. Now with the spic chef taking the fall, what's the issue?"

Ethan hesitated, didn't want to say the words out loud. "There's a recording." He coughed, pushing his chest out. "Of the... incident."

"A recording? Are you certain? How?"

"Our new project, the Data Collection unit. One of the Watchers logged onto your personal webcam. Not sure how it happened. Why I keep telling you to use your executive login, it's scrambled."

Sinclair waved this away. It was useless telling him. He was too old. Too set in his ways. He thought he was bullet-proof and maybe he was, but Ethan had to make him see this wasn't going away so easily.

"And I'm recognisable in this recording?"

"Oh yes," Ethan replied, kicking at a pile of leaves. "I've seen it. It's you all right, strangling that hooker. Jesus, Sinclair. What happened? Too old for you, was she?"

"Actually, yes. I was after something younger. But my usual facilitator was out of town, so I made do with an escort agency." He made a face. "Bad idea. The girl was playful at first. Good company. But then she started getting sassy. You know the type – didn't know when to keep her damn mouth shut. Two Viagra down, and if I'm still having problems that's on her, not me."

Ethan didn't flinch, by now he was used to the old man's candour. "So, what? You thought if you couldn't fuck her you'd kill her?"

"I saw red. I snapped. But the recording is no more, yes? Everything's taken care of?"

"With any luck."

"With any luck? What the hell does that mean?" He narrowed his eyes at Ethan. "You know, I wouldn't put it past you to use this. Is that what's happening here? Payback for the photo?"

Ethan picked up a thin birch twig and twirled it around his fingers. "Don't worry. I've hired someone to take care of the rogue Watcher, and to retrieve all copies of the recording."

"Take care of? You mean…?"

Ethan looked away.

"Well, shit, son. You might have gone up in my estimation. Grown a pair at last."

"Thing is, I messed up initially. Hired some cheap goon. It seems you get what you pay for, even with hit men. But don't worry, I've done more research. We've got the best in the business working on it. It'll be done. Next day or so."

Sinclair threw his hands in the air. "Then why in heaven's name are we freezing our nuts off out here?" He looked at his watch. "Come on, man. As far as I can tell, there's nothing more to talk about. It's done. Taken care of."

Ethan turned to Sinclair. "This can't happen again. You

hear me? Jesus, once the keynote goes out we'll be the number one tech company in the world. That means more scrutiny, not less. More people gunning for us."

"Yes, I am aware of this fact. What do you take me for?"

Ethan sighed. The problem with Sinclair Whitman was he was old money. Never had to work a day in his life, never had to strive. Not like Ethan. He'd come from nothing. He hadn't been able to bribe people, have Daddy pay his way to the top. Sinclair believed he was untouchable, and perhaps he was, but Ethan had seen enough seemingly untouchable people destroyed these last few years.

"Don't fret, son." Sinclair patted him on the shoulder. "I promise I'll be more careful from now on. I'll get rid of every fucking computer in every house I own, if that helps. Consider me told." He held his one hand up limply and slapped it with the other. Then he placed both hands on his hips and peered at the clear blue sky. "All righty. Well, the sun's far enough over the yardarm. What's say we head back and you crack open that bottle of fifty-year-old single malt I bought you for your birthday?"

And with that, the CFO of Cerberix Inc. was off, striding back to the house with a spring in his step and not a care in the world.

Ethan watched him for a few moments. Maybe he was right. Maybe he was making too much of this. But tell that to his indigestion. Tell it to his irritable bowel. He should be on top of the world right now. Gearing up for full celebrity status, hailed as the new Jobs, the next Musk. Yet here he was with his asshole twitching nervously as he followed on behind. Still, Sinclair was right about one thing: money talked. You could always buy yourself out of a hole.

Problem was, now Ethan had started down this path – covering up murders, hiring hit men – he couldn't help but think it would be a tricky road to come back from.

Chapter Fifteen

Acid had climbed into bed the minute she got home, and fell asleep the second her head hit the pillow. She hadn't even had the energy to get undressed. Fourteen hours straight through. It might have been a record. But that's what happened when your nervous system was at breaking point.

Once showered, she sat at the kitchen table with a strong coffee and a blueberry and chia seed muffin. Ready to book that holiday. Ready to escape her life for a few weeks. So when she opened her laptop and a notification informed her of a message from Caesar, she almost threw it across the room. She logged into the Annihilation portal and clicked on the message informing her of a rat infestation that needed her attention.

"Fuck off. Are you kidding me?"

She thought about replying, but it was pointless. When a message came through you dropped everything and reported in. What it meant was a new job.

What it meant was Caesar not playing fair.

Acid shut down the laptop and hired an Uber.

Then she threw the blueberry and chia seed muffin across the room.

———

THE FINE GRAVEL of Kennington Place's driveway crunched under her boot as Acid got out of the taxi two hours later and slammed the door. It was ten past one in the afternoon. She should be on a plane now, Sipping at a large G and T.

She walked around the back of the mansion and down the metal steps that led to the secure entrance. Caesar had given no clues why he'd ordered her return. Not even in the six text messages that had pinged in quick succession once Acid had turned her phone on. He'd given the order and, like always, she had to obey. Acid would never use the word 'pimp' in Caesar's presence, but some days it felt like it.

At the bottom of the steps she removed her sunglasses and looked into the eye-scanner next to the door. With a hydraulic puff, the door slid open. Acid marched down the corridor and took the lift to the top floor.

"You have got to be bloody joking." The doors has opened to reveal Alan Hargreaves sitting on the leather bench outside Caesar's office.

"Acid Vanilla. What a treat."

Acid despised Alan Hargreaves. Always had done. He might have been a crack shot and one of the best snipers around, but he was also a total creep and an abject moron to boot. You only had to consider how he'd misread the codename system to see that. Caesar let his operatives choose their own name, based on their original initials. It was the only part of their past they hung on to. As Hargreaves' real initials were A.H. he could have chosen anything: Atomic Hammer, Anvil Hex. Even Airplane Hangar would be better. But no, the stupid prick had gone for Alan Hargreaves. Zero imagination.

Acid flicked her shades back on and joined him on the bench. Her day was getting worse by the second. The pressure in her head was intense. "Don't tell me, Caesar's put us on a job together."

Hargreaves sniggered. He was a small, weasel-like man with an eternally moist top lip and a comb-over that was fooling no one. "We can but hope. We haven't worked together for such a long time. Do you remember Venice?"

Acid rolled her eyes. How could she forget? Stuck in the penthouse of the Belmond for nine long days, waiting for Hargreaves to get the right shot.

"I'm not sure why we're here," he went on. "I got a message from Caesar this morning, asking me to come in as soon as possible. You?"

"Same."

Hargreaves sniggered. "The plot thickens."

"How long have you been waiting?"

He looked at his watch. "Twenty minutes. I'm sure he'll call us in soon."

Caesar liked to make people wait. It was a power move. Acid leaned her head back against the wall and closed her eyes, trying to zone out as Hargreaves reminisced about the Venice job as though it was some romantic holiday they'd shared. Her mind drifted to white sandy beaches and palm trees, a blue, tranquil ocean. She wouldn't let this setback derail her. Whatever Caesar wanted, she'd get it done. Quickly and without fuss. Then she'd be away.

The door creaked open and Ethel's head appeared. She beckoned Acid and Hargreaves inside. They followed her through to where Caesar stood looking out of the window behind his desk. He didn't turn around. Ethel gestured for them to sit, before joining Doris on an antique chaise longue on the far side of the room.

"What's this about, boss?" Acid asked. "I'm supposed to be on hiatus."

"Yes, well, circumstances have changed." Caesar turned from the window and closed his eyes, pained. "I can no longer agree to time off. Not yet."

Acid clenched her jaw. "But we agreed. This is best for everyone. Two weeks. That's all I want."

Caesar's eyes stayed closed. "I understand, but no."

"No? What do you mean?"

"I mean you can't have a damn holiday." He opened his eyes and glared at her. "We've had a new job come in and I need you on it. You're still one of my best operatives, Acid. Even on a bad day. This is an important job. A high-profile client."

"Ah shit." She sat, already resigned to it. "Go on then, hit me. Is it a tricky one?"

"No. But it has to happen fast. Next few days. The client is Cerberix Inc." He paused, nodding as it sunk in. "Yes. Exactly. High profile as hell. Some IT bod saw something they shouldn't have, and the bosses want rid. Want it to look like a suicide but are happy for an accident. As long as it's done quick. You're to recover a file as well. Some recording. It'll be on the mark somewhere, most likely a thumb-drive."

Acid looked at Hargreaves. "What about him?"

"He goes with you. Backup. You might need a long-range option. The mark is in the wind. Cerberix panicked and hired the first cheap freelancer they could find. Some thug. And wouldn't you know it, he fucked up. Got himself killed. Not only that, he tipped the mark off and Raaz believes they're now on their way to Paris. She has them on CCTV buying a ticket for the Eurostar this morning." Caesar finished talking and stared at Acid. A bead of sweat ran down his forehead.

"Fine. I'll do it. But on one condition."

"Go on."

"I work alone. Solo mission. And before you say anything, if they want this done fast, sending two of us will muddy the waters. I can get you a suicide. Can definitely get you an accident."

Caesar narrowed his eyes and breathed heavily down both nostrils. "All right. We do it your way. Hargreaves, your services won't be required. Ethel, Doris, show him out and debrief him."

Hargreaves turned to Acid. "Spoilsport. I was looking forward to working together again."

She ignored him. The Sinister Sisters appeared either side and led Hargreaves out. Acid waited a beat, then turned back to Caesar.

"I do this job. Then I want a whole month off."

"You've a bloody cheek, girl. But all right. Where will you go?"

"Not sure yet, somewhere hot and out of the way."

Caesar sighed. "Right then. Get this done. Then take a month. You can fly out from Paris. Raaz will send the job details over to you within the hour."

Acid glanced at her watch, her mind racing with flight times and connections. It was a few minutes after two. If she was going on holiday straight after the job, there was something she needed to do first. She slid her sunglasses on and told Caesar she'd see him in a month.

Chapter Sixteen

It was a stretch calling the place where you landed in Stornoway an airport. A strip of tarmac with a café would be nearer the mark. Only, today the café was closed. Acid made her way through security and called a cab from a payphone. There was no taxi rank outside. There was barely a road. A lot of sheep, though.

It was a bad line but the woman in the office confirmed there'd be a taxi there in five minutes. Acid hung up and went outside, wishing she'd brought a more suitable coat than her trademark leather bomber. It was always so much colder in the Hebrides. The thought came to her: maybe she should look for another home, somewhere closer to London. But, as before, she tossed the idea aside. This was the safest option.

The taxi arrived a few minutes later. A beat-up Skoda in silver with an orange stripe down each side. The driver opened the boot and Acid hauled her holdall inside. Then she climbed into the backseat and gave the gruff man behind the wheel the address.

"Foiseil Blar House, please. It's near the Old Mill."

Ten minutes later they pulled up. "Here y'are, hen," the driver mumbled. "Call that fo' punds."

Four pounds. It was another world up here. Acid shoved a ten through the gap in the Plexiglas and told the driver to keep the change. After retrieving her suitcase from the boot, she stood in front of the large building for a few minutes. Like she did every visit. Readying herself for what she might find inside. It never got better. It always got worse.

She ventured inside and up the stone steps to her right that led into the reception area. A window led through to a small office space where a rotund, white-haired woman sat reading a tattered paperback. She was here every time Acid came. Mary, she was called. She had a kind face and thread-vein-flecked cheeks that dimpled when she smiled. She looked up as Acid approached.

"Oh, hello there, dear. Are you visiting someone today?"

Acid leaned on the thin ledge and spoke through the holes in the glass. "I'm here to visit Louisa and pay her invoice for this quarter."

"Of course, the lovely Louisa. And you're family?"

"Yes. We've met before. I always pay in cash. Do you remember?"

Always cash, always in person. Nothing to tie them together. No electronic trail.

Mary licked her finger and sorted through a pile of receipt books. "Of course. And you have payment with you today?"

Acid leant down and zipped open the front of her suitcase. She pulled out a zip-locked bag containing a bundle of notes and slid it across the counter.

"Lovely. I will have to count it. Do you want to go see her in the meantime and I'll do you a receipt?"

Acid looked over at the large double doors to her left. "Yes. Why not?"

"Lovely. I just need to see some ID, then I can buzz you through."

Acid went back in the suitcase, double checking for the correct passport.

"It's a bind, I know," Mary said. "But we need to be careful these days. It's the rules. Health and safety or something."

She'd mistaken Acid's pout for annoyance. People often did. Truth was, Acid appreciated the checks and extra security, it was why she'd chosen Foiseil Blar House. That and the fact it was in the middle of nowhere.

She located the passport. "Here you go." She handed it over and watched as Mary scanned it and typed something into a computer. Acid closed her eyes. Tried to make peace with the situation.

"Here you go, dear." Mary returned the passport. "Now if you can stand by the doors, and when you hear the buzzer push on through."

Acid did as instructed. Then made her way along the dark corridor that led to room five. She'd made this short journey many times these last six and a half years, but it didn't get any easier. As she neared, she saw the door was open and peeked her head around. Sometimes Louisa was asleep. Sometimes she was in the TV room with the rest of the residents. But today she was awake and in her chair by the window. Acid went in.

"Hi Mum," she said. "How are you?"

The woman didn't respond. She didn't even acknowledge she'd heard. Acid ventured further inside and sat on the chair opposite.

"Louisa?" she tried again. "Are you there?"

This time the old woman turned and her face broke into a smile. She looked well. She had colour in her face and her eyes sparkled in the light. She looked like herself again, the person she had been.

"Oh. It's you," she said.

"Yes," Acid said, wiping her eyes. "It's me."

The two women sat looking at each other for a short while, nodding their heads in agreement.

"Do you know who I am, Louisa?"

Louisa fiddled with her hands. "Yes. You're the girl from next door. I always thought you had a lovely way about you. How are your mum and dad?"

Acid sniffed. "They're fine. How are you doing?"

"Can't complain. I'm going into town later. I've got a few bits I need to get before the party."

"A party?"

"You'll come, won't you? I'd love you to be there."

Acid went to hold her hand but stopped herself. "Yes. I'll be there. I'd like that."

"Excellent, we'll have a ball."

Acid stood and went to the window. Grey sky and fields as far as the eye could see. "I'm sorry I've not been to see you for a long time," she said, out the window. "I've been working too hard."

"That's okay, darling. I understand. You're busy. We all are."

Over on the horizon Acid could make out a herd of cows. Those long-haired ones with the horns.

"I'm going away for a while. On business and then a holiday." She turned back to Louisa. "I wanted to see you before I went." Returning to the chair, she took hold of the old woman's hands. They were ice cold. So unlike the soft, warm hands that had held her all those times. She was about to say something else, when there was a bustling in the corridor and a nurse walked in carrying a black bin bag.

"Oh, I'm sorry. I didn't realise anyone was here." She spoke to Acid, then turned to Louisa, raising her voice, giving it the whole bit. "Well, apart from this one. How are you today, trouble? Still breaking hearts?"

Louisa giggled girlishly and waved the woman away.

"I won't be a second, then I'll leave you to talk." She bent over and picked up the waste bin, emptying out a single balled-up tissue. "I'm Mel," she said. "You the daughter, are you? You can tell. Good genes with you two."

Acid looked at the old woman in the chair.

Good genes. Jesus.

The bats gnawed at her nerves.

"Oh, heavens, no. I didn't mean... I mean, it's not always genetic, is it? Only a small percentage and—"

"Don't worry. I know you didn't mean that."

"No. I was only saying, you know, same bone structure."

"Thanks." Acid stood and went over to her, lowering her voice. "How's she been?"

Mel sighed, serious now. "She has her good days. But they're getting fewer and far between, I'm afraid." She stared at Louisa as she spoke, and Acid could see real concern in her eyes. Compassion, you might call it. "We've had to calm her down a few times. She gets scared, angry. I caught her slapping someone in the TV room a few weeks back. An old fella in his nineties. Poor old sod, he hadn't a clue what was going on." Acid laughed despite herself, and after a few seconds Mel did too. "She's a feisty one, I'll give her that." She looked Acid up and down. "I'd say you take after her in that regard as well."

Acid stared at the woman, trying to gauge where she was going with this.

"Well anyway, I'd better get on. It was nice meeting you. And don't worry, your mother is in good hands."

"Thanks."

Mel left and Acid turned to face the old woman. She'd gone offline once more. There were bursts of consciousness now and then, but mostly when Acid visited she was like this. Staring at nothing, unresponsive.

"I've not been doing too great, Mum," Acid whispered, sitting down. "It feels like my past is catching up to me, and I've run out of places to hide."

Acid would never have said this to anyone else. Not even her own mother if she'd been compos mentis. But it helped. She brushed a strand of hair from Louisa's face and tucked it behind her ear.

"Anyway, I have to go now, Mum," she said. "It'll be a while until I see you again. Take care of yourself. They're good people here. They'll look after you." She stood and kissed Louisa on the head. She smelt like soap. "Don't be going around hitting anyone, all right? Unless they deserve it. In that case, give them hell."

She moved to the door. She had to get out of there. The walls were closing in. Leather wings battered at her psyche. She had one foot in the corridor when Louisa called out.

"Alice? Is that you?"

She spun around. The woman was looking right at her.

"Yes... Yes, Mum. It's me." She hurried over and knelt in front of her, held onto her bony hand. "It's Alice."

Louisa's face opened up. "You're such a good girl. I never meant for any of this."

Acid put her hand on her cheek. "Any of what?"

"If they ever touch you, you'll tell me, won't you? I never wanted this for you, my darling."

"It's not your fault, Mum. I know it isn't." Acid held

onto Louisa's hand with all she was worth. A bond that stretched out beyond illness and pain. Beyond the darkness of their shared past.

Louisa coughed. "Well, I should get going. My daughter will be home from school soon and I need to get some groceries. Will you see yourself out?"

Acid laughed joylessly to herself. "Sure, Louisa. I'll see you later. I've got somewhere to be myself." She walked to the exit and paused a moment in the doorway. It was time to be that cold-hearted killer Acid Vanilla again, time to get focused. It might have been her current state of mind, but something told her this new job wasn't going to be as straightforward as she first thought. She took a deep breath, cracked her knuckles, and left her mum's room.

She didn't look back.

Chapter Seventeen

In the end it took Acid two planes and three large G and T's before she felt like herself again. Whatever the hell that meant. But now on the final leg of her journey – in business class on her way to Paris – she was at least ready for her mission. She pulled out her tablet and shifted in her seat, putting the plane window behind her as she logged into Annihilation Pest Control's dark web portal. Once again it was running as slow as an arthritic sloth.

"Bloody hell, Raaz, pull your finger out." The skin on Acid's neck bristled as she tapped at the login button, as if doing this ever speeded it along. It was usual for the Annihilation portal to take longer than regular servers (something to do with the secure hosting and firewalls), but this was ridiculous. She refreshed the browser window, using the web link in her bookmarks to access the site. The URL was a series of numbers, letters and symbols, meaning no one would ever simply happen upon the site. Unless, perhaps, they sat on their keyboard the wrong way. But even then all they'd find was a forum for crypto-trading, with a membership area that they'd be unable to access no matter how hard they tried.

Eventually the login screen appeared and Acid typed in her details, hit submit. Once inside she was met with a direct message from Raaz Terabyte, as expected. Acid clicked on the zip file attached and opened up a folder of photos and some intel on the mark. The usual stuff. The body of the message read:

New assignment. As discussed with Caesar. Client is high-ticket so don't mess this up. The Albanian will meet you tomorrow in Paris, usual place.

No *hello*. No *how you doing?* Acid enlarged the first photo in the file. A headshot, most likely ripped from the passport database. The woman was in her mid-twenties, mixed race, though it was hard to tell from the photo. That was the problem with the passport database, you never got a great likeness. Acid opened the next file. A better photo, but older. From a US college yearbook, by the looks of it. In this one the mark was smiling. Underneath the scan was a name: Spook Horowitz.

"Oh, come on. That's got to be bullshit." She said it out loud and a man two rows in front turned and glared at her. "Sorry," Acid mouthed at him, tapping her earphones. "Podcast."

Acid returned to the tablet and clicked open the main document to see the mark's real name was indeed Spook Rosella Horowitz. It also said she was twenty-seven. The only child of Michael and Fariza Horowtiz, both deceased. Born in Columbus, Georgia. She'd attended the Michigan Institute of Technology from 2012 to 2015 and majored in Computer Science. Then a stint in Silicon Valley. Then a relocation to London, to work at Cerberix Inc. UK. It was an impressive CV.

"Why are you on my hit list, little Spook?"

Acid carried on reading. The report said the girl had seen something she shouldn't have and was blackmailing her bosses. Raaz had included CCTV images taken a day earlier in Paris. Acid flicked through the photos. The so-called tech-wizard had been picked up on four cameras in the Boulevard Saint-Germain area. One of these was on the corner of Rue des Sèvres, the same street that contained a grocery store where the mark's credit card had pinged twice in the last twelve hours. So that was where Acid was heading first.

She clicked open a new browser window and searched properties in the area. Her eyes widened as she saw who owned one of the apartments on the same street.

"Bloody hell, Spook."

Sinclair Whitman, Chief Finance Officer and co-founder of Cerberix Inc. A quick Google search told her he was back in the States but, regardless, if Acid's hunch was correct – and her hunches often were – this was a bold move on the mark's part. A good plan, truth be told. If someone wants you dead, hide in the last place they're likely to look. The only problem for Spook Horowitz was she hadn't factored in the depth of knowledge available to Annihilation Pest Control.

But Acid still had work to do. Had to ensure her theory was correct before she struck. Plus there was the recording to retrieve – an imperative part of her mission, the report said. The word, *IMPERATIVE*, written in capital letters. Acid sat back in her seat. Whatever's on that recording must be damaging as hell if they're going to these lengths.

Also in the pack was Acid's reservation information under her current alias: Melissa Font. She was to stay at a small boutique hotel in Montparnasse, a short distance from where she suspected the mark to be hiding out. Acid clicked open the invoice. She was booked in for three nights. Not long for a job like this. She bit her lip, sensing Caesar's heavy presence breathing down her neck. He wanted it done in three days. It'd take her two. She'd be lying on a beach by the weekend.

Acid closed the laptop down and pressed the call button above her head. They were scheduled to land in thirty minutes. Time enough for one more drink.

Chapter Eighteen

Hiding out in Sinclair Whitman's Parisian apartment was a huge gamble. Spook knew that. But so far, so good. She'd even found a spare key once she'd gotten in through the fire escape, so could come and go as she pleased. Not that she was in the right headspace to visit the sights. She'd been lucky with the masked man. But the threats weren't going to stop. Not while she still had the recording. She was sure of that.

She had, however, risked a few trips to the café on the corner. For supplies. To stop herself going stir crazy. Which was where she was heading now. With her collar up and a beanie hat pulled down low over her eyes.

"*Bonjour. Ça va?*" the owner sang, as Spook approached the counter.

"Yeah, um, *bonjour*. Can I have *deux* croissants?" Spook tried. "*S'il vous plaît.*"

The man didn't seem to mind her terrible attempt at speaking French. He lifted a see-through cover on the counter and picked out two large croissants, placed them in a paper bag.

"There you go, *mon ami*. Six euro."

Spook handed over the money and stuffed the croissants in her rucksack, checked her laptop was still there. It was. : Just as it had been in the elevator five minutes earlier.

"*Au revoir*." Spook pulled her beanie down and stepped out onto the street. It was a nice day out. Peaceful. A small park lay opposite Whitman's building and Spook scurried over there. It was stupid, but she needed fresh air. She'd only stay a few minutes.

She found a bench over to one side with tree cover all around. No chance of anyone sneaking up on her. She took out one of the croissants and gnawed on it greedily. It tasted good. The pastry was flaky and buttery with a hint of salt. It was true what they said, they did taste better in France. Though now Spook wished she'd bought herself a coffee to go with it.

She was considering going back to the store, when a man entered the park on the opposite side. He was mixed race, with short afro hair that faded to skin at the back and sides. He wore a dark grey pea coat, with a green scarf wrapped around the bottom half of his face. This wasn't unusual for the time of year, but along with his notable height it gave him a sinister edge that Spook didn't like. The man didn't look at her directly but meandered around the half circle of grass and sat on the bench positioned to the right of her, next to an old lamppost in dire need of a paint job. Spook watched him out the corner of one eye, croissant frozen in her grasp as her mind flicked through a list of possibilities and likely outcomes.

If he was here to kill her then he'd have done it by now. There was no reason he'd toy with her like this. The place was deserted, and the tree cover meant no one from the surrounding apartment blocks could see much of what was going on. But if he had been sent to kill her and hadn't done so yet, what did that mean? Most likely he'd have instructions to retrieve the recording. He'd need her to lead him to it. Spook put her arm around her rucksack and pulled it close.

"Stay cool, dude," she whispered to herself. "He's a regular guy. Probably lives around here."

The man pulled his scarf from his face and stared over at her. A stare that would make anyone shift uneasily in their seat. Even if people weren't trying to kill them. Spook took in the deep scar running down one side of the man's face.

Shit.

Was this it? Had he come for her? She didn't take her eyes off him as her breath froze behind her ribs and her knuckles whitened around the straps of her rucksack.

The man reached for something inside his coat and Spook let out a small yelping sound. This was it. She screwed up her eyes and tried to make peace with the fact that, in a second, the man would pull out a gun and splatter her brains all over the cherry blossom tree behind her.

An image flashed across her memory. Her parents at her graduation ceremony. They were both so proud. So full of love for her. She'd let them down and now she was going to die here. Alone. On a cold bench in a deserted Parisian park, so far away from home.

She tensed every muscle and waited. Nothing happened. She opened one eye. The bench opposite was empty. The man nowhere in sight. With a shaking hand, Spook shoved the last of the croissant into her mouth and stood to leave. She felt sick. What was it her *nenek* used to say to her when she was being bullied? *Hendak berani berlawan ramai.* It was an old Malaysian saying, meaning: If you want to be brave, you must face your enemies head on.

Spook couldn't go on like this. The paranoia. It was making her ill. If someone was coming for her, she had to know who it was. Otherwise she'd be looking over her shoulder forever and that was no way to live. She swung the rucksack on her back and hurried back to the apartment as fast as she could.

Once inside, she locked and bolted the door. Then she drew the curtains and took her laptop into the bathroom, the only room with no windows, and locked that door as well. She nestled down on a pile of towels in one corner. This would take some time.

She opened her laptop and logged onto her Watcher portal. She had a passing worry that Cerberix would have deleted her profile. But no, she could still access all the information she needed. Including Ethan Clarkson's email address. She bashed out a short piece of C-Sharp code on a text editor: a simple Brute Force attack that would sift through hundreds of thousands of password combinations to gain access. Or so she hoped.

Spook could write this type of code with her eyes shut but the process took time. She pasted the source code into the compiler and went to get a drink. Hacking was thirsty work. So was being on the run from a killer.

In the kitchen she selected a glass from a cupboard above the sink and filled it to the brim with cold water. She wondered briefly if the water in Paris was safe to drink but dismissed the thought, it was the least of her worries. She was about to take a long drink when there was a banging on the door.

Shit.

She tiptoed over, listening carefully.

"*Bonjour*," a voice said from the other side. A man's voice. "Sinclair? Are you home? I heard footsteps."

Spook stared at the door, hoping somehow it would give her some answers. The man knocked again, his voice friendlier now. "Come out, Sinclair. I know you are home. You are avoiding me?"

He wasn't going to let up.

"Hello?" Spook tried, putting her face near the door. "Can I help you?"

"Who is this? Where is Sinclair?" he said, sounding less playful.

Spook put the glass of water on the small key table beside the wall and brushed herself down.

"I'm so sorry," she said, opening the door and putting on her best smile. "My name's Shauna. Shauna Whitman."

The man in the doorway was short, with thinning dyed-black hair greased back in a ponytail. Going by the sagging skin on his neck and hands, Spook guessed him to be in his late sixties. His face, however, told a different story. Or tried to at least. It was stretched taut in a perpetual rictus. The result of many facelifts.

"*Mon Dieu*. I was expecting Monsieur Whitman." He held up his hands in mock surprise.

"I'm Sinclair's niece," Spook said. "From California. I've got my finals coming up in a month and my dear uncle said I could stay here a few weeks, to study. Away from distractions."

The man sniffed. "I see. I live over the corridor. Your uncle and me, we are acquaintances from a long time. Or we were. I have not seen him for at least three years." He looked away. If his face wasn't so rigid, it might have had a look of sadness.

"Well, thanks for stopping by. I'll let my uncle know you said hello. Mister…? *Monsieur*…?"

The man was staring off into the middle distance. He blinked. "Please tell Sinclair that Clement said hello. That will do."

"Sure will," Spook told him, making to shut the door.

"Very well. *Au revoir*, Shauna Whitman."

Did he give her a weird smile as he said that? Like he knew something? Spook brushed it off. She was being paranoid. Same as in the park. She closed the door and locked it. Locked all the bolts. Put both chains on. Then she picked up the glass of water and downed it in one go before returning to her laptop.

The program was still running. And as Spook waited, her mind drifted again to the poor woman in the video. She hadn't been able to watch it again since that first time, but the images, the actions, were imprinted on her memory. *Uncle Sinclair.* That evil bastard. He'd pay for what he did. They all would. The whole stinking lot of them. Whitman, Clarkson, whoever sent that guy to her apartment. Spook was determined now. She'd show the world what they'd done. If it was the last thing she did.

The laptop screen flashed and Spook's stomach did a somersault. She was in. Clarkson's personal email account. Jackpot. She settled herself in front of the screen and perused the information on offer. Nothing immediately stood out. No emails from anyone called Top Secret Assassin Network or anything similar. She read a few threads. One from an accountant. One from a Victoria Secret model Clarkson had been trying to date. One from his brother. But nothing from anyone even remotely resembling a hired killer. She looked in the recycling bin, but it was empty. She was starting to give up hope, when she clicked on his *Sent Items* box and there it was. Clarkson had archived the thread from his inbox but it was still there – an email exchange between the CEO of Cerberix Inc. and a man calling himself Beowulf Caesar.

Spook read through the emails and a shiver ran down her spine. They were written in coded language – talking about an infestation, a rat problem that needed taking care of – but the message was clear. They were arranging for Spook to be killed. For a pest to be eradicated. One email from Clarkson in particular spoke of him having someone mess up and how he now needed the issue rectifying. As soon as possible.

Spook read on. In the final part of the thread this Caesar guy was telling Clarkson that he'd send his top operative to handle the situation. Would have it done by the weekend. Spook swallowed. Today was Thursday. She stared at the name of the operative mentioned:

Acid Vanilla.

"Okay," she whispered to the screen. "Let's see what you're made of, Acid Vanilla."

She cracked her knuckles and opened a new browser window. Now the real research began. And if she was going to survive the next few days, she had to work fast.

Chapter Nineteen

The handsome Frenchman had a strange expression playing across his swarthy Gallic features. Conceited, you might call it. Overconfident. Acid had met him – Lucas – at the train station a day earlier, when she'd accidentally spilt her take-out coffee all down his front. He was incredibly sweet and charming, playing the incident down and asking if he could buy Acid – or Melissa Font, as she introduced herself – a replacement coffee. And now here they were, in the middle of the day, writhing around naked on his bed.

Lucas rose up from kissing Acid and cast her with a crooked smile, placing a soft hand on each of her bare knees. "You will like very much," he told her. "I am expert." His voice was deep and gruff, and he seemed to be both smirking and pouting at the same time. No mean feat. His large trapezius muscles rippled in the light from the window as he eased Acid's legs apart and, not breaking eye contact, slowly lowered his mouth between them.

Acid groaned, playing her part as best she could. But her heart wasn't in it, and her mind certainly wasn't. She squirmed about, groaned some more, ruffled Lucas' thick wavy hair, but all the while she was thinking about her current mission. About Spook Horowitz.

"Melissa? This is okay?" Lucas asked, popping his head up.

"Oh yes, it's wonderful," Acid lied. Truth was, even if she hadn't been so distracted, Lucas wasn't the crowd-pleaser he clearly thought himself to be. In fact, he was typical – in Acid's experience – of most good-looking men his age, who seemed to believe a mere eagerness to perform would cut it.

"You do not like?" Lucas' thick eyebrows met over his fine nose.

"Yes! You're amazing," Acid purred, upping her game. "Don't stop, will you? Please."

As Lucas returned to slobbering about like an overeager puppy, Acid turned her head to look out the window, watching the building opposite. The reason she was here – the reason she'd orchestrated the coffee spillage and the boozy lunch that had led them to Lucas' apartment – was that his front room was directly opposite Sinclair Whitman's residence. From her vantage point on the bed, Acid could see straight into his open-plan lounge and kitchen. The curtains, shut since she arrived, had recently been opened and now she saw movement behind the glass, a round face at the window, with black hair and glasses. It was her. Had to be.

"Got you," Acid whispered.

Now the mark's whereabouts were confirmed, Acid could move. The client had specifically asked for a suicide, but they'd have to make do with an accident. No way they'd want the mark's body found in that particular apartment. Acid felt a ripple of relief flow through her. She'd do it today. Somewhere outside. Wait until the mark left the building and push her in front of a passing Metro train. Then she'd get the next plane out of here. The Maldives perhaps, or Mauritius.

"*Mon chéri*. You are ready for me?" The Frenchman came up for air. No staying power these youngsters. He blew his fringe from his eyes. "Now we make love, yes?"

Acid sat up and put her hand on his chest. "Listen, sweetie. We'll have to stick a pin in this, I'm afraid. I've got to go meet someone."

Confusion furrowed Lucas' brow. "But you say you not know anyone in my city?"

"Yes, I did, didn't I? But they're arriving today. Now in fact." She swung her legs over the side of the bed and slid off. "We'll do this again though. Promise." She grabbed her phone from the nightstand and moved to the window, firing off a few shots with the zoom function on the camera. The mark was peering out on the street below. The idiot. She was face on and the light was decent. Despite the distance, Raaz could get a match.

"What are you doing?" Lucas asked, standing beside her.

Acid held up her phone. "Oh, you know, sweetie. Insta-gram and all that. Beautiful view, right?"

Then she scooped up her clothes and made for the bathroom.

"But what about me?" Lucas whined, gesturing forlornly at his wilting penis.

Acid spun around, holding up an imaginary watch on her wrist. "Sorry, sweetie. You sort yourself out if you need to. I have to freshen up."

As she closed the door to the bathroom she heard Lucas

huffing loudly, the way only the French can do. Lucky escape, she thought, as she locked the door and got dressed.

An hour later, back in her hotel room and freshly showered, Acid logged onto the Annihilation portal to find three messages. The first was from Raaz, telling her CCTV had picked up the mark entering Sinclair Whitman's building three days earlier.

"Super, thanks for that now. You could have saved me a garlic douche."

The next message was from Caesar, moaning about how she was taking too long, how this was an important client, a new account. Acid deleted the message without replying. And the next one, also from the boss, more of the same. She was about to log off, when a direct message window popped up. He wasn't letting up.

CAESAR: What the hell is going on? Where are you?

Acid's first thought was to ignore it. But he could see she was online. She typed back.

ACID VANILLA: In Paris! As arranged. Now have confirmation on the mark's location. Will happen today. Let you know when complete.

She had hoped that would be the end of it, but no. A reply appeared almost instantly.

C: Make sure you get proof. Video or photo. The client requested it. Also, what the hell is taking so long?! Not like you. Should I be worried?

Acid chewed her lip. She could do without the lecture.

AV: No. Nothing to worry about. Give me one day. It's done.

Then she'd be free. For a while, at least.

C: Fine. Report back the second it's done! I mean it!

Acid reached for the blister pack of Paracetamol that lay on the nightstand and forced two capsules through the foil backing. She was about to log off for a second time, when yet another message box popped up. What the hell did he want now? But as she returned her attention to the screen, she saw it wasn't Caesar. Or Raaz. Or anyone she recognised.

555p00k: Acid Vanilla. Need to talk.

Acid sat upright on the bed and lifted the tablet onto her knees. The message portal was secure. Annihilation operatives only. Her first thought was it was Banjo messing around.

AV: Talk about what?
555p00k: Your assignment. I'm the person you've been sent to kill.

Acid let out an audible snort. It had to be Ethel and Doris. Testing her loyalty. The old witches had form with this sort of thing.

AV: Don't believe you.

She cracked her knuckles and waited. Whoever it was, they were taking their time. Proof she'd guessed right – Acid had long had the Sinister Sisters down as single-finger typists. Not a euphemism. A minute later the reply appeared:

555p00k: Name is Spook Horowitz. I know you've been sent to kill me because of what I saw Sinclair Whitman do. You've been hired by Cerberix. Your code name is Acid Vanilla and you're in Paris. Near me.

Acid paused. Read the message again. Then she typed back:

AV: How are you contacting me? This is a secure network.

555p00k: Piece of cake for me. I hacked into the White House database when I was 13. Your system doesn't compare. Tell Raaz Terabyte she needs to sort out the backdoor in your code. The reason I'm doing this is I need your help.

Acid paused. If this was the mark, she wasn't bold, like she'd first thought. She was just plain old crazy. Or grasping at straws.

AV: I'm here to do a job. Why would I help you?

Acid picked up a glass of water from the nightstand and took a long drink. She watched the screen. Something felt off.

555p00k: Because I'm being framed. Because an innocent woman is dead. Someone who links to your past. Once you know the full story you'll understand. Meet me face to face. I'll explain. You'll want to hear this.

Once more Acid snorted out loud. Who the hell did she

think she was dealing with? She stared at the words, wishing she had the wherewithal to close the laptop and get on with the act of killing. But she couldn't. *Links to your past.* What did she mean? Something weird was going on and Acid needed to know what. Besides, if she got the mark out in the open she'd get the job done quicker than she hoped.

AV: Fine. Will meet. But I'm not promising anything.

555p00k: Understood.

AV: Where?

555p00k: Top of the Eiffel Tower. Midday. Come alone.

Acid glanced at the ceiling. Nothing like being dramatic. She finished her glass of water and replied to the message, telling the mark she'd be there. Then she shut the laptop and closed her eyes. Whatever this Spook had to say, she'd hear her out. But after that, she was a dead woman.

Chapter Twenty

Spook gazed up at the imposing metal structure of the Eiffel Tower and sipped a take-out coffee, holding the paper cup against her lips and letting the steam warm her nose and cheeks. Was this the dumbest idea ever – meeting face to face with someone who wanted to kill you, and who was set to receive a lot of money once they'd killed you? Well, possibly. But right now it was the only play Spook had.

She looked at her watch. It was a few minutes after twelve and the park here at the base of the tower was a sea of couples. Each one clinging to the other, fighting the chill of the fall air so they could be here. Together. In Paris. Underneath the famous monument. As if in some way this would make their love more special. More real.

Spook finished her coffee, throwing the empty cup in a bin. She had no time for loved-up couples at the best of times, but when you were being hunted by the world's top female assassin it did tend to highlight your sense of aloneness somewhat. Still, right now the more people that were around, the better. From everything she'd discovered about this Acid Vanilla character, Spook believed she'd stick to her word, didn't think she'd pull anything so gauche as to bump her off without hearing her out first, but she wasn't taking any chances. She joined the short line of people waiting to ride the elevator to the top, and took her place behind a man and woman, getting as close as possible in an effort to fox any sniper that might have a sight trained on her. She scanned the crowds and wondered if her would-be killer was already here. Hidden. Watching her. Would she even recognise her if she saw her? All she had to go on was an old photo, found after a long trail and a lot of dead ends.

Bouncing quickly from foot to foot as the line filed down, Spook went over what she was going to say to this terrifying enigma who wanted her dead. She only had one shot at this, she knew that. But from all she'd discovered about Acid Vanilla, it was a shot worth taking. The similarities were there. Now if she could just sell this the right way, and tug on the old heartstrings enough, she might just pull it off. The problem was, the whole plan relied on Acid Vanilla being capable of empathy and compassion, and that was in no way a certainty, but it was all Spook had. She had to try.

She got to the front of the queue and showed the man the e-ticket on her phone, bought from the website earlier. It had cost twenty-five euros for access to the top. Twenty-five euros to meet the person holding your fate in their hands.

The man waved Spook into the elevator and she took her place along the back wall, waiting as more lovebirds climbed aboard. She counted eight couples in total, all of them staring doe-eyed at each other, probably a few vin rouges down, eager to get to the top and have their Amazing Romantic Paris Experience. None of them noticed the small, mixed-race oddball standing in the corner, with an oversized bobble hat pulled down over her eyes and an expression not dissimilar to that of an old family pet who's just realised this particular trip to the V-E-T is one way.

The elevator quaked and juddered as they travelled the three hundred metres to the top. The couples were still at it, snuggling up to each other, obsequious in their union and oblivious to everyone else. Spook wondered how many engagement rings were being held nervously in pockets, how many men here were mentally rehearsing the next half hour. She couldn't blame them, of course. She'd been mentally rehearsing the next half hour all morning.

They reached the top of the tower and the doors slid open to reveal a vista of unbroken blue sky. Spook hung back a few seconds, allowing all the couples to vacate before stepping out herself. The air was a lot colder up here, with more of a breeze. She pulled up the collar of her vintage ski jacket and burrowed into it as she walked over to the side and looked out across Paris. Even someone as cynical as Spook had to admit it looked kind of beautiful. If she was here for any other reason she might have even enjoyed it. As it was, all she could think about was finding Acid Vanilla and saying her piece. After that, it was down to the gods. For the second time this month Spook said a prayer to herself, still feeling a phoney but thinking it couldn't hurt.

She made her way to a gold-plated telescope that pointed out over the river. There were fewer people on this side and her plan now was to wait. Acid Vanilla would have a more up-to-date image of her to go off, so the ball was in her court. Hell, it had been from the start. Spook shoved her hands deep into her pockets and waited. Around the other side of the viewing platform a woman shrieked, making Spook jump. But it was a happy shriek. A shriek of excitement from the first of today's future brides.

"You know, I'm such an idiot sometimes."

Spook spun around on hearing the voice. A woman stood next to her, staring out into the sky's endless blue expanse. This woman was a few inches taller than her, but still smaller than she'd imagined, with thick, dark brown hair. She had the collar up on her leather jacket and her large sunglasses hid most of her face, but Spook knew straight away it was her.

"I was looking out over Paris, thinking it didn't seem right," she went on. "That something was missing. Then I realised, it's because I can't see the bloody Eiffel Tower."

Spook stared up at her. "Is it… you?"

"Yes. It's me. At least I think so." She – Acid Vanilla - was more well-spoken than Spook had expected, with a heavy undercurrent of British sarcasm in her tone. "So, you've got me up here," she continued, brusquely, "but I'm not waiting around. It's bloody freezing. Say what you need to say, quickly. But like I told you, I'm here to do a job."

"I understand what you're saying," Spook stammered. "But my hope is when you hear the full story, you might change your mind."

Acid shifted her stance, as if to get a better look at her. "You're still not telling me anything."

Spook looked around. "Is anyone with you? That man?"

"What man? I'm here alone."

"In the park the other day. He was watching me. And then today I saw him as I was coming to meet you. He followed me but I lost him."

Acid frowned. "What did he look like?"

"A tall, black guy. Jamaican, maybe. He had a scar down one cheek."

Acid was quiet for a moment, staring out over the city.

She had a perfect pout, Spook thought. Perfect cheekbones, too. Menacing, but striking.

"Who you're describing sounds like Barabbas Stamp," she said quietly. "But that's impossible. Like I say, I'm working alone."

Spook scrunched her nose up, squinting into the bright sky. "He was a scary looking dude. Could have been the guy that you know."

"No," Acid said. She looked at Spook, her face still rigid with tense coolness. "Well, if that's all you came here to tell me..."

"No, wait. Please. I didn't mean to be watching Sinclair Whitman I was drunk. Being stupid. But then I saw him kill that poor girl. They said it was his private chef who did it. But it was Whitman. It's so messed up." She spoke fast, the words pouring out of her. "He killed an innocent girl and now they're paying you to kill me so they can cover it up. You okay with all that? Do they know I've got a copy of the recording?"

"They know. I'm to recover that as well. I'm guessing you haven't got it on you right now." Spook shook her head. "Well, don't worry, I'll find it. It's what I do. Blackmailing these people was a stupid move, you do know that?"

Spook scowled at her. "I'm not blackmailing them. I wouldn't know how to start. Geez, I'm running for my life here."

Acid sighed. "Sorry, kid. But you're not selling this, and I've got my own shit to deal with. I'm going now. I'd say I'm sorry, but I'm not."

She turned and stuffed her hands in the pockets of her jacket before striding towards the elevator.

"I've got skills," Spook shouted after her, despair rasping

at her vocal cords. "I found you, didn't I? I could help you. Work for you. Or something."

Acid kept on walking but Spook followed her. This was her last chance.

"She was a sex-worker," she cried, then lowered her voice as people looked over. "The girl, I mean, the one Whitman murdered. She was an innocent girl, down on her luck. Trying to support her young son." Acid stopped. She turned to look at Spook. "It's true. Her name was Paula Silva. She was a high-class escort. Wrong place, wrong time. With the wrong client, I guess. Her little boy's name is Alex. He's four years old. There's no one else at home, so he'll grow up an orphan, passed around the system. All because of what that bastard did. And you're going to let him get away with it."

Acid was silent for a long time, her face rigid and expressionless, eyes hidden behind sunglasses that reflected back nothing but blue sky. It was an unnerving sight. And when she eventually spoke, her voice was quiet but emotionless. "What are you asking me?"

"Not sure," Spook said, as adrenaline surged through her system. "To let me live. To maybe help get back at those murdering pricks."

"Fucking hell. This gets better. Are you totally insane?"

"Think about it. You don't have to kill me if the person who hired you is in jail. Or dead."

"Aww. But I like killing people."

Spook couldn't tell whether she was being sarcastic. "Come on. I know who you are. What you do. But you know more than most how hard life is for people like Paula Silva. For her son. Don't they deserve justice? Help me, please."

Acid tilted her head, dropped her weight to one hip.

"Do you know how preposterous that sounds? If my boss knew I was even talking to you he'd be apoplectic. If I do what you're suggesting, he'd be putting a price on my head. And I wouldn't blame him." She looked away. "Sorry, kid. Can't help you."

The elevator doors pinged open and Acid climbed aboard.

"Please," Spook tried again. "You aren't all bad. I know it."

Acid kept her head down. The elevator was filling up. Spook was desperate. If Acid left, it was over.

"Alice. Please."

Her head snapped up. "What did you call me?"

"Alice," Spook said again. "I know all about you. You don't have to do this."

As the elevator doors slid shut, Acid Vanilla looked into Spook's anxious, pleading eyes. "Yes," she said. "I do."

Chapter Twenty-One

"Idiot." Acid punched the wall of her hotel room as the door closed behind her. "You stupid bloody idiot."

She went at it again, slamming her fist into the hard plasterboard over and over until her knuckles left bloody imprints. Only then did she slump, no less angry, onto the bed and closed her eyes. She wished for sleep, some blessed respite from these chaotic thoughts of hers. But her heart was pounding and her nerves were far too raw for that.

Her phone vibrated in her pocket. A text from Caesar. In it he sounded angry and impatient, his default setting these days. It was sad, but Acid hardly recognised her boss from the ambitious, erudite man who'd taken her under his wing all those years ago. Back then he'd been a gentleman killer with a simple goal: to create the best assassin network the world had ever known. And he'd achieved it too. But he'd become power-hungry in the process. Obsessed with staying number one at any cost. Back in the day he'd have trusted Acid to complete a job in her own time. She was a craftswoman, after all. An artist. She shouldn't be expected to rush her work. But now it was all about pleasing the client. All about money and deadlines and bottom-end.

She rolled over and grabbed for her holdall, hauling it onto the bed and pulling out her tablet and a litre bottle of Grey Goose from Duty Free. She turned the rough-textured bottle over in her hands, feeling the weight. The bats willed her to crack open the top, take a few swigs. Everything would look better soon enough, they told her.

She put the bottle on the nightstand and swiped open the tablet. A quick search and she'd opened up several news sites from around the world, those running the miserable tale of the dead girl and Sinclair Whitman's private chef. She read each article in turn. All the same. Murdered woman, chef in custody, Whitman nowhere near the scene. Only *The London Standard* had mentioned her by name – Paula Silva – but the article brushed over what she was doing there. There was a small photo of her at the bottom of the page. Almost as an afterthought. She was young and nice-looking, but with a sadness to her. Acid recognised that look. Had seen it many times.

The article didn't mention her age either, but Acid would have guessed she was around thirty-five. The same age as Louisa when that vicious bastard almost killed her.

Acid stared at the screen. The mark had called her Alice. She knew about her. Knew about her past. But wasn't that impossible?

She threw the tablet on the bed and walked through into the white-tiled bathroom, where she turned on the tap and leant down to splash water on her face. It was ice cold and she opened her eyes into it, an attempt to wake herself. It made sense now – why the mark had risked meeting with her.

She straightened, meeting the glare of her own reflection in the large mirror above the sink. She had the look of a startled beast, and could tell just from her eyes she was slap bang in the middle of a major episode. Not good. But what was that phrase...? *If you're going through hell, keep on going.*

Except Acid saw something else as well, as she considered herself in the mirror. Something she hadn't noticed before. It was there in the slightly odd twist of her mouth, in the tiny lines at the corners of her eyes, there most of all in her current expression: a mixture of pain and anger – but also humanity, compassion even. That flirtatious nurse was right. She did look like her mother. More so, she looked like her mother had done when Acid was young. Before Oscar Duke. Before destiny ripped both their hearts out and danced all over them. An image flashed across her mind, her mother lying in a pool of her own blood, her face almost unrecognisable it was so swollen. Then she thought of Paula Silva. Already forgotten. A postscript to a much bigger conspiracy. There'd be no justice for that poor woman. Acid swilled water in her mouth and spat it violently into the sink. The pressure in her head was too much. The bats. Always the bats. The high-pitched chatter she'd quelled these last few days was now cacophonous.

This was her story, they told her. Her cross to bear.

She looked up from the sink. Looked herself dead in the eye. "No. No way. Don't you fucking dare."

Back in the bedroom she picked up the bottle of Grey Goose. She now had zero qualms about screwing off the cap and taking a long swig, hoping to drown any crazy notions with the strong, viscous liquid. She drank again, imploring the alcohol to do its work, to transport her to a place where none of this mattered. Where she was carefree and without conscience. A place that, although not comfortable, was a place she recognised.

She was Acid Vanilla, for Christ's sake. One of the best assassins in the world. If not *the* best. She was highly trained in many disciplines, had killed people on six continents - drug barons, African despots, government officials. She'd been tortured, shot at, had broken nearly every major bone in her body. Yet right now her hands were shaking and she had a tightness in her chest.

Shit.

Tears now?

She punched the bed by her side.

"You are a bloody professional," she yelled, emphasising each word with another fist to the mattress. She was here to do a job. That was all. Nothing special. She'd done this type of mission hundreds of times before.

More images flashed across Acid's prefrontal cortex. Faces and voices she hadn't thought about in so long. Memories buried deep inside of her. Marcia, on her knees and weeping. Begging for mercy. Telling Acid how there'd been some mistake, that she was an innocent pawn, a mule. Then that car journey to hell. With Marcia in the boot howling all the way, inconsolable after finding her boyfriend strung up by his intestines.

Acid took another drink. She could see it all in front of her, as clear as the bloody knuckles that now clutched the bottle of vodka. The hotel suite covered in blood. Marcia's severed hand on the bed. And then Caesar, albeit younger, slimmer, standing there with a shit-eating grin across his face, telling Acid this is how it was, how it would be from now on. The message was simple. Do not get involved with a mark. Do not listen to their stories. No matter how well they paint their picture of innocence.

"You exist for one reason and one reason only, my dear," he'd told her. "To remove the mark. To eradicate the problem for the client. You aren't a judge or a jury or a fucking do-gooder. You aren't paid to have opinions. You aren't paid to have a heart. You are a hired killer. That is what you do. And this," he gestured at the severed limbs, the pooling blood, the suitcase of unmarked bills in the corner, "this is what happens when you let your guard down and allow yourself to get attached."

Then later, in the back of Caesar's Beamer, with Davros Ratpack driving. Caesar friendly now, telling Acid how valued she was. Good cop, bad cop, all rolled into one. Devil and angel.

"You'll learn," he'd purred in her ear as he put his hand on her leg. "You're young. You're new to this game. Let this be a lesson and move on. It's a steep learning curve. But learn you will."

Wasn't that the truth?

So what the hell was she doing, sixteen years and many kills later, still falling for the old sob story. Letting herself get emotionally attached.

"No." She sat bolt upright. "Not going to happen. Won't let it."

She got to her feet and moved over to the bureau opposite the bed. She slid the top drawer open and removed the Glock and a spare magazine. She pocketed the spare and stuffed the pistol into the waistband of her jeans. Then she ran her fingers through her hair, took one final slug of vodka, grabbed her jacket and card key, and left the room.

It was time to finish this.

The only way she knew how.

Chapter Twenty-Two

For those wishing to experience the famously laid-back attitude of the native Parisian, the traffic-heavy Boulevard Saint-Germain on a late Friday afternoon was not the place to go. Cars and vans lurched erratically along the wide dual carriageway as drivers leant on their horns, making their presence known, and switched lanes every few minutes in a futile attempt to try and beat the system. The boulevard was a long, slow road at the best of times, but today the side on the Left Bank had roadworks half-way along and was down to one lane. Tempers were already frayed, but were exacerbated somewhat by the small American girl who was weaving her way through the traffic and getting in the way of just about everyone.

Cars braked and swerved to avoid Spook as the drivers wound down their windows and yelled French obscenities in her direction. She bowed her head, raising her hands in show of an apology as she scurried across the road as fast as her short legs allowed.

Once over the other side she stopped and looked back,

scanning the crowds of people – tourists and locals alike – glancing from one face to the next, like a watchful meerkat on the lookout for a predator. The man wasn't anywhere to be seen. But that didn't mean he'd given up the chase. Didn't mean she could relax.

Things had gone from bad to worse for Spook since Acid Vanilla left her at the top of the Eiffel Tower. Initially she'd been frozen there with fear, as her imagination ran wild. Was the enigmatic assassin now waiting for her at the bottom of the tower, ready to slit her throat as soon as she left the elevator? For this reason Spook had taken the stairs, in the hope she might slip out the back exit undetected.

There were over a thousand steps down to ground level and it had taken it out of her. But it had also given her time to think. To plan her next move. Which was to get back to Whitman's place, get her stuff and get the hell out of Paris. She'd take the first plane she could get. Put it on her credit card. Somewhere far away. Somewhere even Acid Vanilla couldn't find her. But as Spook turned the corner towards Whitman's apartment, she saw him. Sat in the park, same bench as before. The tall man with the scar on his face. She jumped behind a bus shelter but it was too late. He rose from the bench and walked slowly but intentionally towards her. Her first thought was that his composed and sinister gait reminded her of the T-1000 unit from Terminator 2.

Her second thought was to run.

Fast.

And she hadn't stopped running since. Leaving the Boulevard Saint-Germain behind, she headed down the side of a Louis Vuitton store, zig-zagging through the hordes of people coming in the opposite direction. At the end of the next street, she skipped up onto the step of a doorway for a better look over the throng. Given his height, she'd be able to see him from a way off, even with all these people. She narrowed her eyes. Nothing. But this was not the time to get complacent. Whoever this man was, he meant business. Plus she still had Acid Vanilla to contend with.

Spook stepped down from her vantage point and cut down the back of an old church. A grand and beautiful building with a tall spire and ornate pillars. She might have taken a passing interest if she wasn't running for her life. The end of the street opened out onto the wider Rue De Seine and Spook quickened her pace, moving with purpose, praying the street would lead to the river as it suggested.

She pushed on, running past expensive boutiques and tiny art galleries, past pavement cafés and exotic restaurants. She hardly noticed any of them. Her eyes were on the horizon and the blue skies above. A hundred metres or so in front was a gated area, a small square where the street she was on intersected with another. A growing tightness in her chest had now turned into a terrible stitch that was slicing her in two, and she wondered whether she might rest there a few minutes. She glanced back over her shoulder.

And her heart stopped.

There he was. About a hundred metres down on the opposite side, making big purposeful strides. Not running, still serenely ominous, but he was gaining on her. With the stitch adding to her already aching legs and lack of any real direction, he'd be on her soon enough.

She pushed on, grimacing against the pain and heading down a narrow alley that ran between two art galleries. Drainpipes dripped on her from above, and she had to wind around piles of stinking garbage bags to get to the end. There were footsteps behind her. Walking faster now. Closing in. Spook took a left down the next street. Another narrow road that ran behind a row of shops. It was also deserted. Not a good place to be. Though, if you were planning on killing someone in the middle of the day in Paris without being seen, it might have been the perfect spot. The footsteps were closer now and had fallen in time with her own. She picked up her pace, running as fast as she could towards the adjacent street where she could see people and traffic. Ten more steps, twenty maybe, and she'd be safe. He wouldn't kill her in front of people, would he?

But she wasn't quick enough. She felt a hand on her shoulder. It grabbed her and pulled her back. She went to scream but another hand covered her mouth. Then her attacker hustled her into an alley and shoved her against the wall. The impact knocked all the air out of her and she slumped to the ground. Adrenaline soared through her system, but it was useless, she knew that. She had nowhere to run. No fight left in her. She was going to die here. Scared and alone. She tried one last time to scream, but a hand grabbed at her cheeks and squeezed them together. Then a face loomed at her out of the darkness. A mess of hair and dark glasses.

"Stop yelling," Acid Vanilla rasped. "I'm trying to bloody well save your life here."

Spook's scream transformed into a strangled, confused yelp as Acid released her grip.

"What the hell?" Spook said, fighting for breath. "That man. With the scar. He's coming. He's following me."

Acid's face was stern. "I know, I saw him. I've been following you. But he didn't see us come down here. We'll stay a few minutes. Give him the slip."

"Who?" was all Spook could manage. The adrenaline was still pumping around her body and she was worried she might wet herself.

"Barabbas Stamp," Acid whispered. She looked over her shoulder, then back to Spook. "He's bad news. All I can think is Caesar got impatient with me not taking you out sooner and sent him along to finish the job. You're kind of a big deal, you know that?"

Spook scowled. "So, what? You wanted to finish the job yourself?"

"No, it's not like that." Acid bowed her head. "I've been going over what you said. About the woman who was murdered. I believe you."

"He killed her for nothing," Spook said, putting emphasis on the word nothing.

Acid moved closer. "Okay, now listen. I can't help you. Not the way you want. I'm sorry, I know that's not what you want to hear but my boss would kill me. I'm crazy even for doing this, but no news there." Spook opened her mouth to speak but Acid shushed her down. "I'll help you get you out of Paris. Away from Barabbas. But then you're on your own, all right?"

Spook swallowed. "Thank you."

Acid held Spook by both shoulders. "You ready to get out of here?"

Spook sure was, but before she could answer a third presence appeared in the alley. The man. Spook cried out as Acid spun around to face him, her gun drawn. But it was too late. She heard a whistle of air, a dull thud, and Acid stumbled forward. Spook tried to catch her but she was a dead weight and fell to the floor, unconscious. Spook watched her drop, letting out a terrified wail as she gazed up into the pitiless face of the man who'd been chasing her. And for the third time that afternoon, a hand clasped around her mouth.

Chapter Twenty-Three

Coming around, it was the smell that Acid noticed first. A dank mustiness permeating her nasal canal as she blinked blearily into the dark room. But she picked out another smell too, behind the damp. It was heady, spicy, reminded her of childhood. She opened her eyes and tried to make sense of her situation. From what she could tell, she was in some sort of underground chamber. The only source of light came from a small window, translucent with grime and dust and cut into the raw stone wall to her left.

"Here she be," a deep voice bellowed. "I thought you was never coming round."

Acid squinted through the gloom, making out the unmistakable form of Barabbas Stamp. He was standing in the far corner of what she could now see was an old crypt. That accounted for the smell: frankincense.

"What the hell are you playing at?" she asked, attempting to stand up and realising she was strapped to the chair she was sitting on, her hands fastened with cable ties. "Are you fucking kidding me?"

Barabbas walked over to her. "Calm it down, girly. All will become clear soon enough." He was holding her sunglasses and put them on. "Do they suit me, *cher*?"

Acid didn't answer. She was already sizing him up. Barabbas Stamp was tall, with a relaxed swagger and long, wiry limbs. From Haiti originally, and that was all Acid knew about him. If she had to guess, she'd say he was in his mid-thirties. Though the long, bulbous scar that started below his eye and disappeared around the angular curve of his jawbone made him look older. They'd worked together only a handful of times over the years and Acid had always found him difficult to talk to. He was guarded, like they all were in this profession, but it was more than that. He was nasty, spiteful, loved to inflict as much pain and suffering on his marks as possible.

Barabbas removed the sunglasses and tossed them on the ground.

"Caesar not thrilled with you. At all." He held up a mobile phone. "Not after I shows him the video I took – your romantic rendezvous at the top of tower. Meeting with a mark, Acid? Oh dear. She got to you."

Acid followed Barabbas' eyeline over to the far corner where Spook was also strapped to a wooden chair.

"Hey." Barabbas landed a stinging blow across Acid's face with the back of his hand. "Don't look at her. Look at me."

"Watch yourself, pal," Acid said, staring up through her fringe. "Why am I tied up, Barabbas? Why are you even here?"

"Caesar sent me. He's worried you've lost your way, taking too long to complete the job. He's worried you've lost your mind too." He walked around the space as he spoke, pausing every so often for effect. He stopped behind Spook's chair and placed his hands on her shoulders, smelled her hair. "Looks like he was correct. Seems this little missy has gotten to you."

"Not true. I was getting the job done. My way. I needed more time, that's all."

Barabbas sniffed. "Time's up."

"What? So you're here to kill us? Okay then – bloody well get on with it."

"Woah." Spook now, glaring over at Acid.

Barabbas chuckled to himself. "I'm here to clean up your mess. Do what you were sent here to do." He flipped open his phone. "Soon as I connect to Terabyte's feed, I can record my handiwork. Proof for the client. Then my orders are to take you back to Caesar. Alive. Boss wants to deal with you himself."

Acid struggled at the ties. "You expect me to simply walk on a plane with you?"

"Tsk, *cher*." Barabbas pointed over to a wheelchair in the corner. A large syringe rested on the seat. "The celebrated Dr Florestine will be returning to England from a business trip. With his poor paraplegic wife in tow."

"I see." Acid gestured at the syringe. "Muscle relaxant?"

"Deadly Nightshade. But don't fret yourself, I got the antidote, you'll be fine. Until you get to Caesar, at least."

Acid rolled the idea around in her head. "What about her? The client wanted a suicide or an accident."

Barabbas pulled out a gun, a Sig Sauer, from his belt. "Client just want it done. Same as Caesar." He spun the pistol around his finger and scowled at the phone in his other hand.

"The system's still playing up," Acid called over. "But listen, Caesar doesn't have to doubt my motivation. Or my commitment to the job. I can speak to him. Sort this out."

Barabbas ignored her. Acid glanced at Spook and gave her what she hoped was a reassuring nod, although she wasn't sure she managed it. Truth was, she was stumped. She'd been trying to get her hands free from the moment she regained consciousness, but they weren't coming off without a blade. She shuffled on the chair, judging the weight and structure. It was old, rickety, the joints where the separate pieces met were loose.

Barabbas moved closer to Spook, but keeping his eyes on Acid the whole time as he traced the gun down the side of the young American's face.

"Me think you *pale kaka*, *cher*. Playing for time. But we done here."

He stepped back and straightened his arm, pointing the gun at Spook's head, making her emit a soft, wailing cry, reminiscent of a dying cat. Barabbas snickered humourlessly. That look of terror in a victim's face, it was like vitamins to him. His finger quivered on the trigger. Acid closed one eye, bracing herself for Spook's brains spattering up the crypt wall.

"*Fout tonè!*"

Acid opened her eye. Barabbas was shaking the phone, his ire growing as he waited for a connection. She relaxed a notch. Barabbas might have been a malevolent butcher, but for now it seemed he was following his orders to the letter. Acid could only imagine Caesar had them all on a tight leash since she went AWOL.

"Wait," Acid called over, seizing the opportunity. "Spook is a computer genius. Like, a bona fide genius. She's got real value. Caesar could make good use of her at HQ." She paused, letting the words land. "Come on, Barabbas, we both know Raaz is limited." She nodded at his phone. "Case in point."

133

Barabbas looked as if he'd smelt something rotten. "You think the boss would want this *bounda plat* working for him?"

"Yeah, Acid, what are you saying?" Spook whimpered.

Acid chewed the inside of her cheek. "It's your only play, kid. It might not be what you planned on doing with your life, but you're out of options. We both are." Then, speaking to Barabbas. "Seriously, she's one of the best hackers in the world. She managed to hack into the White House, for heaven's sake, and she was only a kid."

The Haitian looked impressed. He turned to Spook. "This true?"

"Uh-huh," Spook said, between sobs.

"Well, ain't that something. Little girly has skills." He went for it again with the gun, stroking it across Spook's forehead. Then he stuck it under her chin and tilted her head back. "Not a bad looking *koko*, truth be told. Up close and all. Sweet little missy. So what you suggest, Acid? We take her back with us and she become part of the team?"

Acid leaned forward, shifting her weight onto her feet. "Caesar would welcome her skillset. I know it. We can say it's your idea."

Barabbas licked his lips. "What about the client? Can't be letting *salopri* go free when it suits. That bad for business."

Acid stuck out her bottom lip. "What? Are you saying the boss can't handle an angry client?"

"No. Not what I'm saying. Ah, here we are." He held his phone up as a wide grin cracked his face in two. "At last. We got a connection. Looks like this is the end for you, girly."

Acid watched helplessly as Barabbas dragged a stone plinth from out of the corner and set it up a few feet from Spook. Then he placed the phone on top, taking a moment to set up his shot.

"Now we ready to make a movie." He glided over to Spook and continued to trace the gun up the side of her head, taunting her, playing to the camera. Acid looked at the floor. She knew Barabbas used jacketed, hollow-point rounds. There'd be no mistaking the job was done when the client saw the footage – at that proximity the hydra-like spread of the bullet would decimate Spook's entire head.

Acid closed her eyes and waited for the shot. But it didn't come. Instead she heard Barabbas yell out like a wounded banshee. She snapped her head up to see that bold little American biting down onto the fleshy part of Barabbas' hand and him dropping his gun.

It was the distraction Acid needed.

She rocked forward onto her feet then ran backwards as fast as she could, smashing the chair against the stone wall of the crypt. It broke up on impact with a loud crash and splinter of wood. Barabbas had already managed to pull his hand free from Spook's jaws and was reaching for the Sig Sauer. She only had seconds. Acid pushed away from the wall, realising that a part of the chair was still attached to the cable tie on her wrist. It was a sturdy piece that had been part of the back support, with a sharp point at one end. She closed in on Barabbas and leapt forward, shoving the makeshift spear into the side of his neck.

He screamed out in pain as the jagged wood tore through flesh and sinew and muscle. The force of the attack sent them both toppling over onto stone floor. Acid landed on top and was able to shove the spike deeper still as Barabbas let out a deep, guttural wail. His eyes bulged at her, full of hate and madness. They both knew he wasn't walking away from this, but he wasn't going without a fight either. He lashed out with his long, bony arms and grabbed a handful of Acid's hair, wrenching her head back. She leaned into it, twisting the wooden spear, grinding it against severed nerve endings. Barabbas released another rasping howl and loosened his grip. That was enough. Acid leant forward and yanked the wood free. It was time to finish this.

With blood spurting into her face from the open wound, she stabbed down again, pushing the bloody spear through Barabbas' ribs and into his heart. His whole body went stiff and he made a sound like someone letting the air out of a balloon. Then he was limp. Barabbas Stamp was no longer a threat. He was no longer anything. With a gasp, Acid collapsed onto the cold floor of the crypt, fighting for air.

"That was crazy," Spook cried. "You killed him with a wooden stake through his heart. In a crypt. Wow. Thank you."

Acid turned her head to look at her. "Don't thank me yet. Now we have to get away from here. Fast." She rolled over and got to her feet.

"But you saved my life."

"Maybe. For now." Acid looked down at the lifeless body of her colleague. "But I can't help but think I've just signed a death warrant for the both of us."

Chapter Twenty-Four

Acid knelt next to Barabbas' bloody corpse and patted him down, finding car keys and a butterfly knife. She cut through the cable ties on her wrists and found Barabbas' phone, which had been knocked to the floor in the melee. She released Spook and handed her the phone.

"Can you get into this?"

Spook turned it over in her hands. "Not sure. I'd need special equipment."

"Nah, it's not worth it." Acid grabbed it back and examined the screen. "Raaz will have been tracking us all. She'll know Barabbas had us here. We need to move."

Spook got up, rubbing at her wrists. "Where will we go?"

Acid retrieved her Glock and leather jacket from the corner of the room. "Away from here. Caesar will know soon enough that Barabbas has failed, that we're still in play. And I wouldn't be surprised if there were more operatives after us." She was walking towards the door, but stopped. "Wait a second. How did we get here?"

Spook removed her glasses and cleaned them on her shirt as she spoke. "He dragged you to his car and bundled you in the back seat. He was parked at the end of the alley."

"Yes, and what about you?"

She put her glasses back on. "I went in the front."

"Why didn't you run?"

"Umm, he had a gun pointed at me."

"What, the entire time? Whilst he was bundling me into the back seat?"

"I don't know. Guess I sort of froze."

"You sort of froze?" Unhelpful waves of nervous energy pulsed down her spine. "Whatever. Let's get out of here."

Acid pulled a silver compact from her jacket pocket. She flipped it open and examined herself in the mirror, pulled a face. "Jesus. You got a tissue?"

Spook picked up her rucksack and rummaged around inside, handed her a packet.

"Cheers. I look like a bloody serial killer." She spat on the tissue and proceeded to wipe the blood spatter from her face. "There we are. Okay, let's move."

"But where will we go?" Spook asked.

Acid put her jacket on and popped the collar. "Well, Spook, I don't know about you, but I need a bloody drink."

They found the way out and hurried up the steps of the crypt, blinking into the bright normality of a typical Friday afternoon in central Paris. The benign mundanity of a working city. It was jarring.

Acid put her sunglasses on and considered the streets a moment, getting her bearings, then she set off along the Rue Bonaparte. There was only one place she wanted to go right now.

"Shouldn't we hide?" Spook whispered, skipping along beside her.

Acid didn't look at her. "We are doing. In a way. But I also need to work out what the hell to do next. I need a plan. And I don't know about you, but I plan a lot better when I'm a tad lubricated."

They walked down the street in silence. Down the next one too. Every hundred yards or so, Spook opened her mouth to speak – in the hope, perhaps, some choice words might appear – but thankfully they never did, and each time she shut it again. It was a good move on her part. Acid was veering dangerously close to the edge. One wrong word and she was likely to put a bullet in the kid herself.

They got to the river and Acid pulled the two phones from her pocket, Barabbas' and her own. She removed the batteries and SIM cards and threw them as far out as she could into the flowing depths of the Seine. Then she stamped the phone casings against the kerb and tossed these in two separate litter bins.

She turned to Spook. "Give me your phone."

"What? You serious?"

"Yes. Give." She held out her hand as Spook reluctantly handed over her phone, a brand-new iPhone 8.

"You won't get to the battery," Spook told her.

"Want to bet?" Acid knelt down and smashed the casing to pieces with the butt of her pistol, then she threw the SIM and what remained of the battery the way of the others. "Now let's get going."

They set off across the Pont du Carrousel and through the gardens that held the famous glass pyramid of the Louvre and, over to the left, the Arc de Triomphe. Impressive scenery, but Acid paid no attention to any of it. She'd been here many times over the years, but even if she hadn't it wasn't the time for sightseeing. As they got to the Madeleine district of the city, the streets opened out into the large square of the Place Vendôme and Acid slowed her pace.

"Here we are." She gestured over to the grand building that spanned along one side of the square.

Spook squinted at the signage. "The Ritz Hotel? Woah. We can't hide out here, can we?"

Acid sniffed. "Why not?"

"Well, isn't it incredibly expensive and sophisticated? And, you know, we're kind of scruffy-looking."

"Hey. Speak for yourself." They both looked down at Acid's scuffed boots, at her jeans with the rip in one knee and covered in crusty flecks of Barabbas' blood. "All right, fair enough. But don't worry. They know me here. Trust me."

She set off towards the impressive entrance and old Pierre – the reassuringly brusque and tight-lipped doorman that had worked the door for the last twenty years.

"*Bonjour, monsieur*," Acid called out, but the stoic Frenchman didn't let on. As they got nearer, he leaned over and opened the large glass door so they could enter. Acid removed her sunglasses and gave him a wink. "*Merci.*"

With Spook following on behind – making the sort of irritating noises people often did in places of extravagant splendour – Acid made her way down the long corridor that led off from the main reception area. Above her head, ornate chandeliers dangled crystal droplets, and along the wall, plush velvet curtains finished with gold lamé stitching framed ten-foot-high windows. At the end of the corridor Acid took a left, heading through the short lane of glass-fronted boutiques that led to her destination.

"Here we are." She slowed her pace. "Bar Hemingway. The best bar in the whole world."

She stepped inside the small but perfectly formed cocktail bar and breathed the place in, pleased that it smelt the same as always. Of leather and gin and good times. Of past glories and decadence. Of history.

"Bar Hemingway?" Spook repeated, looking around at the newspapers on the wall, the pictures of old Ernest. "Bit lame, isn't it?"

"He used to drink here," Acid told her. "And he helped liberate it from the Nazis. So, no. It's not lame."

She walked up to the bar and ordered her usual. Gin Martini, dry as a bone. "What's your poison?" she asked Spook. "My round."

Spook didn't answer. Just stared at her.

"What is it?" Acid asked.

"I've just noticed your eyes."

"Oh, that."

"They're different colours."

"Yes. I was aware. Did you not discover that little morsel of information whilst researching me?"

Spook kept on staring. "They're amazing, so striking."

"So they tell me."

"They're like David Bowie's."

"Really?" Acid said dryly, brushing it away. It wasn't the time. "Anyway, back to the important matters. What do you want to drink?"

Spook squinted at the cocktail list, twisting her mouth from side to side. "I'll just have a Coke," she said.

"You're not having a bloody Coke," Acid told her, then turned to the bartender. "She'll have a Martini. In fact, make hers a Clean Dirty."

The barman bowed in agreement and began the alchemy, picking up a large bottle of gin and solemnly making the drinks.

"What's a Clean Dirty?" Spook asked.

"Wait and see. Why don't you go sit down and I'll bring them over?"

Spook hesitated a second, then did as she was told. Acid watched as she sauntered over to a table along the back wall. Despite her compact size and cute appearance, she was ungainly. Like an awkward teenager. Not Acid's first choice for someone to help her out of this awful mess.

"You certainly can pick them." She slid onto a bar stool to wait for the drinks, noticing a bearded, prime-era Hemingway looking down on her from an old *Time* magazine cover on the wall.

She scowled back. "Don't look at me like that, Papa." His eyes were sad. Like they understood what she was going through. "Yes. I know, I'm screwed."

She couldn't spin this. She'd killed one of her own. One of Caesar's top operatives. You didn't get to walk away from something like that. Not even her.

"What would you do?" she asked him. "Fight? Run away? Blow your head off? Actually, don't answer that."

Acid knew what she had to do – leave everything behind and disappear. For good. South America perhaps, or Asia. Somewhere they'd never find her.

She glanced up at Old Ernie. His face said it was risky. It said they could still find her.

"Well, what else can I do?" she said. "I mean, I could try reasoning with Caesar. We do go way back, and I am sort of his favourite – or I was – but I don't know, that seems even riskier."

The only other option of course was to kill them first, before they got to her. But that would mean taking on the whole of Annihilation Pest Control, Caesar included. Even the thought of that made Acid's head hurt. She glanced up at Hemingway and shook her head. It was a ridiculous notion. A suicide mission.

"*Voilà, mademoiselle.*" The barman placed the Dry Martini down in front of her, along with a small silver pedestal that held small bowls of shiny, pitted olives and salted peanuts.

"*Merci beaucoup.*" Acid took a long drink. It was strong, dry, ice cold. Perfect. And so needed. The barman returned a few seconds later with Spook's drink, the same as Acid's but with the addition of a single ice cube made of pure olive juice.

Acid told the barman to keep the tab open and took the drinks over to Spook, who was fiddling with a coaster. "Put that down," she said. "I need you to concentrate."

She took the seat opposite and sipped at her drink as Spook continued to peruse the décor. Neither of them spoke for a few minutes. A rare moment of serenity, here in the eye of the storm. But it also brought the realisation they were total strangers.

Acid regarded a Hemingway print over Spook's shoulder. "You know he killed himself with a rifle he bought from Abercrombie and Fitch." She raised her glass. "Let's hear it for America."

"Hey. We're not all like that, you know," Spook mumbled. "Some of us think they should ban firearms."

Acid rolled her eyes. "Oh god, you're not one of those, are you?"

"What? Someone who doesn't like innocent people – school kids – getting killed? A liberal snowflake? Yeah, I guess I am. I guess you're not."

"I'm a rebel, sweetie. A libertine." Acid ran her finger round the edge of her glass. "I just think gun control – politics, even – those are concepts for people who believe life is supposed to have rules." She took a long sip of her drink. The kid looked disappointed, but what the hell did she expect? Twelve hours earlier she'd been ready to kill her.

"What about actual laws?" Spook asked. "Are they pointless too?"

Acid puffed out her cheeks. "Laws are made by rich old men to benefit other rich old men."

"Oh really?"

"Yes. Really. Like those ready to pay a quarter of a million dollars to have you killed." Spook's eyes widened. "That's right, you heard."

"Okay, wow. But still, you can't put them all in the same boat. Laws are made to protect the innocent. You know, like... don't kill people."

Acid leaned forward, pointing. "Most of the people I kill deserve it. You don't usually get a price placed on your head unless you're into dodgy stuff yourself."

Spook tilted her head. "Not *everyone* deserves it. Do they?"

"You're an exception." Acid gripped the table with both hands. "People in power don't give two shits about the likes of me or you. They deserve everything they get."

"Is that what you tell yourself, so you can sleep at night?"

"Piss off." Acid picked up her drink. This was why she didn't mix with civilians. She was better off with her own people. Where she didn't have to think too deeply about her choices.

"Don't forget it was me who bit that dude," Spook said. "I know you finished it but... well... I'm not some wet-behind-the-ear loser."

Acid was about to respond but thought better of it. Instead she drank as another silence fell between them.

Longer this time. It was Acid who broke it a few minutes later.

"Go on then, the suspense is killing me. How did you know?"

"Know what?"

"About my mother. The way you threw that out as I was leaving – Whitman killing the sex-worker – that was your big play. Which tells me you know about my mum. About me. You called me Alice."

Spook took a sip of her drink and pulled a face. "Jesus, that's strong." Acid glared at her. "Okay, what do you want to know?"

"All of it."

"I'm a hacker. I'm good at finding information on people."

"Even people who are supposed to be dead?"

"I guess. You've got an interesting back story."

Acid looked around. But no one in the small cocktail bar was interested in them. "I was told all records of who I was had been erased," she said. "Caesar has his best people working on it."

"Maybe his best people aren't as good as they think they are."

Acid thought of Raaz Terabyte, and how much she'd like to be there when she found out this geeky American – with her timid demeanour and terrible fashion sense – had bested her.

"I knew it was a gamble, meeting face to face," Spook continued. "Or idiotic. But I also knew I had to humanise myself to you. Make me more than a target. From every-thing I found out about you, I hoped you might still have a soul in there. Somewhere."

"Is that right?" Acid said. "You think I'm some bleeding heart, do you? Because you're wrong. I kill people."

Spook swallowed. "Yeah. But here we are. You were coming to help me get away. You said so before that guy arrived. I'd say my gamble paid off."

Acid lowered her voice. "All right, say that's true – you haven't answered my question. How did you know about my mum? How did you know that would change anything?"

Spook shifted in her seat. She paused, as if readying herself to answer the question in a way that would be agreeable. In a way that wouldn't get her head blown off.

"I've been a hacker since I was nine years old," she began. "I can get in anywhere, find anything. You must have done your research on me. I was one of the youngest people to get accepted into the MIT, aced all my classes, could have walked into any job in Silicon Valley."

"So why London?"

Spook shuddered, dropping her gaze to the glass, running her thumb down the stem. "I went through a bad break-up. I had to get away from the States for a while. I know it's a cliché, but there you go. And I liked London, and the Cerberix job paid well. I knew it wouldn't be forever. The whole point was we were training the AI to do the job."

Acid finished her drink and gestured for the barman to start up a second. "A break-up so bad you had to put four thousand miles between you? This guy must have been a real piece of work."

Spook narrowed her eyes. "Who says it was a guy?"

"Oh? I see." Acid paused. "But I still don't get how you found out about me. Like I said, they deleted my entire past."

Spook sat up straight. "Nothing is completely deleted

these days. If you know what you're doing. First thing was to work out who was coming for me. So I hacked into Ethan Clarkson's personal emails. Found a thread between him and your boss. That's Caesar, right?"

"Correct, Beowulf Caesar. A great man. Once. Still is maybe. To some." She caught herself and waved it away, gestured for Spook to continue.

"Well, he spoke highly of you as well. His most deadly operative, he said. Didn't help my anxiety at all. But he mentioned your name, Acid Vanilla, so I hacked into the Annihilation portal and downloaded your profile. Then I built a rudimentary spider program to scan the web, analysing old news articles, censuses, police and hospital reports. Any information fitting your profile. I also ran some facial recognition software I've been developing that examined any relevant photos it found. After that I had it search through files that had been superficially deleted. Those in trash cans and Time Machine software. That's where the gold is if you know how to access them. And I know how."

Acid was impressed. But didn't let on.

"*Bonjour, mademoiselle.*" The waiter appeared at the side of the table. He placed down Acid's new drink and picked up her empty glass.

"Do you want another?" she asked Spook.

"No." She put her hand over her glass. "I'm still drinking this one."

"Cheap date."

"I just want to keep alert," Spook mumbled. But her cheeks were red.

"Go on then. You found photos of me?" Acid asked, once the barman had left them.

"It took some time. But I found an old article stored on a library's internal server. A newspaper report, about a young girl who got sent to a young offender's institute for killing her mother's attacker. Alice Vandella."

She looked at Acid as she said the name. But if she was waiting for a response, she'd be waiting a long time. Acid sipped her fresh drink.

"The article had a photo – of young Alice. I downloaded it and imprinted it over your photo from the Annihilation Pest Control portal. Perfect match. So then I delved deeper, found out Alice's mother, Louisa, had been hospitalised many times over the years. Broken bones, bruises. Seems to have got herself mixed up with some bad men. Plus there were regular STI tests. Once every month or so. I didn't need an algorithm to put two and two together. She was a sex-worker, right?"

"All right, enough," Acid said. She had a sudden urge to flip the table over.

The bats said, *Do it.*

"S-sorry," Spook stammered. "I didn't mean to—"

"It's fine. Shush." She held her hand up and Spook did as she was told.

Another long silence. Acid drank as the surroundings faded away. Her eyes darted left and right. Speed-thinking.

"I was able to download a list of names – Annihilation Pest Control operatives," Spook whispered. "Raaz Terabyte needs to up her game. Or should I say, Rona Tabet does. Her real name, if you didn't know. I take it operatives use their real initials to come up with their codename?"

"That's correct."

"Well, that confirmed it for me. A.V. Alice Vandella. Acid Vanilla. It's poetic. I'm guessing you chose it because acid is something abrasive and harsh, juxtaposed with something sweet and pleasant."

"Not quite, but nice theory."

"What I couldn't find out," Spook went on, "was how you went from being in the young offender's institute to working for Caesar. That part is dark."

Acid put her drink down. "Story for another time," she said, sitting back. "Right now we have to work out how the two of us are going to stay alive."

Spook twisted her mouth. "Is it that bad?"

"Yes, Spook, it's that bad. The fact Caesar sent Barabbas means he was already doubting me. Once he finds out I've killed him and I'm helping you, he'll throw everything he's got at us."

"You can't talk to him? Try to explain?"

"Explain what? That I've gone rogue? Defied his orders? That I can't even think straight with all the noise in my head? That I feel like swallowing a bullet myself?"

Spook picked up her glass and took a large gulp. "Sorry, I just meant... I don't know... I'm way out of my depth here."

Acid took a deep breath. "I know Caesar. He'll take this personally. He'll want blood. Not only that, Cerberix are a big client."

"What do we do?" Spook asked.

Acid zipped up her jacket. "*We* don't do anything," she said. "I'm sorry, kid, I said I'd help you escape Paris and I will -we'll get to London and I'll sort us out new aliases and passports - but then you're on your own. I suggest you go far away, somewhere no one can find you." She pointed at Spook's drink. "You finishing that?" Spook shook her head. Acid picked up the glass and drank it down.

"But where do I go?" Spook asked. "And what about Whitman? What about getting justice for Paula?"

Acid sighed. "I don't do vigilante work. Not my bag. I'm officially retired as of now." She reached over and touched

Spook on the arm. "You'll be all right. But we need to move fast. The longer we stay in Paris, the more dangerous it's going to get."

"I need to get my stuff," Spook said. "From Whitman's place."

"No. Can't happen."

"But my passport is there." Spook's voice rose and an old man on the next table looked over at them.

Acid spoke through gritted teeth. "Why the hell did you leave it there?"

"I was going back to get it. But I didn't get chance, did I? Barbarella was waiting for me."

"Barabbas."

"Whatever. Plus there's a thumb-drive in the flat that contains a video of Paula Silva getting murdered. I don't know about you, but I think it's kinda of disrespectful to leave that lying around."

The hairs on the back of Acid's neck pricked up. She got to her feet.

"Fine. We'll get your damn passport." She took out a hundred-euro note and placed it under one of the glasses. "But from now on, you keep your head down and you keep your mouth shut. You hear me? Because the way I'm feeling, I'm ready to kill you and then myself. In that order."

Chapter Twenty-Five

Sinclair Whitman wasn't even trying to hide his scorn. "Man alive, will you cheer the hell up? For Christ's sake."

"Don't blaspheme, Sinclair. You know I don't like that." Ethan turned from peering out the airplane window. "And I don't need to cheer up, I'm fine."

"Tell that to your face, will ya?" Sinclair raised his glass as whisky sloshed over the side. Ethan wasn't counting, but it was at least his third since they'd set off. "What's the matter with you? We're about to become number one. Globally."

Ethan forced a smile, not easy with this tension headache he'd had since yesterday.

"Come on, Ethan, you're even making me depressed. I know the keynote is a big deal, but you're a whizz at this kind of thing. Always have been. That's why I knew you were the man to invest in all those years ago. Here, have one, will you?" Sinclair picked up the cut-glass decanter and poured him out a large scotch.

"Thanks." He accepted the glass and took a sip. It left a satisfying burn across his lips and down his throat.

"Go on, son, what is it?" Sinclair asked. He wasn't going to leave it.

"I'm just concerned," Ethan replied. He placed his glass down in the centre of a round leather coaster. "I've not yet had concrete confirmation that the… bug in the system has been removed." He held onto the glass and twisted it round as he spoke.

"Bug in the system? What the hell are you talking about?"

Ethan lifted his eyes off the glass and glanced around the cabin. It was his private jet and only the two of them travelling out today (even Marcy, his die-hard PA was on the next flight out from San Fran) but after everything that had happened, he was inclined to be jumpy.

"The people I hired to take care of your – our – little problem. They've not yet confirmed the recording has been recovered. Or that they've taken care of… well, what needed taking care of."

Sinclair took a large gulp of his scotch, finishing it. "You said it was all sorted."

"I thought it was. They assured me they had it under control. But it's been five days and I've not heard from them."

Sinclair sat back in his seat, his usual cocksure deportment slipping into something approaching unease. Or was he plain old pissed? Ethan couldn't be sure.

"We can't have this hanging over our head, son. Hell, in ten days we're going out live to thirty countries on that webcast and you need to be bringing your A-game." He slammed his fist into his open palm.

"Yes. I am aware of this, Sinclair. Which explains why I'm antsy right now."

"No need to shout, Ethan."

"Well, you asked."

"Yes, and now I know." He paused a moment. "Call them. See what the hell's going on. If they can't, or won't, solve this problem for us, then we hire someone else."

Ethan considered it. "So, what? I say, 'Hi, I'm just calling to find out whether you've managed to kill our employee and retrieve the recording of our CFO strangling a hooker?'"

Sinclair was pouring himself another scotch. "Why not?"

"Well, for one thing we don't know who'd be listening. That's why we're in this mess. What if someone hears, records me? Then we're both fucked."

Sinclair sat forward. "Pull yourself together, Ethan. For Christ's sake."

"Hey. What did I say?"

"Oh, come off it. This is not the time to be pious."

Ethan finished his scotch and handed his glass back for a refill. "Maybe I can call via a different route. Mask the IP."

"There we go, it'll be fine." He was smiling now. He handed Ethan a full glass. "You're overthinking it. Get some answers, and if it's not what we want we hire someone else. Someone who'll get it done. Today. I'm yet to find a problem where money can't buy you the answer. There's always a way. Now, cheers."

Ethan didn't answer. He didn't drink either.

"He said not to call him – the main man, Beowulf Caesar – he said he'd call me. Was adamant."

Sinclair belched. "Fuck that, we're the ones paying this shmuck, we decide what happens." He gestured to the phone, moulded into the arm rest of the seat opposite. "Call him. We touch down in London in five hours. We need this done. Agreed?"

Ethan moved over to the seat with the phone. "Agreed."

Chapter Twenty-Six

Caesar had been eyeing up a particularly tricky long-range putt when he heard the gentle knocking on the door of his office. Although, really, it was more of a soft tap than a knock – almost apologetic – as if whoever was knocking didn't want to be heard. He glanced over at the Sinister Sisters, both drinking chamomile tea on the far side of the room. They hadn't heard the door, or if they had were pretending they hadn't.

Caesar ignored it for now and returned to his shot, bending over his new Ping Sigma G putter – with its lightweight elastomer shaft – and eyeing up the hole. He had to get this one in.

Had to.

Every single shot today had veered off into the skirting board and he was about ready to kill someone.

He adjusted his grip on the club and eased back on his swing as the door went again and Raaz Terabyte put her head around. "Caesar, I'm sorry to bother you but— Oops!"

She'd swung the door open as he took the shot and the door clipped the ball, sending it scuttling across the carpet. Another skirting board job.

"Bloody, bleeding shit. That was going in." Caesar leaned back from his swing, putter in hand.

"S-Sorry," Raaz stammered. She looked down. "Wait. Is that a Barbie doll head with no hair?"

"I was out of golf balls," Caesar said. He gripped the club in both hands. "Let's have it, then. Have we heard from Barabbas?"

Raaz shut the door and moved over to the side of the room, her eyes on the golf club. "In a way."

Caesar glanced over at Doris and Ethel, who shook their heads in unison. Something was wrong.

"What do you mean?" he asked Raaz. "Stop being bloody cryptic."

"From what I can see, he was logged onto the system about thirty minutes ago." She paused, swallowed. "He had a problem connecting, by the looks of it. But I didn't notice straight away because I was on the line with Magpie. She's over in Hanoi and—"

"I don't give a flying tit about Magpie," Caesar yelled. "Tell me about Barabbas. And Acid."

"I think Barabbas might be dead," Raaz stuttered.

"Excuse me?"

Raaz backed away. "I checked his feed – he managed to sign in and was recording the job. There's footage of the mark tied up. Barabbas readying himself to eradicate her. But then – well – it's sort of unclear, but I think the mark bit him. Then there's some sort of commotion, and his phone hits the floor and switches off."

"I do not bloody well believe this." Caesar's first impulse was to wrap the putter around Raaz's head, cave her skull in. It was the least she deserved, and no one would blame him for it. No one in this room, at least. But he needed her if they were to remedy this. "I take it you followed this up?" he growled.

"Yes. I checked on Acid Vanilla, but her phone was dead too. So I did a comparative search and, as I suspected, the triangulation had them all at the same place. Barabbas, the mark and Acid. I got CCTV footage from the area. Saw them all entering the basement of the Saint-Germain-des-Prés church." She went quiet, her voice breaking. "Three go in, but only two come out. Acid and the mark. I assume Acid killed Barabbas and…" She trailed off as Caesar held up his hand for silence.

"Right. Everyone shut up." He paced up and down in front of his desk. "We can still get in front of this. Where is Alan Hargreaves right now?"

"Belgium, I think. I can check. But that's not all, boss. Sorry. It gets worse."

"Worse? How the chuffing fuck can this get any worse?"

Raaz fidgeted with a leather bracelet on her wrist, her eyes still fixed on the golf club. "I've had a call come through on the protected line. Ethan Clarkson. He says he wants answers. Sorry, boss, I told him that's not how it worked. That he shouldn't be calling us. But he's demanding to speak to you."

Caesar clenched his fists around the club. He could do without this. His whole organisation seemed to be crumbling around him. The deadliest assassins in the world and they were all acting like clowns.

He selected another Barbie head from a bowl on his desk and dropped it onto the carpet. "Fine. Put him through. I'll talk to him."

Raaz moved over to the desk and pressed some buttons, patching the call through to Caesar's phone.

"Okay, boss." She stepped away and mouthed the words, "You're live."

A voice crackled out the speaker, "Hello, is anyone there? Can you hear me?"

Caesar composed himself, getting into character. "Loud and clear, old boy. Everything okay in the old US?"

"No, it's not. I've been on hold for twenty minutes. What sort of half-assed operation are you running over there?"

Caesar didn't flinch. "Mr Clarkson, I presume?"

"Who am I speaking with?"

"You know who I am. You called me." He eyed the angle of his shot, sticking his tongue out in concentration.

"Whatever. I suppose you know why I'm calling?"

"I said I'd call you when the job was complete."

Clarkson scoffed audibly. "Well, we kind of needed that to be yesterday. Hell, we needed it to be last week."

"Yes, my apologies. We did have a few issues, I'm told. You have to appreciate, dear boy, that these sorts of jobs are a little... unpredictable, shall we say. But we have it all in hand. I assure you."

"I was told you were the best. That you'd have it done in a couple of days."

"We are the best." Caesar closed one eye and took his shot. The bald Barbie head bobbled along the plush carpet, missing the raised hole by a few inches. Caesar grimaced, but held it together. "Like I say, there were a few unexpected hold-ups, but it's done."

The voice on the line went muffled, like the mouthpiece had been covered and another conversation going on. Then louder, crisp again, the voice returned. "We can be certain of this?"

"Yes. It's done." Smiling through gritted teeth. "You have my word."

Back on the line, the voice sounded cheerier. "Well, that is good to hear. Can you also confirm you have the recording? I mean, we wouldn't want that falling into the wrong hands."

Caesar looked at Raaz. "Don't you worry, my friend. The problem has been eradicated, and all items have been recovered. Which means, of course, you can now release the second half of our fee."

The phone went silent, more muffled voices. Then, "Tell you what. You send me the recording first – proof – then we'll release the money. I'm going to be in London for the next three weeks so you can courier it over. I'll email you the address."

"Excellent." Caesar scowled at Raaz. "Is that everything?"

"Sure," Clarkson said. "I look forward to receiving the package. I'll see you later." He hung up.

"Bloody bollocks!" Caesar yelled into the ceiling.

Raaz started. "Why did you tell him that—" but he cut her off.

"What else was I going to say? That our operative is helping the mark to escape? Jesus." He lumbered over to his desk and sat. "Okay, get Alan on the blower, Banjo too. Tell them to drop whatever they're doing and get to Paris. I need that fucking mark eradicated. Today. Tell them I'll double their normal fee. And they're to bring Acid Vanilla to me." Raaz stood there a moment. "Well, go on then, piss off." Caesar blasted the words in her face and threw the putter against the wall as she ran from the room. "Jesus-bloody-pissing-hell."

The Sinister Sisters did little to hide their thin-lipped smiles. They loved it when people messed up. As Annihilation Pest Control's top clean-up squad, it was their bread and butter.

Caesar picked up a jewel-handled letter opener from his desk and held it up in front of his face, balancing it between his fingertips. "What the hell is Acid playing at? After everything I've done for her. The stupid, ungrateful bitch." He threw the dagger down. "You know, I should have seen it coming. All this talk about holidays. The sloppiness on recent jobs. She's lost her edge."

Everyone suspected Caesar had a soft spot for Acid Vanilla, and maybe he did, but he would not stand for this reckless disobedience. Favourite or not, she'd killed a fellow operative and now, for some senseless reason, she was helping a mark to escape. That was too much. Far too much.

Caesar turned to the sisters. "This won't be a concern for long," he growled. "Hargreaves and Shawshank will get the job done. The client never has to know. Then Acid is going to pay for this. You mark my words." He sat back and put his hands behind his head, an outward show of bravado to try and dampen the niggling voice in his head. "Leave me," he told Doris and Ethel.

The old women looked at each other, then placed their cups and saucers down and quietly shuffled out of the room, shutting the door behind them.

Caesar waited a minute, made sure they were far enough down the corridor, then let out a loud groan.

"Shit!"

He looked at his watch. Alan and Banjo would be in

Paris by this evening, ready to do what was required. They'd get it done. He was sure of it. He had to be. With any luck, news of this tremendous fuck-up would never get out. His reputation would be safe.

Yet, even as he told himself this, even as he left his desk and strode confidently around his office, a small voice whispered in the back of his mind. He tried to ignore it, puffed his chest out, raised his head high. But the voice kept on. Growing louder. Becoming incessant. And what it was saying was clear:

Do not, under any circumstances, underestimate Acid Vanilla.

Chapter Twenty-Seven

Acid opened her eyes and sat bolt upright on the large velvet couch, unsure where she was but sensing it was vital for her to be awake. Across the room she could make out blurred red numbers. The cooker's digital clock display. She peered around. Other objects came into focus: the large bay window that looked out over Paris, the basic but expensive décor, the original artwork on the walls. It was Whitman's apartment. She narrowed her eyes at the clock. 8.35 a.m.

"Shit." When the bats were around, Acid didn't need much sleep. In fact, she couldn't sleep most nights. But she must have dozed off. That wasn't good.

She padded over to the kitchen and filled a glass with water, drinking it down in one go. She examined the room, happy to find that old sop, Clement – Whitman's neighbour from across the hall – was nowhere to be seen. He must have slipped away after Spook disappeared into the bedroom and Acid's feigned tiredness turned into actual sleep. That would have been around five. She remembered because every hour that ticked by had felt like another nail in her coffin.

The plan after leaving Bar Hemingway had been to grab Spook's passport and get the hell out of Dodge. Annihilation knew they were here, together. They were sitting ducks. But after logging onto the airline, the first flights available weren't until the following evening. Her next idea was going to a hotel – somewhere off-grid so they could lie low until it was time for the flight – but whilst getting Spook's stuff, a drunk and tearful Clement had appeared at Whitman's door with a bottle of expensive vodka and invited himself inside. He hadn't shut up until he'd literally sent them both to sleep.

Still, Clement was an interesting enough guy, full of amazing tales. As his tongue had gotten looser, he'd told them how he'd been a decent photographer back in the day, had albums heaving with candid shots of Paris nightlife and exotic parties. After that he didn't take much convincing to show them his collection, and with all the drink and exuberance inside him he hadn't noticed Acid as she palmed one particular photo into her jacket pocket.

She took it out now and examined it in the cold light of day. A young Ethan Clarkson, taken in Whitman's apartment, maybe ten years ago. At some seedy party he'd been throwing. Acid curled up her lip in disgust at the image. The more she found out about these bastards, the more she wanted to put a bullet or two in them.

No.

She pushed the thought away and stuffed the photo back in her jeans. Right now she had more pressing issues. Like getting out of Paris alive. She put down her glass and went to locate the American, finding her in the main bedroom, face down on the super-king-size bed.

"Hey. Wake up." Acid rapped her knuckles on the door. "We need to move."

"Ugh." There was a hint of movement from the bed, a muffled grunt, but that was all.

"Spook! Get up," Acid yelled. "You are being hunted by trained killers, remember? Not the time for a bloody lie-in."

Spook sat up. "Crap. What time is it?"

"Don't worry, it's still early," Acid told her. "But we need to get a wriggle on."

"Yeah, sure, but where?" Spook asked, feeling around the bed and locating her glasses under a pillow. "We need to hide, right?"

"Yes. But we'll call at my hotel first," Acid said, looking around the room. "Get your stuff together and let's get out of here. How many bags have you got?"

Slowly Spook got to her feet. "An overnight bag and my rucksack. I've been staying in the small room, they're in there." She sniffed at herself and pulled a face. "Eugh. I need a shower."

"Later," Acid said. "We were stupid staying here last night. We'll find a hotel, somewhere off the beaten track – we can wash and rest up there. Our flight's in nine hours."

Spook rubbed at her eyes and stumbled across the hallway into the smallest of the three bedrooms. Acid took a deep deliberate breath and followed on behind.

"Bloody hell. What have you been doing in here?"

Spook was stuffing clothes and books into a small suit-case on the bed. She stopped and looked up.

"How do you mean?"

Acid gestured at the toilet rolls and comic books littering the floor. The half-eaten croissant on the nightstand. The piles of wires and hard drives on the bed. "It's like a teenager's den in here."

Spook picked up a small black thumb-drive, held it up triumphantly.

"Is that it?"

"Sure is."

"Well, there you go. Have you made a backup?"

Spook slipped the thumb-drive in the front pocket of her rucksack. "This is the backup. The original is on my laptop."

Acid walked over to the window and peered through a gap in the curtain. "And you're still thinking of leaking it?"

"I have to."

"Well, be careful," Acid told her. "Get somewhere safe first. And don't leave any trace to your whereabouts."

"I'm not stupid, you know," Spook replied. "I mean, it'd be easier with a partner…"

"Don't," Acid told her. "We've been through this." She picked up a dog-eared copy of Iron Man from the bed and flicked through it. Why anyone on the run from a hired killer needed this many comic books was beyond her.

"But after everything we talked about," Spook said. "With your mom. Don't you want to get justice for that poor girl? What was it – powerful, rich white men not caring about people like us?"

Acid shot her a hard look. "Stop it."

"Help me expose them, Alice."

Acid was over there and on her in a second, jamming a sharp fingernail into Spook's chest. "Do not ever call me that. You hear me?"

Spook gasped as though her breath had frozen in her throat. Then, without speaking, she side-stepped away from Acid's white-hot rage and finished packing up her stuff. Acid watched her for a few more seconds then strode back into the kitchen, punching the wall in the hallway as she passed through.

In the kitchen she filled up the kettle and flicked it on, locating a jar of instant coffee from one of the cupboards. It was a nice place Whitman had here. Modern, is what you'd call it. Stark. The kitchen appliances were as unused as the guest bedrooms. The toaster was box-fresh. The kettle too. Acid made a cup of hot black coffee and as she drank it, hip resting against the counter, she peered around the rest of the apartment. The more she looked, the more she saw. Or rather, didn't see. No family photos, no ornaments, no shelves rammed with books or DVDs. Not even a cupboard in which to throw those things when visitors came calling. It didn't look like an apartment that was lived in, nor even one that was used as a second home. It looked like a showroom. Or a backup plan. An if-all-else-fails hideaway. In her experience, there were only certain types of people who had that kind of security. And they weren't to be trusted.

Acid finished the coffee and went back to the bedroom. She leaned against the doorframe and rested her head on the wood. "Look, I'm sorry for being a cow."

"It's fine," Spook said. "I get it."

"I'm stressed right now, that's all. And I need you to focus. These are professionals, Spook, and they mean business."

Acid watched the young American as she absent-mindedly stuffed an old jumper into her suitcase. Then she stopped and sat on the bed, stared out the window. As though she had all the time in the world.

"For heaven's sake, kid, get it together. We need to move."

"Sorry, yeah. I'm done."

Spook zipped up her bag and slung her rucksack over

both shoulders, then went out into the lounge area. Acid gave the room a final once over before following her out. Spook was stretching in front of the window.

"Nice morning, isn't it?" she said, not turning around. She'd opened the curtains and was gazing out on one of those autumn days where the air felt good. Cold, but crisp.

Yet something else spiked the air this morning. Acid sensed it as she joined Spook at the window. Something she couldn't quite put her finger on. The bats were already awake, chattering across her synapses and prickling her nerve endings. She looked out the window, scanning the bare trees down the side of the boulevard and in the small park, registering the piles of dead leaves, crunchy and brittle, that covered the pavements and pathways. Then, as her eyeline rose, she took in the tall buildings opposite. One building in particular stood out from the rest – a white stone apartment block with fine neo-classical pillars and ornate balconies up one side. It was next door to Lucas' place. But that wasn't the reason for her racing heartbeat. Something had caught her eye. In a window. Two-thirds of the way up.

Was that…?

She narrowed her eyes.

"This is the sort of Paris day you dream about," Spook was saying. "Like an old movie. Paris in the Fall. You can imagine Marlene Dietrich or someone kicking about in the leaves. Don't you think?"

Acid didn't answer. She was only half listening. Her senses were on fire and she was certain now. She'd seen something. A flash of light in the room across the way. Sunlight reflecting off a watch maybe, or someone's spectacles.

Or the telescopic sight of a sniper rifle.

"Shit. Move!"

Acid pushed Spook with all her strength, sending herself flying backwards the other way. They fell either side of the window at the exact moment the glass cracked, and a bullet splintered the granite worktop a few feet behind them.

"Get over here."

Everything slowed down as Acid's focus dilated from macro to micro. She scrambled to her feet and dived at Spook, tackling her over the back of the couch as a second shot took out an art deco lamp a few inches from her head.

"Stay down," Acid yelled as more bullets thumped into the thick velvet couch. She dragged Spook to the side of the room where they were able to edge around the back of a large cabinet. It was unlikely the shooter had a clear shot at them here, but Acid didn't want to find out how near he could get.

"Okay, Spook, listen to me," she said, fixing the young American right in the eyes. "If I'm not mistaken, that sniper is Alan Hargreaves. One of my lot. If that's the case, he'll have got that rifle from The Albanian."

Spook stared at her open-mouthed. "Okay, and…?"

"The Albanian has access to the German military, so I'd bet on that being a Blaser rifle he's using. Now, I counted four shots so far, meaning he's got one shot left before he has to reload." Acid picked up a cushion off the couch. It was a simple move, but it might just work. Either way it was all she had. "On the count of three, I'm going to throw this cushion. When you hear him shoot, run as fast as you can towards the door, okay? He can reload in a few seconds. So that's all we've got. Seconds. You understand?" Spook's mouth hung open. Acid clenched her teeth. "Say you understand."

"Yes," Spook said. "I understand."

"All right, so he shoots, we run. Ready?"

"What about my case?" Spook asked.

Acid eyed it across the other side of the room. "You'll have to leave it. You've got the recordings in your rucksack?"

"Yes. But my clothes? My comics?"

Acid gave her a hard stare. "That man shooting at us wants to put a bullet through your brain. Forget your damn comics. Now, are you ready?"

"I'm ready."

With that, Acid tossed the cushion high across the room and the two women held their collective breath, poised like sprinters, ready to move as soon as they heard the gunshot. They watched as the cushion arced through the air, rising up over the middle couch. Acid tensed, waiting for the familiar sound of shrapnel puncturing glass and preparing to make a dash for the door. Then the cushion landed softly on the couch and bounced off onto the cream carpet.

"Bollocks."

Spook looked at her. "Why didn't he shoot?"

"Because he's good at his job," Acid said. "To be honest, I thought that was a long shot. Excuse the pun."

Neither of them laughed.

"What do we do now?" Spook asked.

Acid closed her eyes. "Plan B," she said. "Same as before. The second you hear that gunshot run as fast as you can. And don't stop until you're on the other side of that door."

"But there are no more cushions."

"I know, it'll be fine."

"But how are we going to distract him?" Spook asked, then seeing the look on Acid's face, "Oh. Oh no."

"Yes," Acid told her. "It's all we've got."

She braced herself. She could do this. Every cell in her

body told her she could do this. Her eyelids twitched. The bats echoed around her soul.

They said, *Do it.*

They said, *You're invincible.*

They said, *What have you got to lose.*

You never hear the bullet that kills you.

Acid launched herself at the door at the other side of the room – over the trenches, into the no-man's-land of the apartment. A heavy-metal band played in her head as she tore across the hardwood floor, the bass drum pounding a deep rhythm that reverberated into her chest and the heavily distorted guitar shredding the edges of her vision, focused only on the door in front of her. Every muscle in her body was tense, ready for death.

You never hear the bullet that kills you.

Time slowed again as she skidded past the first couch, pushing off against it and diving into a forward roll, hoping to confuse Hargreaves' aim. She came out of the roll and lurched for the door, had grabbed the handle and was pulling it open when she heard the shot, felt the searing pain in her shoulder.

"No!" Spook cried out from the other side of the room as Acid spun around to glare at her.

"Bloody well run," she shouted, falling through the open doorway.

For once, Spook didn't need telling twice. Acid watched as she pushed back against the wall and sprinted across the apartment with her head down. She had seconds to make it. Already Alan Hargreaves would be loading the next five rounds into the rifle. Taking aim.

"Come on. Nearly there." Acid held out her hand and Spook grabbed it as a bullet arrived right on cue. The shrapnel splintered the wooden doorframe above Spook's head as Acid dragged her to safety.

"Oh my god, did you see that?" Spook asked, as Acid helped her to her feet.

"Yeah, good effort," she rasped. "But don't get cocky. This is far from over."

Spook raised her head. "What do we do now?"

"Now we run, Spook," Acid told her. "We run."

Chapter Twenty-Eight

They were running fast through the back streets of Paris. Running faster than Acid had run in a long time. Maybe ever. "Come on. Keep up," she yelled at Spook, before cutting down an alley that ran between two cafés.

"I'm going as fast as I can," Spook said. "But I'm not so good at this sort of thing."

They got to the end of the alley and Acid looked both ways before taking a right down a narrow, cobbled street. "What sort of thing?" she asked, as Spook caught up with her.

Spook grimaced. "Sports. Athletics. The physical stuff was never pushed on me. Gifted child and all that." She gasped for breath. "My folks said I didn't need to be athletic when I showed such promise in math and computer sciences."

"I suppose so," Acid panted. "Until you find yourself running for your life, hey?"

"Where are we heading?" Spook whined. "I'm getting a stitch."

"Not sure," Acid replied. "But we need to stick to the back streets. Away from CCTV. Away from Raaz Terabyte."

They got to an intersecting road, just as narrow and winding as the one they were on but empty. They took a quick left and Acid slowed her pace, stepping into the deep arch of a doorway for cover. She grabbed hold of Spook and pulled her close.

"Come on. We can rest here a minute. Gather our thoughts."

Spook huddled into the cramped space. Her face was bright red. "Are you hurt?" she asked Acid, pointing at the bullet hole in her jacket.

"Nah. It's just a flesh wound. Keeps the game interesting, doesn't it?"

"Game? Is that what you call it?"

Acid looked up the street. "I think there's a Metro station round the next corner. Means we'll be exposed, but only for a short while. It's our best bet if we want to get away from the centre."

Spook looked down, fidgeting with the straps on her rucksack.

"What's wrong now?" Acid asked.

"Am I ever going to be safe?" she asked.

Acid sighed. "Short answer: I don't know."

"Okay. And what's the long answer?"

"I definitely don't know?" Acid put her hand on Spook's arm. "One step at a time, kid. We're in this together. For the time being, at least." She cast Spook what she hoped was an empathetic smile. "You know, I am pretty good at this sort of thing."

Spook scrunched her nose up. "What sort of thing?"

Acid shrugged. "You know – evading death, killing people."

Spook zipped up her coat. "Fair enough."

They set off again and came out on a short street that led onto Rue des Saints-Pères and then joined the busy thoroughfare of Boulevard Saint-Germain. Acid stopped at the corner and stood on her toes to better see over the sea of people. The Metro station was a few hundred metres away. They crossed the road and made their way over to the stairway that led down to the underground. Acid stepped back, allowing Spook to go first, and cast an eye over her shoulder. Her skin bristled with white heat energy. The vein in her neck buzzed like a neon tube.

"Okay?" Spook asked.

"Yes, go. I'm right behind you." She could see no immediate threat, but that meant nothing. Stealth and secrecy were Annihilation Pest Control's trademarks – and Caesar didn't hire any old thug. He'd handpicked an elite network of assassins to help him realise his vision. The best of the best. Why Acid had always prided herself on her work.

How strange it is, she thought now, that life can change so radically in a matter of days. But yet she shouldn't be surprised. This wasn't the first time it had happened. She shook it off and followed Spook down to the platform.

"Where are we going?" Spook stage-whispered, as Acid joined her by a large map of the Paris underground system.

Acid squinted at the station names. Times like this she had trouble processing so much data. Her mind was filled up with chatter, her mood too in the red to focus.

"Let's follow this nice pink one all the way to the end," she said. "Porte de Clignancourt. That'll do. I'm sure we can disappear there."

Spook followed her finger on the map. "Ah, the Sacré Cœur. I always wanted to visit."

Acid bit her tongue. "Perhaps some other time. I don't know if you remember but we're kind of in deep shit at the moment."

As if to highlight this, she'd spotted someone over on the stairwell. Someone she recognised. He was in disguise, dressed like a cartoon version of a Frenchman. Complete with a limp black beret hanging over one eye. But the stoop was unmistakable. As were those piggy eyes.

"Ah, shit."

"What is it?"

Acid chewed her lip. "Seems Alan Hargreaves fancies his chances close range."

"How do you mean?" Spook asked, spinning around.

"The guy coming down the stairs, see? The little guy with the beret, holding the umbrella? That's the man who was shooting at us. But I don't know how the hell he managed to find us so quick."

Spook looked over. "He doesn't look like an assassin."

"Takes all sorts. He's our best sniper." She squinted down at the hole in her jacket. "Though I guess he's having an off day himself. But don't misjudge him, Spook. He's a vicious little prick. I've seen him do horrific things to people."

"Well, he can't kill us with an umbrella, can he?"

"I wouldn't be so sure."

They watched as Hargreaves made his way down, stopping every few steps to inspect the crowds below. He knew they were there, Acid was sure of it.

"He can't kill us now, surely," Spook whimpered. "Not here. Too many people around."

"You'd think," Acid replied. "But having a lot of people around is useful. You want crowds. Look around you, no one here is taking the blindest bit of notice of each other. I could walk up to someone, slit their throat open, and then disappear into the throng before anyone even noticed."

Overhead a station announcement chimed the arrival of the next train.

"Okay, get ready," Acid whispered. "We can make this. Stay low and follow my lead." She grabbed Spook's hand and led her over to the edge of the platform. The arrivals board overhead said the train was two minutes away. Nearly there. Acid bounced from foot to foot as they waited. Crowds. She hated being hemmed in. Hated it philosophically, metaphorically, but most of all she hated it physically. She slipped her hand inside her jacket and felt for the reassuring weight of the Glock. The bats screamed for her to take it out and end it all. They wanted a bloodbath, here and now. It could be glorious.

She flipped her collar and risked a glance over at Hargreaves. His lips were moving, like he was talking to someone. Then he pressed his finger into his ear and that confirmed it – an earpiece. No doubt Raaz Terabyte was on the other end, giving him instructions, real-time data on their whereabouts. Acid dipped down behind a tall Frenchman as Hargreaves looked out over their platform, mouthing the word, *Where?*

The intercom chimed again. One minute. They were almost safe. Hargreaves had reached the bottom of the steps and was casting his beady eyes left and right, frantically searching them out. Acid could feel the rumble of the train's arrival. Could hear the screech of brakes in the dark tunnel.

They'd made it.

Thirty seconds more and they'd be out of there.

And that's when Alan Hargreaves turned around, looked Acid Vanilla dead in the eyes, and mouthed the words, *Got ya!*

Chapter Twenty-Nine

Alan Hargreaves bristled with keen excitement as he hurried down the last few steps. "Right then, you treacherous bitch. Let's have it."

He pushed onto the platform as the train pulled into the station, gripping the umbrella tight and bristling with excitement. His new toy. It had cost him the best part of two grand on the dark web, but it'd be worth it if he pulled this off clean like Caesar wanted. Yes indeed. Doing what Acid Vanilla wouldn't do, what Barabbas Stamp had failed to do, would elevate his position no end, grant him access to the bigger jobs, the better money. Two lousy grand was nothing compared to what this device would earn him. The way Alan Hargreaves saw it, you had to think of these things as an investment.

The order from Caesar had been clear – eradicate the mark as soon as possible and retrieve the recording, which Alan surmised to be in the rucksack on the girl's back. Easy pickings. Now the only person standing between him and victory was that blasted woman.

Alan Hargreaves hated Acid Vanilla. Had done ever since they got back from Venice and he found her and Banjo Shawshank laughing about him. It wasn't his idea to get locked in a room together, nor was it his fault he'd misunderstood the codename system. When he started at the firm, no one explained to him properly how it worked. Once he'd realised and come up with a more exciting name it was too late, Raaz had already uploaded the Alan Hargreaves profile onto the system – so that's who he had to become. But in his head, he'd always be Aryan Hungwell.

All the dismissive asides and put-downs he'd endured from Acid over the years spurred him on as he elbowed his way deeper onto the platform. Not only was she nasty and vindictive but she was a traitor, a dirty little turncoat. She'd put the organisation in jeopardy and Alan was determined to make her pay. Caesar had told him in no uncertain terms that he wanted to deal with Acid himself, that he was to bring her back alive. That is, he'd said, unless circumstances meant Alan had to kill her to get to the mark. Well, wouldn't you know it, something told him those circumstances would most likely be present today. Yes, he was going to eradicate the celebrated Acid Vanilla. What a joy.

The thought buoyed him as the train doors hissed open and he shoved his way onto an already packed carriage. He could see Acid and the mark boarding the next carriage along but in the same section of the train. Around thirty people were crammed into the space by the doors where Alan waited. Same in the next carriage. Alan let out a quiet snigger to himself. What a couple of mugs. They clearly thought they were safe, that he wouldn't risk attacking them in such a public place. Alan pulled the rubber stopper from the end of the umbrella.

Safe they were not.

Far from it.

For once in his life Alan's short stature was an advantage as he made his way through the carriage, hiding from sight. But half-way down he got stuck behind a tall woman in her early sixties. "Excuse me, ma'am," he drawled as the woman turned and looked down her nose at him. "Can you move, please?"

The woman was attractive, what Alan would call handsome rather than beautiful. She was prim, well-dressed, a typical Parisian. She shifted over a few inches but not enough to allow him to pass. Stupid cow. She was pushing her luck. All he had to do was jab the end of the umbrella into her arm and a few seconds later she'd be shitting out her guts. A minute after that and her heart and lungs would collapse.

Aconite – that was the magic ingredient. Otherwise known as Monkshood, otherwise known as Wolf's Bane. Administered via the tiny spike on the end of the umbrella, it would leave the victim to die a horrible death.

Alan peered around the side of the woman. Up ahead he could see them, the mark and Acid Vanilla. She was looking his way. Laughing at him.

Alan held up the umbrella, mouthed, *I'm going to kill you!*

Acid Vanilla pulled a face as if impressed. But he knew she was mocking him. She blew him a kiss and ducked behind a group of teenage boys.

Alan gritted his teeth and barged past the woman. He had to move fast. In less than a minute they'd be pulling up to the next station and Acid and the mark would vanish. He might never get this chance again.

He pushed on through the carriage and into the next one, holding the umbrella out in front of him. Poised.

Ready. Every muscle in his body was tense and rigid. But this was it. A few more steps and he'd have them.

So long, Acid Vanilla.

His only obstacle now was a fat sweaty man about the same size and shape as him. Alan gave him a hard stare – meaning, *get out of the way* – but the man didn't budge. Alan pushed past him regardless, though looking up saw only the space where his prey had been moments earlier.

Shitting hell.

They'd disappeared into the last part of the carriage. Hidden by the crowds. His heart sank, but he pulled it back. They had nowhere to run. Sitting ducks to his alpha fox.

He imagined the hero's welcome he'd receive back at HQ. Him single-handedly saving Annihilation Pest Control from embarrassment. Caesar would love him for this. They all would.

A single bead of sweat formed on his top lip and he wiped it away with the back of his hand. It just meant he was ready, pumped, in the zone. He was going to finish this, once and for all. The train was approaching the next station but it didn't matter. He had them. Passengers swayed with the movement of the slowing carriage, revealing the mark a few steps in front. She gazed at Alan, a pathetic expression on her face. This was it. Alan advanced on her, holding out the umbrella like a medieval lance. He couldn't see Acid Vanilla but no doubt she'd be further up the carriage, searching for an escape route. Saving her own skin. It didn't matter. He'd take them one at a time.

"Not so fast, sunshine."

A dark shape lunged in from below and caught Alan off guard. He felt a sharp pain in the back of his knee and his leg buckled, sending him lurching into the metal bar by the train doors. Passengers glared at him – as if it was him being the nuisance. He spun around grabbing hold of the bar to correct himself, but Acid Vanilla was on him. In a flash of leather and hair she grabbed the umbrella with one hand and applied pressure at the base of his thumb with the other.

Shitting shit.

Alan gnashed his teeth and tried to fight it, but it was a classic move and rendered his grip powerless. He watched in horror as Acid twisted the weapon from his grip and jammed the poison spike into his own thigh. She dodged around the back of him and twisted his arm up his back.

"It's done, mate," she whispered in his ear. "It's over."

Alan peered down at the spike protruding out of his leg, a numb sensation already spreading though his groin, into his feet. His muscles quivered. "I'm… going to… kill… you…" he wheezed.

As the train pulled into the station, Acid lowered him into an empty seat at the end of the carriage. "No. You aren't, are you?" she sneered.

Alan's guts churned as his whole body went into shock. He tried to scream but no sound came. Tried to move but he couldn't. It was reminiscent of those times when he'd fall asleep on his arm and wake up with it feeling dead, not his own. Only now it was his whole body. And it was dying for real. His head was numb. His vision was cloudy, a fog of grey seeping in from the sides. Where were the bright lights? The chorus of angels?

"Don't worry," he heard Acid purr in his ear. "I'll tell Caesar you gave it your all."

Then, with a lurch, the train stopped, at the same moment Alan's heart did the same. The last thing he saw was Acid Vanilla helping the mark up from the floor. Then the train doors opened, Acid shot him a final look, winked impishly, and they were gone.

Chapter Thirty

Acid raced up the steps and out of the Odéon Metro station with Spook following close behind. They hadn't travelled far – one stop, in fact – and it didn't bode well for their escape.

"That was crazy," Spook said, catching up with Acid at the top of the steps. "It all happened so fast. You were amazing."

"Yeah, well, I do this for a living, darling." She looked about her. "Okay, change of plan. This area is going to be swarming with police as soon as they find Hargreaves. I reckon our best move now is to walk to the Sorbonne and jump on a Metro there."

It wasn't the best plan, but it'd do. Out west would be far enough away from danger that they could lie low until their flight. It would give Acid time to rest and consider her next move.

They got to the Sorbonne with no issue and rode the line to the last station: Pont de Saint-Cloud. After a quick assessment of the locality, they happened upon a small hotel a few hundred metres from the Metro, imaginatively named

The Hotel Saint-Cloud. Acid gave it a quick once over – taking in the old sign covered in mould and bird shit, the warped and rusty Juliet balconies, the paintwork not tended to in years. It was a real dump, but it was also innocuous. The sort of place you'd walk straight past even if you were looking. Perfect for their current requirements.

The two women approached the entrance in silence. Acid noticed Spook seemed thoughtful now. The giddiness of the last few hours had faded and had been replaced with something darker. That was a good sign. It meant she was grasping the enormity of her situation.

The interior of the hotel was no better than the outside. After creaking open the main door, Acid and Spook found themselves at one end of a long narrow space with a metal lift to their right and a small reception area at the far end that consisted of a counter window and, beyond that, a larger room. Acid detected a faint smell of cabbage as they walked the length of the dingy room, flanked by racks of information leaflets advertising bus tours, museums, places of interest. The reception area was empty, so Acid leaned on the counter and put her head around the window. The room was a real mess, with worn orange carpets and two battered filing cabinets along the wall. An ancient, tobacco-yellow computer sat on a desk below the reception window and on the wall opposite a framed print of Monet's Water Lilies was even more washed out than usual. But no sign of any life. Acid leaned back and dinged the brass bell on the side of the counter.

"Will we be safe here?" Spook whispered. "Why don't we go straight to the airport?"

Acid didn't answer. Mainly because she didn't know what to say. At times of heightened stress the bats took over. So far she'd put on a good show, but now she felt herself unravelling. Maybe that was fair enough – it wasn't every week you killed two of your colleagues and got a price put on your head by your boss. Well, ex-boss. Though he was more than that. He was her mentor. Her friend. Hell, Acid might have once used the term father figure. Not anymore. Caesar was good to those who worked for him, but he was also a vicious and vindictive man. Killing two of his operatives was bad enough, but helping a mark to escape, defying his orders – he'd take that as a personal insult. He'd want blood. He'd want her head on a spike.

"Where the hell are the staff?" Acid banged her palm on the bell a few more times, then turned back to Spook. "Airports are too busy," she told her. "I can't relax in crowds. We'll be safe here until it's time to go."

"But I thought—"

"Well don't, all right?" Acid went for it again on the bell. "Let me do the thinking."

"Yes, okay, I am here." A woman appeared on the other side of the counter. A small, wiry woman with thinning, hennaed hair that gave her a look of late-period Paul McCartney. She didn't smile when she asked, "Can I help you?"

"We'd like a room," Acid said. "*Merci.*"

"Just the one?" The woman curled her mouth and a row of tiny wrinkles formed on her top lip. A smoker. "For the two?"

Acid beamed. "Yes, that's fine." The woman's eyes drifted to the hole in Acid's leather jacket, the dried blood on the sleeve. "It's supposed to be like that," Acid told her. "You know, fashion."

The woman held her gaze. Then she sighed dramatically and shuffled over to the computer, tapping in a few details. "We only have a double room, no twin."

"Yes. We'll take that," Acid said. "A double is fine."

The woman looked down her nose at them. "*Mais un seul lit!* Umm… one bed?"

Acid pouted. "One bed is perfect, isn't it, darling?" She sensed Spook bristle next to her. "We are in Paris, after all. The city of love."

The comment received a loud sniff from the other side of the counter. The woman typed something into the computer and handed Acid a key without looking at her. "Breakfast is served from seven until nine."

"Thank you. We'll try and make it." Acid winked at the woman. "If we're not too exhausted from all the sex." It helped, being like this, playing another role. It was only ever a temporary fix but it worked, escaping her problems inside her own twisted psychology. She put her arm around Spook. "Come on, sweetie. Let's get you upstairs."

They rode the rickety old elevator up to the third floor in silence and Acid yanked open the stiff metal concertina doors. Still in silence they zig-zagged down four short corridors until they reached their room, 11.

"Here we go," Acid said, handing Spook the key. "Inside, quick."

Spook unlocked the door and went in. Acid gave the corridor a once over and then entered herself. She shut the door and locked it.

"Geez. It's freezing in here," Spook whined, pulling her coat around her.

Despite the season, someone had left the window all the way open. A flimsy net curtain flapped in the breeze, revealing the hint of a view and the rusting frame of a Juliet balcony on the other side.

Spook walked over and looked out the window. "Oh, real nice."

"What's wrong?" Acid asked, checking the wardrobe, checking under the bed.

"The view," Spook told her. "I hope you like air-conditioning units and garbage bags."

Acid joined her and they both paused a moment to take in the run-down building a few metres away. In the alley below, a small cat snaked its way around piles of food waste that had spilled out of two industrial bins. It was safe to say this wasn't the nicest hotel in Paris. But then, they weren't on holiday.

"Wait a minute," Spook said, spinning around. "Where's the bathroom?"

"There isn't one," Acid told her. "I saw a communal one down the hall."

"A communal bathroom? Gross." Spook lowered the window to within an inch closed and moved over to the bed. "Where the hell have you brought me?"

"Calm it down, I can still change my mind about you." She watched as the cat pulled at something white sticking out of one of the bins. "Anyway, we aren't staying long."

"Woah, there's a bunch of posts on Twitter about Whitman," Spook cried, from inside the room. "Consensus is, he did it. He killed Paula Silva and Cerberix are covering it up. Nice. That's got to work in my favour, right?"

Acid didn't reply. She watched the cat as it struggled to remove whatever it had found.

Spook kept on, her voice rising excitedly. "He might have to put out a statement at this rate. What do you think?"

With one violent tug, the cat released its prize, which turned out to be the curled-up handle of a white bag. It came flying out and split open on the floor of the alley. The cat ran off as a pile of shitty nappies spilled out. Story of my life, Acid thought, turning back to the room and registering what her companion had just said.

"What the hell are you playing at?"

Spook was lying on the bed with an iPod Touch resting on her chest, the screen illuminating her face as her eyes darted about the screen.

She looked at Acid. "Huh?"

Acid was on her in a second, snatching the device from her hands. "Why didn't you tell me you had this?" Spook opened her mouth a few times, trying to form words. She looked confused. "Are you stupid?"

Spook blinked. "It doesn't have a SIM card," she said. "I leapfrogged onto the Wi-Fi from some café down the street."

Acid closed her eyes. "Doesn't matter. They can still track us. Triangulation? Wi-Fi hotspots? Ring any bells? I thought you were supposed to be a genius."

Spook stared into her now empty hands. "I wasn't thinking," she mumbled.

"Right, well say goodbye to it." Acid smashed the iPod against the corner of the windowsill, breaking it up enough to remove the battery components.

"I'm sorry," Spook offered.

Acid didn't look at her. "Stay here," she growled. "I'll be back soon."

Spook sat up on the bed. "Where are you going?"

"I need to get rid of the battery. Plus I need a dressing for my shoulder." She looked around the room. "Maybe a towel and some soap."

"Eugh. You're going to use the communal bathroom?"

"I've been in worse places. I'll be about an hour. Lock the door behind me and keep it closed. Do not open it to anyone but me." She craned her head to make eye contact, make sure Spook was listening. "Do you understand? No one but me."

"Yes. I'll be fine."

Acid considered Spook, marvelling at the girl's naïvety. But maybe it was her own that worried her. She couldn't blame Spook too much. It was her who'd fallen for the sob story. Who'd let her heart rule her head. She grimaced at the thought. She was losing the plot. It wasn't even lunchtime and she'd burnt every bridge available to her.

She flipped her sunglasses on and swung the room key into her palm. It was pointless worrying about it now. The die was cast. All she could do was keep on her guard and try and stay alive. One day at a time. She gave Spook a final nod. Then she let herself out the room and locked the door behind her.

Chapter Thirty-One

Beowulf Caesar pressed a fat, heavily jewelled finger down on the intercom button. "Ethel? Doris? Can you come back in?" He walked over to the window and rolled his neck around on his shoulders. He hadn't slept since yesterday, but he was too angry to feel tired. Every sinew in his body was taut. Every muscle tense with rage. How could she do this to him? After everything he'd done for her.

"What's going on? Tell me," he said, as the old women shuffled into the room. "Have we heard from Hargreaves?"

Doris drew a bony finger across her throat.

"What? Dead?" Caesar slammed his fist onto the desk. "And it was Acid?"

The sisters nodded.

"Maybe now you'll see sense," Ethel wheezed, in a rare vocal moment. "You know we never saw eye to eye with that one. She was far too impetuous, too full of herself. I always said you let her get away with murder." She laughed. A husky spluttering laughter that made her entire body sound hollow. "I'm not telling you anything you don't already know. She's been a liability for far too long. Yes, it's true, we don't like her, but I'll be the first to admit she was good at what she did. The best, even. But something's changed in her, and she needs to be put down. Eradicated. Before she does any more damage to our reputation."

Caesar sat. He didn't want to admit it, but Ethel was right. Acid Vanilla had run out of last chances. Going off script like this wasn't only *career* suicide.

"I don't understand what the bleeding shit she thought she was doing. What was she hoping to achieve?" He swivelled the chair around until he faced the window. "You know, I've had Ethan bastard Clarkson on the phone again this morning. He's an annoying prick, but he's got a right to be angry, don't you think? We've messed up royally and we're still bloody doing it. He wants the recording in his hand, he says. Can't understand why he hasn't got it."

"What have you told him?" Ethel asked.

"What do you think I bloody well told him?" He spun back around to face them. "I fed him the party line as before. 'It's all taken care of. Not to worry.' But I can't keep that up forever, can I? He hired us because he wanted this doing quickly and efficiently. With no fuss. And what does he get? The fucking mark still in the wind. Protected by our top operative. Jesus bleeding Christ. And now you're telling me she's killed Barabbas Stamp and Alan Hargreaves? Are we certain?"

Ethel nudged Doris, who pulled a photo from her handbag and slid it across the desk at Caesar. He snatched it up and squinted at it. With today's technology it annoyed him how blurred and useless most CCTV captures were. Raaz had once explained that the reason the quality was so bad was due to storage capacity and financial costs. Wasn't it always? In the end everything came down to money. The image was clear enough, however, to make out the prone form of Alan Hargreaves.

"Useless prick." Caesar pulled at his bottom lip. This was too much. He was losing face and that would not do. Acid Vanilla might have been someone he valued, even liked, once upon a time. But this wasn't a fairy tale. Ethel was right. She had changed. She'd belittled him and everything he'd built, and he needed to send a message. Not only to her, but to the whole organisation. To the world.

He thumbed the intercom button. "Raaz? Get me Banjo Shawshank on the line. I need to speak to him. Now."

Chapter Thirty-Two

"Are you sure this is a good idea?" Spook asked, sniffing the contents of the plastic cup and pulling a face. "Don't we need to stay on guard?"

"Yeah, well, I need a drink as well. So, cheers." Acid raised the plastic cup, sloshing the green liquid over the side.

Spook sat on the edge of the bed with the cup in her lap. "Fine, I guess. Cheers." She took a long drink and looked out the window, trying to hold back the inevitable.

"Aw shit, no. Don't do that." Acid sighed. "It's going to be okay."

Spook wiped at her eyes. "How the hell do you know? You're going to abandon me the minute we get back to London. What then?"

"You get a one-way ticket to somewhere far away. Start a new life. It is possible."

"Great. Thanks. What a help."

Acid sat upright on the bed and crossed her legs. "Listen, I need you to do something," she told her. "I found a payphone while I was out and rang Tariq, my forger, about getting new aliases. Passports. It'll take him a few days, so if I give you a secure email address, is there a way we can upload what he needs without giving away our location?"

Spook sniffed. "I can leapfrog onto the café's Wi-Fi from my laptop. Set up a Tor – an anonymous network. No one could trace us in the time it takes to upload a few photos. Even if they could, they'd get a false reading."

"Wonderful. Can you set that up, like now?"

"No problem."

Spook went to her rucksack and pulled out her laptop. It took her less than fifteen minutes to set up the Tor. Then another five to upload the photos – using the ones she'd already found of Acid, and one of herself. She created a secure email account and uploaded the files to the address Acid gave her. Then she deleted all evidence of the mailbox and the network. It took her about thirty minutes and neither of them spoke the whole time.

"Good work," Acid said, once she'd finished. "I mean it."

Spook forced a smile as she slid her laptop back in the rucksack. "All in a day's work."

"Another drink?" Acid held up the bottle, ready to pour her one.

"I'm good," Spook said. "I've not finished this one." She took a long drink and shuddered. Absinthe. It tasted rank. Like Dr Pepper if someone had extracted all the nice sugary elements and replaced them with pure ethanol.

"Listen, kid," Acid said. "I know all this has been a complete nightmare for you. But it has for me too. I don't know if you've noticed, but I don't feel too special right now. At all." She finished her drink and poured herself another. "I guess what I'm trying to say is, I don't mean to be so harsh with you. You're doing all right."

"Am I?"

"Yeah. You've been brave, considering. Biting Barabbas and all that. I suppose I owe you."

"Careful, that was almost a compliment." Spook joined Acid on the bed, making her shuffle up.

"Well we're stuck here for a few hours now," she said. "Let's try and relax. Take some of this bloody pressure off ourselves." She punched Spook gently on the upper arm.

Spook put on another smile, wondering if she'd ever do so naturally ever again. She turned to face Acid. "All right then," she said. "Since we won't be seeing each other after tomorrow, tell me the full story. How did you get to be the great Acid Vanilla?"

Acid lay back on the bed and stared at the ceiling. She looked sad.

"Sorry, I didn't mean to be a dick," Spook offered. She put her drink down on the carpet and lay alongside her. "You don't have to tell me."

It was pointed, the way she said it – *you don't have to tell me* – but lying here she felt close to Acid. And, sure, she was probably suffering from some messed-up version of Stockholm Syndrome, but she didn't care. There was a darkness inside of Acid that seemed far too dense and heavy for one person to carry.

They lay there together for some time before Acid spoke. "You thought you were clever, didn't you?" she said. "Working out why I'd chosen my codename – all that shit about juxtaposition of concepts." She turned her head on the pillow and Spook did the same. "I mean, I admit, it sounded great. But you're wrong."

Spook narrowed her eyes. "So, is there a reason?"

Acid smiled. A real smile, with none of the pretence Spook had gotten used to these last couple of days. "Acid

Vanilla was what I used to call myself when I was little. So my mother told me. She thought it was cute. You see, I couldn't say Alice Vandella properly and that's the way it came out: Acid Vanilla. Well, more like Asil Van'ella, but you get the idea."

"Aww, cute. Little Acid Vanilla." Spook shifted closer. The absinthe rushed to her head. "Was it just the two of you, growing up?"

Acid snorted. "Yeah. Until it wasn't. You know, what with all her visitors." She rolled her eyes. "Christ. I need more alcohol."

Spook opened her mouth but thought better of it. Acid grabbed the bottle, already two-thirds gone. She poured herself another large helping.

"You can talk to me, you know," Spook said. "I mean, I'm a good listener. It might help to talk it out for once?"

Acid twisted around to look at her. "Calm yourself, Oprah. I've talked about this stuff a lot over the years. Too much. Never seems to help." She took a drink and lay back down, resting the cup on her chest. She was silent a while, before letting out a deep sigh. "My mum, Louisa, she was only doing what she had to. After her fall she never danced again. And there wasn't much other work out there for an Italian immigrant with no family and no qualifications, plus a young kid to look after. I've never thought bad of her for going down that route. She was a fighter. She did it so we could survive."

Acid took another gulp of the absinthe, difficult in the position she was in. Spook watched as a trickle of green liquid ran down her chin onto the smooth skin of her upper chest. She didn't seem to notice.

"As I got older," she went on. "I started noticing the bruises, heard the shouting. One guy in particular was a real nasty bastard. Oscar Duke, he was called. I think he paid to knock her around as much as anything. Took all his inadequacies out on her. Of which there were a legion." She sneered, as if seeing him there in front of her. "I hated him so fucking much. Then one day when I was fifteen, I came home from school and he'd worked her over good and proper. She was laid out in the kitchen in a pool of blood – and him stood over her with a wine bottle in his hand that he'd been shoving up inside her. I thought she was dead."

She took another drink. She hadn't blinked the whole time she'd been telling the story. It was kind of unnerving.

"That must have been awful. Was she…?"

"No. She got over it," Acid said. "But she was never the same after. That made two of us."

"And what happened to the guy?"

Acid shifted her weight, propping herself up on one elbow and resting her head on one hand. "You know what happened to him."

"He was the guy?"

"Yep. He was the guy." She sighed once more. But with no pain behind it. "You see, I was only fifteen. But I was strong, athletic. I did gymnastics and Judo every week. At first it was a way of keeping me out of the flat when Louisa had visitors, but it turned out I was a natural at both. I was even scouted for the Olympics. Before my life went tits up."

Spook stared into those striking, mismatched eyes. "That's awesome," she whispered, immediately wishing she'd said anything else. "I mean, not that your life went tits up… but, well, you know…"

"I lost it," Acid went on. "I walked in, saw her, saw him, and went berserk. I managed to get the bottle out of his hand, and I went for it."

Spook propped herself up, mirroring Acid. "You killed him."

"I killed him all right. Smashed the bottle off the kitchen counter and jammed the broken end into the bastard's neck. Over and over again. I don't remember much about it, but the police said I almost cut his head off. Good. He deserved it."

Spook's voice trembled as she asked, "Your mom called the police?"

"They were already on their way. Some neighbour had heard him beating on my mum and called them. When they arrived I was dripping with blood. Head to toe. Like that scene in Carrie. Pigs blood. Same thing. They arrested me. Sent me to the young offender's institute, as you know. Then came all the therapy and tests."

"Tests?"

Acid finished the drink. "They thought I was a psychopath at first. Said I showed no remorse for my actions." She rolled her eyes theatrically.

"I see." Spook leaned over and picked up her own drink. It tasted better. The medicinal burn less harsh. "Were they correct?"

Acid didn't answer straight away, either she was thinking hard about it or she'd decided the conversation was too much. Spook watched her, pensive now. She couldn't help but notice Acid Vanilla had the most perfect profile she'd ever seen. You could see the Italian heritage, now she'd said it. Her nose wasn't small, but it wasn't big either, and had just the hint of a retroussé end. And those lips. Full. All natural. Stuck in a perpetual pout that made her appear mysterious and intimidating all at once. Spook was just starting on the eyes when Acid looked straight at her and pulled a face.

"You all right, Spook?"

"What? Shit." She'd been slowly leaning towards Acid with her mouth open. She sat up, dragging herself away from the tractor-beam-pull of Acid's enigmatic energy. "Sorry. I was just… I don't know… Go on. Were they… I mean, are you… a psychopath?"

Acid stretched her arms over her head. "Thought I was. For a while. Then my therapist helped me come to terms with what was going on. Helped me with coping strategies and the like. But it didn't end well between us." She sniffed. "Then one day I came to the conclusion: why would I show remorse? That bastard wanted to kill my mum. I'm glad he's dead. I'd do it again in a second. You ask me, that's the reaction any sane person should have. The only remorse I have for killing Oscar Duke was that I got caught. Which is why these days I make sure I never get caught." She chucked the plastic cup at the small metal waste bin on the other side of the room but missed. "Anyway, it seems coping strategies only get you so far. Things have been hard recently. I've felt out of sync with myself. As though something's chasing me – karma, maybe – and I need to put it right." She blew her fringe out of her eyes. "Stupid, I know. But it's lucky for you. Or we wouldn't be here. You certainly wouldn't."

Spook swallowed, unsure of the correct response. "Does your mum know about what you do now?"

It was an innocent question, but she got a sharp look.

"My mum's dead."

"What?" Spook let out a nervous laugh. "No, she isn't. I found her. She's in some convalescent home in Scotland. Didn't you know?"

Acid shut her eyes. "No one knows about that," she whispered. "No one."

Spook put her hand on Acid's arm. "Don't worry, who am I going to tell?"

Acid looked out the window. When she spoke next her voice sounded different. Softer. Like all the hard edges had rubbed away. "I put her in that home three years ago. Before that she was living in a quiet little village in the Midlands. Safe. Away from me. Away from all the horrible shit I have in my orbit. But then I got word from her carer she was getting worse. Needed round-the-clock care. Alzheimer's. Horrible disease. I first noticed it when I was inside, it was only mild then. I've always felt it was my fault. Punishment for what I'd done. My poor beautiful mum, paying for my mistakes."

"I'm not so sure about that," Spook told her. "And you're a good daughter."

"Am I? How can I be when I struggle to be in the same room as her? I hate seeing her like that."

"It must be hard."

"I only visit four times a year, and only then because I pay for her stay in cash. If I didn't, I might never go. After everything she did for me."

"I'm sure she knows you care." Spook was grasping at straws and they both knew it. She was relieved when Acid shifted onto her back. It was easier to talk that way. Less chance of losing herself in those penetrating eyes. "I think the fact you're even saying this means something," she went on. "You ask me, the fact I'm here at all proves you care more about people than you let show."

Acid sneered at the idea but didn't reply. She closed her eyes. A minute passed. Then another. Spook wondered if she'd fallen asleep.

"I should go see her," she said. "A proper visit. Tell her how sorry I am."

Spook adjusted herself on the bed, gazing down at the woman alongside her. She knew her as Acid Vanilla: top assassin, master strategist, ruthless killer. But as she watched the steady rise and fall of her chest, she could see beyond the dark intensity of her persona. Somewhere in there she was still Alice Vandella: Judo lover, gymnast, vulnerable fifteen-year-old. Momma's girl.

"It was a guy, by the way." The words were out of Spook's mouth before she realised she'd spoken.

Acid opened one eye. "Excuse me?"

Spook felt her cheeks burn. "Sorry, I just… You asked me before why I came to England. Well, it was a guy who I broke up with."

Acid shut her eye. "Figures."

"Simon Kaye. He was my first boyfriend. First and only. We met at the MIT as freshmen and fell in love. Or at least I did. Thinking about it now I'm not sure he ever loved me back. We were together for two years. Then he invented this app, *Dolla*, that monitors your online spending – and it exploded. Until that he'd been the perfect boyfriend. He was kind, gentle. But once he got in with the tech crowd he changed, almost overnight. In the end he dumped me by text. Two weeks after my dad's funeral."

"Classy," Acid offered. "Worked out best for you though."

"How do you mean?"

"If you'd married him, you'd be Spook Kaye. Wow, and I thought nothing could top Spook Horowitz."

"Ha," Spook replied. "I never realised that. Never put the names together. Says it all. Deep down I always knew we weren't forever."

Spook mused on the idea. Truth was, she'd hardly thought about Simon since she arrived in England. Even less so since she'd had a price on her head. But it was clear. She didn't care anymore. Simon was part of her past. A simple conduit who'd brought her to where she was. Which was, figuratively, her being a stronger woman. Where it had actually brought her was lying on a bed in Paris alongside the most captivating person she'd ever met.

"So, why so coy?" Acid asked. "Why imply it was a girl who broke your heart."

Spook stroked the bedspread. "I don't know. You're so mysterious. Maybe I wanted some of that too." She grabbed the bottle of absinthe and gulped down a large mouthful without tasting it. "It wouldn't have been a huge leap, I'll be honest. I questioned myself a lot over the years. Don't think I've ever decided one way or the other. People have always thought I was, you know…"

"What? A dyke?" Acid turned to her, grinning mischievously.

"Maybe. I hate that word though," she said. "That's not who I am."

"Semantics." Acid propped her head up. "All right then, if you prefer – todger dodger. No? Muff diver? Rug munch-er?" Spook squirmed, but it only incited more teasing from Acid. She had the devil in her. She leaned into Spook. "Stop me, won't you, if I'm turning you on."

Spook laughed. A little too much. They both sensed it. The giggles quickly faded to a silence that hung heavy in the space between them.

Then it happened.

The thing Spook hadn't stopped thinking about ever since she'd met this unfathomable woman who, in a crazy twist, had gone from being the Angel of Death to Spook's only hope of survival.

And it was happening.

Right now.

Spook couldn't be sure who instigated the kiss. That was why it was so amazing. It just happened. Like in a movie, she thought, as their tongues darted in and out of each other's mouths, wrestling for dominance. And when Acid slipped her top over her head and climbed astride her, for once Spook gave as good as she got. In that dingy Paris hotel room, with the net curtain flapping almost ironically in the afternoon breeze, Spook breathed in Acid's hot body, finding the answer at last to a lifelong question. And this time she wasn't on the receiving end of Acid Vanilla's sharp tongue. Instead what she got was one that was softer. And much more accommodating.

Chapter Thirty-Three

Acid sat on the side of the bed and emptied her lungs of air as the bats nibbled and toyed with her nerve endings. It felt like the worst jet lag she'd ever experienced, coupled with an uncontrollable hit of euphoric energy. A crash was coming. She was certain of it.

She took another deep breath. She'd literally kill for a cigarette right now and she knew what that meant. Her focus shifted to the window frame, seeing details for the first time. The black mould encroaching into the room from the corners of the glass, the yellow stains on the net curtain.

She'd known something had shifted the second she woke. She hadn't even planned on sleeping but there it was. Casual sex – it was a good sedative. It was also a bad sign. She was losing control.

"You bloody idiot," she rasped to the carpet. It was talking about her past that had done it. That never ended well. But she hadn't been able to stop.

She padded over to the window and slid it open a few inches more. The breeze felt good against her naked body and she made no move to cover herself. The building oppo-site looked to be empty, but she didn't care. She didn't care about anything. That was the problem. The bats were here to stay, and they were vampire bats, they had teeth.

She leaned out onto the Juliet balcony. The rough, peeling paintwork scratched at the skin on her stomach and breasts but she welcomed the discomfort. She traced her finger along the raised scar that ran down her left fore-arm, acquired after a run-in with a rival operative, both going for the same mark. That was sixteen years ago, back when she joined Caesar's organisation. Sixteen years of killing people. By anyone's reckoning that was a lot of bad karma.

"Hey, you." It was Spook, stirring sleepily in the bed behind her.

Acid didn't turn from the window. She could hear the American moving around. Could hear the scratching of the sheets. Then a contented sigh.

"Listen, Spook," she said, speaking quickly. "I needed that. I think we both did. The release. But it shouldn't have happened."

"Geez." Spook yawned. "How was it for you?"

"Stop it. It's not like that. But that was stupid." Acid left the window and moved over to the two bags of shopping in the corner – the purchases made after disposing of the iPod. She removed a towel from one, along with a gauze dressing and some surgical tape. "I'm going to take a shower and try and freshen up. While I'm gone, you get yourself up and ready. Okay? We have to leave for the airport in an hour."

Spook brushed her hair behind her ears and moved onto her back. "What time is it?"

"Half past four." Acid wrapped the towel around her and gathered up her clothes along with the Glock. "Lock the door behind me. And same as before, don't open it to anyone but me."

Spook grunted in response. For a second Acid had the idea to yank the bedclothes off her. But she didn't. "Keep it together," she murmured to herself, as she shut the door behind her and strode barefoot along the dim corridor. "Not much longer."

The communal bathroom was sparse, but plusher than she was expecting. It was set up as a wet room, tiled from floor to ceiling in dark grey slate. A shower unit overhung one wall, with a toilet at the other side. Along the wall facing the door, a mirror dotted with fine flecks of toothpaste hung above a porcelain sink unit. She placed her clothes, towel and gun down on the sink and twisted the shower dial into the red. The pressure of the shower surprised her and she was glad of the sting from the water as she stepped inside. Her skin felt paper-thin. Raw nerves bristled under the surface.

She closed her eyes and put her whole head under the flow. She hadn't brought soap, but it didn't matter. The water was hot enough to cleanse her soul. For now, at least. She stayed in this position a few minutes, cocooned in the transient safety of the steamy room. Maybe she could stay here forever, she thought. Away from Spook. Away from Caesar. Away from herself.

"*Bonjour?*"

Acid's ears were full of water. So when she heard the voice, followed by a dull banging, she wasn't sure whether she'd imagined it.

"*Excusez-moi.* I need the toilet most desperately." She was certain now. It was a man's voice, speaking English with a French accent. "Are you there?"

Acid put her head back under the water and tried to

ignore the banging. But it was no use. The moment had passed. She yanked the shower off and stepped out, catching a glimpse of herself in the mirror and looking away.

She'd never enjoyed catching her reflection off guard. Something about marrying the external representation of who she was with her internal sense of self. It always jarred. Because who was she? Acid Vanilla? Alice Vandella? Maybe she was Melissa Font or Anastasia Blanco – or any one of the twenty pseudonyms she'd used over the years. More than likely, she thought, as she grabbed the towel and dried herself, she was none of those people. She was nobody at all – a soulless changeling who took on whatever form she needed to stay alive.

Acid's reflection shook its head. It looked disappointed. It also looked a lot like Louisa.

"Please," the voice called out again, more desperate now. "Are you almost done?"

Acid placed her towel down on the cold tiles and stepped onto it, drying the soles of her feet before slipping on her underwear.

"Open the door. Please."

Acid stood upright as a dark thought hit her in the guts.

"You bloody idiot," she whispered at the mirror. She'd been so absorbed in her own internal confusion she'd let her guard down. This person could be here to kill her. She didn't recognise the accent, but that meant nothing. Annihilation operatives were trained in accent-work. She grabbed the Glock off the sink and moved to the door.

"Who is it?"

"Please," the voice whined again. "I think I may wet myself."

Acid gripped the handle of the gun as a million

thoughts flashed through her mind, not one of them helpful. More banging from the other side. More pleading. They certainly were making a lot of noise for a trained assassin. Slowly Acid reached over and slid the bolt out of the latch. Then in one fluid movement she swung the door wide open and stepped back, gun raised.

"*Merde! No, s'il vous plaît*"

Acid looked into the face of a short man in his late fifties. He stared at the gun, then at Acid's naked form. He looked like he might wet himself there and then.

"Please, I am so desperate." He was wearing a beige polo-necked sweater and brown trousers belted far too high around an extensive gut.

Acid leaned out, grabbed him by the shoulder. "Come on then. Don't just stand there." She pulled him into the bathroom and slammed the door shut. Then she gestured at the toilet bowl. "Quickly. Do whatever it is you need to do."

The man's eyes almost popped out of his head. "But I am afraid... You are... I need the toilet."

"Yes, and I'm letting you," Acid said, turning back to the mirror and placing the Glock on the sink. "But I've not finished. So do your business and then leave me in peace."

The fat Frenchman paused a moment, but his bladder won out. He shuffled over to the toilet in the corner and unzipped himself. He let out a satisfied sigh as a loud cascade of piss splashed into the bowl.

Acid gripped the sides of the sink and dipped her head, snorting heavily down both nostrils. In, and out. It was an old trick her therapist had shown her. It was supposed to calm her down, but it never did.

"*Mademoiselle?*" the man offered. "You are okay? You need a doctor?"

"I need something," Acid whispered into the sink. She

turned to the man. "Do you have a mother? I mean, is she still alive?"

The man's eyes widened. "Well, yes. But she is ancient." He smiled, despite himself.

"Do you visit her?" Acid asked.

"Of course," he replied. "Poor woman. She gets confused. I have to do lots for her now. But it is fine, you know. I don't mind."

Acid scoffed. "Yeah. You don't mind."

"Well, it is the least I can do after everything she has done for me, *non*?"

It was like a bullet to the heart.

Acid picked up her black jeans and pulled them on. "You know, I told him I needed a holiday," she said. "I bloody well told him. Two weeks away and none of this would have bloody well happened. Wait a second..." The man had zipped himself up and was making for the door, but Acid blocked his path. "Do you tell your mother all that?"

"Tell her what?"

"That you appreciate her. That you love her."

The man frowned. "*Mais oui*. She is my mother."

"Yes. I know." Acid picked her black t-shirt up from the sink and pulled it over her head. "I have to see her, don't I? I have to tell her?"

The man went to reply but Acid had already turned back to the mirror. She scraped her hair into a ponytail and slid on a hair tie from her wrist. Her reflection stared back at her, resolve twitching at the corners of her mouth, the pout fierce with determination.

"You're right though," she told the man. "I have to see her. Before I go away forever I need to tell her how I feel. Tell her I'm sorry. Tell her I love her." She slapped the confused man on the shoulder. Kissed him hard on his salty forehead. "Thanks for the chat, friend. You've been a real help."

She grabbed her towel and the Glock and opened the door. As the stout Frenchman waved a limp hand in good-bye, Acid Vanilla pushed past him and disappeared down the corridor.

Chapter Thirty-Four

The pressure in Acid's head was almost unbearable as she returned barefoot up the musty, hotel corridor. The seventies carpet didn't help – dirty slashes of beige and cream swirling into pink and crimson – it was enough to send anyone insane. But at least she knew her next step. Now she just had to break the news to Spook.

She tensed as she got to the hotel room, noticing the door had been left ajar.

"For heaven's sake," she mumbled to herself, pushing it open. "Spook. I thought I told you to lock this."

"Hello there, Acid."

She was already in the room before she looked up to see Banjo Shawshank over by the window. He was dressed in his usual attire, tweed suit, patent-leather winkle pickers. The large vintage pistol – pointed at Spook's head – finished off the ensemble. In one fluid motion Acid dropped the towel and pulled the Glock from her waistband. She pointed it at Banjo as he grabbed Spook around the neck, using her as a shield.

"I wondered if you'd be next," Acid said. "I would say it's good to see you but, you know, I'd be lying."

"Well, it is good to see you, babe," Banjo hit back. "You're somewhat of an elusive butterfly these days." He squeezed Spook's neck tight and aimed his gun at Acid's head. "A lot of people have been looking for you ladies."

"Yeah? Well, they keep finding us," Acid said. "But then they end up dead. By the way, what the hell is that?" She gestured at Banjo's gun, playing for time. "It looks bloody ancient."

Banjo sneered. "Philistine. This little beauty is a 1902 Luger. An absolute classic. All reconditioned, of course, but antique enough to get through customs with the right paperwork."

Acid considered the angle. The Luger held 9mm rounds and from this distance it would punch straight through her skull and shred her brain matter before she knew what was happening.

"Go on then," she told him. "Do it." Banjo flexed his grip. She could tell he was itching to. "But I don't see a suppressor," she added. "I bet it makes a right old racket. Could get messy."

Derision turned up the ends of Banjo's moustache. "That's rich. Coming from the queen of chaos. What happened to you, Acid? You were the best."

"I am the best. Always will be."

"Nah. You've gone soft. Helping a mark to escape? Killing two of your colleagues. Jesus Christ. How's that search for salvation working out for you?"

"I told you, it's not like that."

"Sure it's not."

Acid closed one eye over the barrel of the Glock. "Put the gun down, Banjo."

"You first."

Neither of them moved.

Acid took a moment to slow her breathing, slipping effortlessly into a well-worn persona – that of a mechanical, stoic, killing machine. In this state she was present, unshakable. To say it felt good would be incorrect, but it hadn't let her down yet.

"Acid. Help me." Spook wriggled in Banjo's grip, pawing helplessly at the wiry arm wrapped around her neck.

Acid ignored her. "What's your play, Banjo? I take it you're here to kill us both. Why haven't you?"

"Caesar would still prefer you back in one piece. Wants to deal with you himself." He flexed his hand on the gun. "But if I have to kill you, I'm sure he'll understand."

Acid didn't flinch. "Why's she still alive?"

"Hey!" Spook cried out.

Banjo gave it a beat. "Well, babe, right now she's a convenient shield. But she's also good bait. Plus, I've orders to retrieve this bastard recording everyone's so stressed about. Soon as I get that, well…" He grimaced. "Problem is, we seem to have found ourselves in a classic Mexican standoff, don't we? Tut, tut. What to do?"

Acid glanced at Spook, then at the floor. She'd noticed something.

"Okay, listen," she said. "Say I surrender, give you the recording. What then? What happens to me?"

Banjo bared his teeth. "I told you. I take you back to Caesar."

"What if there's a better way? For both of us."

"You're bargaining with me? Jesus Christ. Do you think you're in any position to?"

Acid's eye twitched. "Maybe. I know how important this

job is. How important that recording is. My guess is, you take that back to Caesar along with evidence you've eradicated the mark, he won't worry too much I'm in the wind. You see, I can make this easy for you, Banjo. Extremely easy."

No one moved. Even Spook was silent. Her soft whimpering faded away as time slowed. The room bristled with electric danger.

"How easy?" Banjo said.

"I put the gun down. Get you the recording. Then I turn around and walk out that door. Done. You'll never see me again. You can tell Caesar the same."

Banjo grimaced. "He won't like that. You see, the boss has noticed my potential. At last. I go back empty-handed I'll be back in the dog house."

Acid gripped the Glock tighter. "You won't be empty-handed. You'd have the recording. That's what he cares about." Acid glared at him. "I could shoot you right now. You could shoot me. You might even get me first. But you might not." She widened her eyes. "My only plan is saying goodbye to my mum and then get gone. For ever."

Banjo screwed up his face. "Thought your mum was dead?"

"She is. I mean… I'll go to her grave, say goodbye. Then I'm gone. As good as dead. But without all the mess and hassle for you."

Banjo was silent. Looked like he was thinking about it. "Where's the recording?"

Acid kept her aim up. "If we're doing this, I'll get it, okay? No sudden movements."

A beat. Then Banjo jerked his gun for her to move. "Slowly."

Not taking her eyes off Banjo, Acid side-stepped over to

Spook's rucksack. Then, gun still raised, she knelt down and felt for the zip. Once located, she opened the top compartment and stuffed her hand inside. She rummaged around for a few moments before her hand fell on the thumb-drive.

"Here. It's here." She showed it to Banjo.

He held out his hand. "Give it."

Acid edged over to him, holding the thumb-drive at arm's length. Banjo's moustache twitched. He had no free hand. He hesitated a moment, then shoved Spook. She stumbled forward, rubbing at her throat as Banjo snatched the thumb-drive and slipped it inside his waistcoat pocket.

"Don't fucking move," he yelled, moving the gun between the two women.

"You've got the recording," Acid told him. "So I'm going to put my gun down, and I'm going to leave. Deal? Nice and easy. No fuss."

Banjo raised his head. "And you trust me not to kill you as soon as you do?"

"Well, like I said, I don't care. But that monstrosity will make a lot of noise. Draw attention to you." She glanced at the floor. "You don't need that. Let me go, you can handle this in a much quieter way. Tell Caesar you killed me, if it helps. I mean it, you won't hear from me again. No one · will."

"What the hell are you playing at?" Spook rasped next to her.

Acid didn't respond. Banjo's finger quivered on the trigger of the Luger. Seconds passed.

"Fine," he said at last. "Put the gun down and piss off."

Acid gave it a beat, she looked at the floor and closed her eyes. Then she raised her gun in the air along with her other hand. With eyes still on Banjo, she went down on one knee. Then slowly, deliberately, she lowered her gun to the floor, handling it as though it were made of glass. She didn't breathe. A second would be all it took.

"You have lost it," Banjo sneered. "You stupid c—"

He didn't finish his sentence.

He didn't get chance.

Acid grabbed for the bedsheet draped across the floor – the one Banjo was standing on – and yanked it towards her. Banjo flung his hands in the air and released a shot into the ceiling as he toppled backwards. His arms flailed about as he tried to regain his balance but it was too late. As the floor fell away from him, Acid launched herself forward, catching him with a sharp elbow to the solar plexus and barging him out through the open window. He cried out, grasped for something to hold on to but found nothing. Acid gave him another shove before grabbing his legs and flipping him over the top of the Juliet balcony. He looked at her with sheer terror in his eyes as she released his legs and watched him fall.

He screamed all the way down. Three floors.

Seconds later Spook joined Acid at the window and the two women leaned out to see Banjo's broken body lying on a pile of rubbish bags in the alley.

"Three down," Spook said. "How many more of them are there?"

Acid stared down at Banjo. Her friend. "Enough," she said quietly. An image of Caesar flashed into her mind and she wondered how he'd react to this development – another of his top operatives dead by her hands. She almost felt sorry for him. After all they'd been through together, she never imagined it would be her who'd destroy his life's work. She closed the window. One thing was certain, he was about to throw everything he had at her.

It was time to disappear.

217

For good.

Chapter Thirty-Five

Spook stayed at the window for a minute, catching her breath and focusing on not bursting into tears. She'd been uncharacteristically flippant just now – taking a leaf out of Acid's book – but it hadn't helped to alleviate her anxiety. She continued to stare down at the man in the alley. The fourth man who'd tried to kill her in as many days. He looked so weird lying there, with one of his pipe-cleaner legs twisted up behind him. He was reminiscent of a Wes Anderson character, Spook thought, or a Quentin Blake drawing, though much more chilling.

Calmer now, she turned back into the room to see Acid sitting on the bed examining the gun that the man had dropped.

"You know, I almost thought you were going to screw me over," Spook told her. "But no. You saved my life. Again."

"Yeah, well, don't make me regret it," Acid said, peering down the gun barrel, then chucking it on the bed. "Get your stuff together and let's get to the airport. We aren't out of the woods yet."

Acid got off the bed and pulled her black hooded sweat-shirt over her head, followed by her leather jacket. She glared at Spook, still in her pants and t-shirt.

"Jesus Christ. You're standing there like people aren't trying to kill you. We need to split. Now." She moved over to the door. "I'm going to check the corridor, see if there's another way down. Get dressed and meet me outside in one minute."

She paused, about to say something else, but thought better of it. She pointed to Spook's clothes then held up a finger. One minute. Then she slipped out the door and closed it behind her.

The second Spook heard the click of the latch, she collapsed onto the bed and screamed into the pillow – a long, powerful scream that came from deep down inside of her. She wasn't entirely sure what was behind it – frustration maybe, or just plain old fear – but it seemed to help. She sat up and wiped her eyes on the bedspread. Then she gathered up her clothes from where they'd been strewn and put them on.

Acid was at the end of the corridor as Spook exited the hotel room and let the door shut behind her. Unnoticed, she watched as Acid inspected a large window opposite the elevator before sliding it open. A gentle breeze lifted her hair and blew it over her shoulders. Spook let out a long deliberate breath. Then she swung her rucksack onto both shoulders and started down the corridor as Acid climbed out the window.

"We're going down there?" Spook peered over the ledge to see it led out onto an old metal fire escape.

"Woah." Acid flinched, banging her head on the

window frame. "Bloody hell. Don't sneak up on people like that."

"I was being stealth-like," Spook said.

Acid rolled her eyes. "Have you got everything?"

"Got my laptop, but what about the recording?"

"We'll get it now." Acid let herself down onto the fire escape. "Follow me."

"Can't we take the elevator?" Spook asked.

"No," Acid told her. "Someone will have heard that gunshot. We need to get out of here. Fast." As if to highlight this, they heard a loud rattle coming from the end of the corridor – the elevator starting its ascent. Acid gave Spook a stern nod, then disappeared from view.

"Hey, what about my rucksack," Spook yelled after her. "Can you not... Ah, shoot."

She looked out the window. Acid was already half-way down. Behind her the elevator was coming to a stop. Spook picked up her rucksack and pushed it through the window, then climbed out after it.

"Oh man."

She peered down through the gaps in the metal flooring. Three floors up sure seemed a lot higher from this angle, and all at once she felt unstable. Acid glanced up at her, almost at the bottom. She waved at Spook to hurry.

"Yes. I'm coming."

Spook made her way down, not easy when her legs were made of jello. The archaic stairwell swayed and trembled beneath her feet as if any moment the whole structure might crumble beneath her. An apt metaphor for her predicament.

At the final level, she jumped the last few steps before following Acid into the alley. She found her kneeling in front of a large pile of garbage bags – the place where her attacker had landed. Only he was nowhere in sight.

"Where's he gone?" Spook asked. "I thought he was dead."

Acid bowed her head. "Yes. So did I."

"Where is he?"

Acid shushed her quiet and she did as she was told, fighting back the urge to throw up. She stared at Acid, hoping she was about to say something reassuring. But she didn't. Instead she stood and strode purposefully towards the main street on the far side of the alley.

"Hey, talk to me." Spook caught up with her by the side of a busy dual carriageway. "Where are we going?"

"The airport, of course. Like we planned."

"But what about the guy? Banjo or whatever he's called?"

Acid held up her arm as a cab appeared in the distance. "What about him?"

"Well, he's not dead. It's a worry, no?"

"Everything is a fucking worry right now." The cab spotted them and indicated it was pulling over. Acid looked Spook up and down. "Look, I can't think about him. We need to leave." The cab stopped a few feet away from them and Acid walked over to it.

"But won't he still come after us?" Spook asked.

Acid gave her the mother of all eye-rolls. "I don't know. He's got to be injured after that fall. But either way, we need to disappear as soon as possible." She opened the back door of the cab. "Are you coming or not?"

"Yes. Wait for me." Spook ran over and clambered into the cab, shoving her rucksack in the middle seat – a literal barrier between them to match the metaphorical one. Across the other side of it, Acid huffed.

"Didn't think of putting that in the boot?"

"Excuse me?"

"Oh, I'm sorry, I mean the trunk." She said it an American accent, mockingly nasal.

"No. I'd prefer to keep my only proof of what happened close. If it's all the same with you," Spook replied. "I'm going to get justice for Paula, with or without your help."

"Whatever." Acid leaned forward. "Driver, Charles de Gaulle. *S'il vous plaît.*"

Chapter Thirty-Six

Terminal 2D of Paris Charles de Gaulle Airport was an impressive building with a large concrete facade that harked back to the stark brutalist architecture of the sixties. Acid had always found it to be a calming place to fly out from. The check-in area and departure lounge had both been renovated in the last ten years, and she found the vaguely futuristic styling – the white archways, the expansive glass ceiling – both pleasing and relaxing. Though admittedly, on her previous visits she'd been returning home from a job well done. Today, not so much.

It was starting to rain as the cab pulled up outside. Acid paid the fare then went to the check-in desk while Spook used the bathroom. Once reunited they went through security, passport control, all without a hitch, and made their way to the departure lounge. Neither of them said one word to the other the whole time.

The silence continued as they found seats in the vast open-plan lounge and Acid fell into a deep trance of contemplation. Her skin felt like gossamer and a dense wave of restlessness clouded her thoughts. She could have sat there for hours, but she was roused from her stupor by a sharp elbow digging into her ribs.

"Acid? Do you want anything?" The tone implied it wasn't the first time Spook had asked.

"What do you mean?"

"I'm going to get a coffee."

Acid grimaced. The last thing she needed right now was caffeine. She told Spook no, and watched as she sauntered away without a care in the world. Same as always.

A young man in suit trousers and a white polo shirt walked over. "Is anyone sat here?" he asked, pointing to the seat on the other side. He was English and oozed a particular red-cheeked, public-school confidence only accessible to those who'd never had to worry about life.

"No, mate. You go for it." Acid twisted in her seat, putting her back to him and checking her passport and credit card. They were still in the inside pocket of her jacket where she always carried them. Ready for times like this when she had to leave everything behind. The name on both read, *Melissa Font*. Who she was until she met with Tariq. It could be worse. She pulled the new plane tickets from her jeans pocket and folded them around the passport.

"Did you see? The plane to London is boarding." Spook stood over her, sipping at a Starbucks. "Gate seventeen."

Acid didn't move. "We aren't going to London."

"How do you mean? I thought we had to meet that guy?"

"Not until tomorrow. Sit down. We've got another hour before we board." Spook did as she was told and Acid turned to her. "You see, when I went to the desk before, I booked us on a new flight. To Scotland."

"Oh? Why? Oh…" The realisation hit her.

"Yes. I need to say goodbye to my mum. I might not get chance again. I know I said I'd help you disappear, and I will, but I need to do this first." She paused. "Look. It's been a rough few days. We've both been under a lot of pressure."

Spook giggled. "Sounds like something a married couple would say."

"Don't joke," Acid told her, side-stepping the flirtation. "Listen, Spook, whatever you decide to do with that recording, I meant what I said. I can't help you."

"Can't or won't?" Spook turned and sipped at her coffee. "Sorry, I just hoped you'd change your mind. You know, because of your mom, and what happened. And…"

"Yes. I know you thought that. That's why I'm telling you again. None of this should have happened. None of it."

She didn't turn around, watching instead a young family play together across the far side of the lounge, the mum and dad laughing as their little girl tossed a rag doll up in the air.

"Fine," Spook said. "You do what you have to. Only, I see you, Acid. Sure, you have this sharp, merciless persona. No doubt that helps you do what you do. But there's more to you. I know it." Acid sneered audibly, but Spook went on. "You say you want salvation. How are you going to get it if you ignore your emotions?"

"For heaven's sake, I never said I wanted bloody salvation. That was Banjo."

"Well, what do you want?"

Acid scowled. "Some peace and bloody quiet would be a start."

Spook leaned into her. "You won't get any kind of closure on your past if you keep pushing your feelings down."

"Thanks. I'll bear that in mind." Acid popped the collar

on her jacket and sunk into the seat. "Jesus Christ. Closure. Bloody Americans."

The comment killed the short conversation dead and another long silence endured. It continued as they boarded the flight to Glasgow. Continued as the plane trundled onto the runaway and picked up speed. Continued as they became airborne and the seat belt signs pinged off. They'd been in the air for over ninety minutes before Spook broke the deadlock.

"Where will you go?" she asked.

It was a good enough question. If only Acid had a good answer. "Italy, perhaps. Where my mum was born. Up in the mountains, as off-grid as I can find."

"In case they come looking for you?"

"Well, yes." She looked at Spook. "But more than that, I need to escape. From everything. From Acid Vanilla especially."

"I see," Spook said. "Will you be Alice again?"

Acid gripped the armrest. "No. I've told you about that."

"What does your mom call you?"

"My mother doesn't call me anything. She doesn't know who the hell I am." Then, to herself, "Makes two of us."

Spook twisted in her seat. "What was that?"

"Forget it."

Acid was about to press the button to call the hostess, but she stopped herself. She couldn't handle the disapproving look. She'd get a drink later.

"Will you tell me about your mom?" Spook asked. "I'll meet her soon enough. Is she – was she – like you?"

"What, a sarcastic cow with a death wish?" Acid said. Then quieter, "I don't want to talk about my mother. It is

227

what it is. I just need to see her. Say my piece. That's all I can think about. After that, who knows."

"Fair enough." Spook put her hand over Acid's. "I understand."

Acid snatched her hand away. "What the hell are you doing?"

"You look so sad," Spook replied. "I was trying to be a friend."

"Jesus. We aren't friends, Spook. I don't know if you remember, but a few days ago I was ready to kill you."

"Yes, but you didn't. You saved my life. Three times. That's got to mean something." She moved her head so Acid had to look at her. "And what about yesterday? In the hotel room…'

Acid rolled her eyes. "Here we are, I've been waiting for this. I told you, yesterday was a one-off. It was a symptom of something else. I make bad choices when I'm… when I can't think straight. It shouldn't have happened."

She spat the words out. She was being harsh, but it was true. Acid Vanilla didn't have friends. It was so much easier that way.

"What if I came with you?"

Acid didn't answer. She continued to stare at the back of the seat in front.

"We could hide out in Italy. Then once we're safe, I can release the recording. Show the world what they did."

Acid closed her eyes. "Stop it, Spook. It's over."

"But those bastards have to pay for what they did." Her voice was rising to a shrill roar but she caught herself in time, whispering, "Come on, Acid, they killed an innocent sex-worker, left a young kid without a mom."

"Yes, I know, they deserve to die. And you know what? I

would love nothing more than to be the person to do it. But I can't help you."

"But don't you think it sucks? People like Whitman think they can do whatever they want and get away with it."

"People like Whitman have been my bread and butter." Acid sighed. "I'm no hero, Spook. I'm sorry."

Above their heads the seat belt sign lit up. They were starting their descent into Glasgow. From here they had a two-hour wait before catching their connection to Stornoway. They'd get to Louisa around 9 p.m. From there they'd take another plane to London, meet up with Tariq and then get out of England forever.

Outside, dusk was fading into night. Thirty-thousand feet below them tiny pinpricks of illumination hinted at cities and roads. Acid turned her face to the window. Mouthed, *Sorry*, into the clouds. Though who she was apologising to, she wasn't sure. Her mother? Spook? Paula Silva? Maybe it was all of them. Maybe none.

She sat back in her seat. She was doing the right thing, she told herself. She couldn't save everyone. Hell, she was struggling to save herself. But soon she'd see her old mum, tell her she loved her, tell her she was sorry. Maybe one day she'd go back for her – take her out of that depressing care home and back to Italy. Somewhere warm and peaceful, away from the horrors of the world. Somewhere safe.

Whatever the bloody hell that meant.

Chapter Thirty-Seven

Acid peered out the window as the taxi pulled into the gravel driveway of Foiseil Blar House. Standing there now, in the ethereal glow of moonlight, it looked even more ominous than usual.

"This it?" Spook asked, from the back seat. "It looks kind of deserted."

Acid ignored her, but she was right. Not that the convalescent home ever bounced with merriment, but something about the place this evening seemed off. It was quiet. Too quiet.

"It is late, I guess," Spook went on. "Maybe everyone's asleep?"

"I called from the airport and spoke to one of the carers," Acid replied, twisting around in her seat to look at her. "They're expecting me. I think she likes me, so..."

Spook stiffened. "Oh. I see."

"Oh calm down," Acid told her. "Anyway, you can wait for me outside. I won't be long."

"Erm, no. Scotland's freezing." The taxi came to a stop in front of the stone steps leading up to the main entrance.

"All right," Acid said. "But if anyone asks, you're my cousin, Louisa's niece. It's family only. I made sure of it."

Acid paid the driver and the two women got out, Spook wrapping her arms around herself. "I'm still not sure about this," she said.

"It's fine. Trust me." The taxi drove away and Acid walked up to the entrance, pushed on the intercom. She heard a loud rasping buzz echo down the stark corridor beyond, but no one let them in, no one came to the door. The two women stared through the glass panels at the top of each door, peering into the gloom. There was a light on in reception, and beams of light emanated from each room along the corridor. But no sign of life.

"Do you see anyone?" Acid asked, putting her hand over her eyes to shield the glare of the moonlight.

"Nope, no one."

Acid buzzed again. Nothing. She grabbed the door handle and gave it a twist. It pulled open with ease.

Her heart sank.

"Normally the place is like Fort Knox." She stepped tentatively inside and over to the Plexiglas window of reception. Acid had never visited her mother this late. Maybe this was normal. But she still hoped to see Mary's rosy-cheeked face as she got up to the window.

"Aw, no."

"What is it?" Spook asked.

Acid didn't reply. She couldn't speak. Mary was there all right. Sat where she always was. But rather than the usual beaming smile, she wore a mask of pure horror, her mouth frozen in an eternal scream.

"What is it?" Spook asked again as she joined Acid at the window. "Oh shit."

They stared wide-eyed at the poor woman's blood-soaked blouse. At the blood spatter up the wall. And at the deep wound that had opened her neck from ear to ear.

"Who would do this?" Spook asked.

But Acid was already half-way down the corridor. She yanked a fire extinguisher from the wall and brandished it over her head as she kicked open the next set of double doors. Down the next corridor and to the end room she went as the scene got more bloody. It wasn't just Mary they'd killed. Dead bodies were strewn everywhere. Some had been shot, some stabbed, but all had the same rictus grin of fear painted across their white faces.

Acid scanned each bedroom as she passed. There were young and old, patients and carers alike. Some visitors, too. Families. Children. All dead. All murdered.

She got to the end room and stopped. The door was ajar and the light was on. Acid put her ear to the gap. Listening. Not wanting to enter. No sound came from the room.

She pushed the door open and slowly put her head around.

"Oh Mum. No."

Acid dropped the fire extinguisher to the floor and went to the old woman. She was sat in her usual armchair, facing out over the rolling fields. Her eyes were open, but she saw nothing now. Acid laid her hand on her mum's shoulder. She seemed smaller than the last time she was here, more delicate. They'd slit her throat. The same as Mary.

"You bastards," Acid whispered.

She gently took hold of Louisa's forehead and leaned her forward. It was a futile act. An attempt to close up the wound. She was stone cold. Acid brushed a strand of grey hair from her face and kissed the top of her head.

"I'm so sorry, Mum."

A part of her wished she could cry, but she was glad she didn't.

"Is that...?" Spook, at the door.

Acid didn't look up. "Yes. This is Louisa. My old mum." The words almost set her off. Almost.

Spook came nearer. "Was this...?"

"Caesar. Got to be."

"I thought no one knew about your mom."

"They didn't. But this is him. I know it." She pulled her mother's lifeless body to her. Held her against her chest. "But this is on me just as much. I did this. I let her down." In the silence that followed her words, a grim stillness fell over them. She clung tighter to her mum, pulling her closer. "Wait. What is that?" Acid held Louisa at arm's length. She'd felt something under her clothing. Something hard. She stepped back and pulled open Louisa's robe, fumbling at the thin nightshirt underneath. A small box was strapped around her chest, with two wires protruding from either side of the unit. Acid tugged at them, finding they led down to another larger package belted around Louisa's waist.

Spook gasped as a digital clock flashed up on the small box, startling in bright red LED. It began counting down from ten. Acid grabbed Spook's sleeve, pulling her along as she stumbled out the door.

"Run!" she screamed.

Chapter Thirty-Eight

Spook didn't need telling twice. Head down, and with her breath in her throat, she raced after Acid. Down the corridor they ran, leaping over dead bodies and pools of blood. They reached the end of the first corridor and leaned into the corner, pushing against the opposite wall to quicken the turn.

5...

They sped down the next long corridor and burst through a set of double doors.

4...

Past reception and through the entrance hall.

3...

2...

Outside and down the steps.

1...

They were a few metres clear of the entrance when Spook felt a rush of heat energy, and a huge explosion sent her flying forward onto the sharp gravel. Then it was quiet. As if all the sound had been sucked into a black hole.

Spook stayed low, covering her head with her arms and every muscle tense, waiting for death, for some flying debris to crush her. She waited, but nothing happened. Then, slowly, she lifted her head and looked around.

"You hurt?"

She rolled onto her back to see Acid Vanilla kneeling over her with an incongruous look of concern on her face.

Spook sat up. "Don't think so. What happened?"

"A bomb. Attached to a motion sensor." Acid held her hand out for Spook to grab hold of, and got them both to their feet. "They knew I was coming."

Spook looked over at the burning wreckage, then back at Acid whose eyes were cold once more, her face deadpan.

"Come on, let's get out of here." Acid turned and walked back towards the road. Spook grabbed her rucksack and hurried along after.

"Hey, where are you going?"

"Back to the airport, of course."

She was walking fast and Spook had run to catch up with her. "Wait, don't you think we should talk about what just happened?"

"No. Nothing to talk about."

"But your mom, and all those people…"

Acid stopped and turned sharply. "What do you want me to say? She's dead. They all are. And it's my fault. That what you want to hear?"

Spook took a step back. "I don't think you should blame yourself," she told her. "Maybe we should sit down, process it. I know I could do with—"

"No," Acid said, setting off once more. "There's no time. We need to get to London and meet Tariq."

"But—"

"For Pete's sake, no!" Acid yelled. "There's nothing to

talk about. I just want to get to the airport and get out of here."

They marched on in silence, Acid with a face like death and Spook taking deep breaths and trying to keep calm, knowing any outward show of emotion would only provoke more anger in her companion. But then a terrible thought came to her, and she had to run into the long grass and wretch up a mouthful of bile. It was only a small amount, but it was harsh and sour.

"Sorry," she said, when she was done. "I just need to—"

"Whatever. Can we get going?" Acid had her arms folded, tapping her foot.

"Please. Wait," Spook cried, holding her hand up. "I need to tell you something."

"Jesus. Go on, then. Quickly."

"I just thought. I had all this research saved in my Dropbox account. On you, mainly. But also your mom. About her being alive. About the care home." She spoke fast, trying to get it all out before fear stopped her. "It wouldn't have been hard for a decent hacker to find that information."

Acid stared at her, then sneered and walked away, quickening her pace as she got further down the road.

"Do you understand what I'm saying—"

"Listen, kid. This isn't your fault," Acid said, cutting her off.

"But if I hadn't—"

"I've told you, all right? This is on me. My bad karma. Caught up with me at last." She looked at the sky. "Now, please, let's get to the airport and get out of this depressing fucking place."

For Spook, the next hour felt like an eternity as the two women trudged on in the cold and wet. They got to the airport just after nine and got on a plane thirty minutes later. As expected, Acid took the window seat and spent the whole journey with her forehead pressed against the glass. Spook didn't even try to make conversation. She knew from experience any attempt would only get shot down.

They landed at Heathrow just after eleven. Once through security, Acid stomped through the arrivals lounge and out into the cold night air.

"Don't we need a cab?" Spook called after her, watching as Acid strode straight past a row of waiting taxis.

"No. We can walk from here," she yelled back, turning down a winding road, flanked on both sides by tall trees.

Spook scurried up behind her. "Hey."

"What is it now?"

"Where the hell are we going?" Spook held her arms up and let them drop against her sides.

"Jesus Christ. Why do I have to keep explaining myself to you? Where the hell do you think we're going?"

"I just figured—"

"Well don't figure. All right? We're meeting Tariq by the small reservoir on Stanwell Moor. That's it."

Spook shivered. "Sounds grim."

"It's perfectly safe. I've met Tariq there many times. It's our spot."

"And he knows to meet us?"

"Yes, and we'll be late if you don't get a bloody wriggle on."

They carried on with little else said, getting to the meeting point twenty minutes later where, huddled behind a small cluster of evergreen trees that stood near the water's edge, they waited.

"Where the hell is he?" Acid checked her watch. "I don't get it."

She scanned the vicinity and Spook did the same noting how the trees silhouetted against the night sky gave the place an ominous feel. She didn't want to be here. And Tariq was nowhere to be seen. They waited ten minutes, then twenty, Acid pacing up and down the whole time, occasionally stopping to cast her eyes over the area. This was not like Tariq, she told Spook, he was never late.

They'd been waiting almost forty-five minutes when Acid walked up close to Spook and lowered her voice. "Listen, I don't like this. He's obviously not coming. I think we need to get out of here."

Spook didn't reply. Just then she was too afraid to. She followed closely behind Acid as she led them out of the grassland and back onto the main road.

"Staines station is about ten minutes from here," Acid said. "We'll catch a train from there into the centre."

"Then what? What about my new passport?"

Acid turned to look at Spook, her expression changing from icy blankness to something nearing humanity. "I don't know what happened with Tariq, but you've still got your original one, yes? You'll have to risk it." She stopped walking a second and looked down. "Listen, Spook, once we get into the centre, you're on your own. You know that, right? I am sorry I can't be more help. But the entire world's upside down. I don't know what to tell you."

"What will I do?"

Acid puffed out her cheeks. "If I was you I'd go back to the States. It's a big country. Go somewhere quiet, away from a city. Take on a new name, do cash-in-hand jobs for a few years. You should be okay."

"Should be? Geez, thanks for the reassuring chat. You know, I never asked for any of this, Acid. I've done nothing wrong. Apart from believe you might do right by me."

Acid was in Spook's face in a beat, stabbing a finger into her sternum. "You know what, I should have killed you," she said. "Done everyone a favour. If I had, none of this would have happened. I'd be on a beach right now, Louisa would be alive, and I wouldn't have to listen to that whiny fucking voice."

"But you didn't kill me," Spook hit back. "Because you can see this isn't right, what Cerberix did. You ask me, the person you were before all that bad shit happened to you – she's still in there somewhere. And you know what else I think? You wanted out of this life long before you met me. You just didn't realise it."

"Oh piss off."

"No. Why won't you admit it?"

"Admit what?"

"That you've got a heart. That you're not cut out for killing people any longer?"

Acid's eyes blazed with an emotion that was as difficult to read as it was terrifying. "Yeah? Maybe you're right. So I'm useless to you. Can't help you."

Spook forced herself to hold eye contact. Her legs shook. "What, so you're going to run away?"

Acid paused a second. She looked shocked. "You say that to me, after everything that's happened? Fuck you." She pushed past Spook and strode on without her.

It was all Spook could do just to keep up. And when they arrived at Staines railway station twenty minutes later, it was after yet another typically awkward and conversation-less journey. The departure board said the train to Charing Cross was due in seven minutes. They sat and waited, both staring at the train tracks. Spook glanced over at Acid, wondering if she was thinking the same as her. Her face was tense and stony. Her jaw clamped shut in what could have been anger, or shame or simply annoyance, it was hard to tell.

"Can I still use my credit card?" Spook asked, speaking so quietly she hardly heard herself.

Acid sighed. "Do you have to?"

"Well, yeah. I've got no cash. I need to get a hotel for the night. Something to eat. A plane ticket. Clothes. Everything."

Acid was silent. The clock on the departure board ticked away. Three minutes to go.

"Draw out as much as you can in one go," she said eventually. "But listen, if Banjo made it back to HQ then the client has the recording. They might be happy with that. You might be in the clear. So long as you keep your head down." She looked at Spook and smirked. "But you're not going to do that, are you?"

"I don't think so. I have to show the world what they did."

Acid nodded and returned to staring at the tracks.

The train arrived and they got on, found seats next to each other. All with a heavy tension in the air. A shared awareness that this was it, the end of the line. At Charing Cross they stood on the platform for a few minutes in the cold night air, their breath visible under the harsh halogen bulbs above.

"I guess this is it," Spook said. "So long, Acid Vanilla, I hope you find what you're looking for."

"Oh, don't be so clichéd," Acid told her, then paused, something like uncertainty tugging at the edge of her mouth. "Listen, Spook, I am sorry that I can't do more. Can't – won't – whatever. I mean it. But I wouldn't be any use to you. My head feels like it's been shattered into a million pieces."

Spook pushed her glasses up her nose. "I'm sorry too," she said. "I guess I'll see you around."

She swung her rucksack over her shoulder and, not looking back, headed for the exit. She was terrified, she had no clue where she was going, and on top of that her heart was breaking. But what else could she do? It was clear Acid Vanilla wasn't going to help her. Whatever happened next, she was on her own.

Chapter Thirty-Nine

"Come in. Sit down." Ethan Clarkson opened his arms in a gesture of welcome as Sinclair Whitman strode into his London penthouse apartment.

Sinclair looked around. "I take it you've good news for me?"

Ethan indicated for Whitman to sit on one of a pair of brushed-suede couches that faced each other in the middle of the room. Then he sauntered over by the large window that looked out over Knightsbridge.

"Do you know how much stress you've caused me these last two weeks?" he asked.

Whitman sat, folding one leg elegantly over the other. "I've been concerned myself, son. Tell me – is all well?"

Ethan ignored the question. "I haven't eaten. I haven't slept. Hell, I've got the keynote in five days and I'm totally unprepared."

Sinclair stretched his arm along the back of the couch. "All right, drop the fucking Woody Allen routine, will you? What gives?"

Ethan walked over to the drinks cabinet and picked up a large cut-glass decanter from the polished-mahogany shelf. Twenty-year-old Aultmore. He poured out two glasses.

"We are celebrating?" Sinclair asked, brushing a fleck of lint from his trousers. "Come on, son. Tell."

Ethan handed over the scotch and allowed a beatific smile to play across his tanned features. He was back to his old self – calm, charismatic, with the carefree swagger that came from knowing you were untouchable.

"Yes. All is well," he told Sinclair. "I have the recording. It was couriered over to me this morning."

"About freaking time. Well, cheers." He drank. "What about the other issue? The idiot at the bottom of all this?"

Ethan sat opposite. He wanted to tell Sinclair he was looking at the idiot. But he bit his tongue. "The employee? Dead."

"We sure?"

Ethan swirled the amber liquid around his glass. He didn't think much of this particular blend, but it was expensive, and he liked expensive things. "I have it on good authority. Recording retrieved. Problem eradicated."

Sinclair's shoulders dropped. "There we go. All good."

"Maybe. This time. But you can't keep putting yourself in… precarious situations, shall we say?" Ethan sat forward, stern. He needed the old man to understand. "I know we go back a long way and you're a damn good CFO, but I will not allow you to ruin this."

Sinclair looked down his nose. "Are you threatening me, Ethan?"

"No, of course I'm not. I mean, be careful. Why not take a holiday? That island you like."

He was talking about Paradise Island. A secret resort in the Indian Ocean, only accessible by private jet. A place where rich men could live out any fantasy they desired. Where, for a quarter of a million dollars, you could get a Diamond-Standard room and access to a harem of ten girls. All of them beautiful, all guaranteed disease-free. All of them underage.

Sinclair waved his hand. "Nah, I don't feel like it. It's the keynote in a few days. Don't you want me there?"

Ethan turned and looked out the window, speaking now with his back to him. "I don't want any disruptions, Sinclair. That's all. Don't want anything else to knock us off course."

"I swear. It won't happen again."

Ethan looked out at the night sky. The sun had set many hours ago, but a red hue remained over the city. He wanted to believe Whitman. But he was so close now he could taste it. Once he'd delivered the keynote, the world would know how powerful his new Gen-Z system was. He'd be truly unassailable. And he wasn't going to allow anything to get in the way of that. Not even his old friend.

"Hey. Are you listening to me?" Sinclair appeared by his side. "I said, can I see the recording?"

"You want to see it? Why?"

The old man shrugged. "Curiosity."

Ethan couldn't be bothered to argue. He walked over to his desk and woke the computer with a shake of the mouse. The tell-tale video was still on screen. He'd checked it the second the thumb-drive was out of the envelope. He clicked play and stood back, watching Sinclair view the recording. He was enjoying it, the sick old bastard. Ethan looked away and took another drink.

"Can I have this?" Sinclair asked, once it had played through.

"Excuse me?"

"The recording. Can I have it?"

Ethan Clarkson stared into Whitman's held-out hand. As far as he knew it was the only copy. Surrendering it now would take away any leverage he had.

"Come on, son, give it me."

Ethan held his nerve. "In exchange for the photo."

The men stared at each other for a long moment. Then a smile cracked the stiff lines on Whitman's face.

"Oh you're good," he said. He walked back over to the couch. "But no. Good idea. Best we both hang onto our respective… insurance policies, shall we call them?" He finished his scotch and placed the glass down on the low coffee table. "More fun that way, don't you agree?"

Ethan took a deep breath and held it in his lungs a second. "Fair enough," he said.

"Groovy. Then I'll see you at the keynote." Whitman raised his hand in a mock salute. "You take care until then, son."

He showed himself out, slamming the door behind him.

Ethan stood in the centre of the room, staring at the closed door for a good minute. Then, with a yell, he launched his glass at the wall, not flinching when it shattered into a million tiny pieces.

But now a new idea was forming in that genius brain of his. He'd get the keynote out of the way, get the launch event done, and then – once he'd taken his rightful place alongside the likes of Zuckerberg and Bezos – he'd give Caesar another call. Cut out this cancer once and for all, before it could do any more damage.

He sunk down onto the soft cushions of his couch. He'd long ago made peace with the moral and spiritual dilemma brought on by having someone killed. So doing it a second, a third, or even a twentieth time if the need arose – that would be a walk in the park.

Chapter Forty

Despite Acid's deteriorating disposition, her instincts had kicked in. She approached her building from the shadows. The smart course of action. Yet, even as she skulked in the dark alley opposite and assessed the area, she knew the truth. If Caesar, or Davros Ratpack, or the whole of Annihilation Pest Control was waiting for her, she'd find it hard to put up much fight.

She stayed in the darkness, sheltered behind a large tree. Nothing seemed out of the ordinary. Her kitchen lights were on, but she had them on a timer. She crossed the road and headed for the front door of her building, swiftly unlocking both locks and slipping inside. She scanned the entrance hall. The stairs to her floor. All clear.

Acid leaned with her back against the door and closed her eyes. Her insides felt raw. She hoped Caesar was waiting for her upstairs. She'd have it out with him here and now. Would rip the bastard's throat out. Or die trying. Either option was fine by her.

An image flashed across her mind of her poor mother.

The last time she'd ever see her. She looked so innocent and frail sitting there in her chair, all alone at the end.

"I'm sorry," Acid whispered to the ceiling. But she wasn't. Right now she didn't feel sorry, or sad, or scared, or anything. That was the problem.

She'd realised it as soon as she'd left Spook at the station. The chatter had ceased. The intense mania of the bats replaced by a new presence – one that was altogether more despicable – the lumpen manatee of depression. It slumped heavily across her shoulders, weighing her down as she tiptoed upstairs and unlocked the door to her apartment.

Like always, it was concepts rather than words that plagued Acid's senses. A tingling awareness in the back of her consciousness rather than sheer logic. She wished she could cry. It'd be a release. But she couldn't. She'd spent the last sixteen years hardening herself to concepts like pain and guilt and human connection. Indeed, a huge part of her training with Caesar was learning to push her emotions down. To become callous towards life. Her own included. It was the only way she could do what she did.

She entered the apartment and closed the door behind her. She paused, listening, then called out, "Hello." But nothing. She slipped off her jacket and went into the kitchen. The low-wattage, under-unit lights gave a warm glow to the room, absorbed somewhat by the black granite work surfaces. She yanked open her large stainless steel refrigerator and went straight for a beer. Instinct again. She twisted off the top and took a long swig. It was cold and gassy and the carbonation burnt her throat, but she liked that.

Back through into the front room and over to the stereo, she opted for the iPod rather than messing around with vinyl, hitting shuffle and getting Sabbath's, *You Won't Change Me*.

"Well, shit, Ozzy," Acid sneered. "Isn't that the truth?"

She slumped onto the couch, letting the heavy chords wash over her. She'd been stupid to think she could do anything but kill for a living. This was who she was. Remove that part of her, she didn't exist.

"Idiot. Stupid bloody idiot." She sat up and drained the beer bottle in one go. She'd let Spook get to her, but it stopped this second. Acid Vanilla had to return. The role she'd created for herself all those years ago – that person was strong, powerful, full of direst cruelty. But just as important, that person was a survivor. They didn't mope around feeling sorry for themselves like some miserable, wounded puppy. They sucked it up and moved on. They saw when they were crashing and took a holiday. Like she should have done at the start of this miserable episode. Life would have been so different now.

A new song came on the iPod, Beethoven's Egmont Overture. Acid got to her feet and stumbled into the bedroom as the violins sprung into life. The room was dark. But enough light filtered through from the lounge for her to see the large cardboard box on her bed. She stopped in the doorway. She'd never seen this box before. It hadn't been there when she left for Paris. The gentle lilt of oboes carried through from the stereo next door as she moved over to the bed. A part of her already knew what was inside, but it didn't stop her from being tentative as she opened the lid and peered inside.

"Ah, shit."

It was Tariq. Or, more accurately, it was Tariq's head. He had two passports stuffed in his mouth. She didn't need to look to know who they belonged to.

As the music hit an upsurge of strings and woodwind, Acid closed the box and walked over to her wardrobe. She removed a black holdall and placed it on the bed next to Tariq's head. Then she pulled various pieces of underwear from her chest of drawers – bras, pants, vest tops – followed by a bunch of plain black t-shirts, jeans, leggings. She balled each item as small as possible and stuffed them in the bag. Once she'd packed as much as would fit, she took the bag into the bathroom and tossed in hairspray, bottles of shampoo, her expensive creams, make-up. She returned to the bedroom and opened her large ottoman bed, revealing a sizeable armoury: eight pistols, two rifles, plus silencers, knives, a selection of mobile phones. She grabbed a burner phone and checked it worked. Then she stuffed a new Glock 45 and a Beretta 70S down the back of her jeans and shoved whatever else would fit into the holdall. She carried it though into the lounge and put on her jacket. Then, as the orchestra reached its final crescendo, she left her apartment and slammed the door behind her.

Acid didn't know where she was heading, all she knew was she couldn't stay here. Her home was compromised, and even if Annihilation weren't watching her they'd be back soon enough. She hurried down the steps onto the pavement and dummied out the gate before doubling back on herself and heading down the side of her building. At the end of the alley she cut across a small square and took a right, which opened onto to a wider road that led to the river. It was the least populated area in terms of houses, but a short high street led to a strip of food outlets, late-night bars and – most importantly – taxis. The underground would be too risky, and Acid needed to get as far away from here as possible. She hailed down a passing black cab and jumped in the back.

"Can you head east, please," she told the driver. He was a big man. Typical cockney. He was wearing a flat cap and an expression that said he'd seen everything there was to see in life.

"That's it? Just east?" he asked. "Sounds ominous."

Acid clocked his eyes in the rear-view mirror. "I'm looking for a hotel." She held up the new phone, glad to see it had data and a signal. "I'll let you know in a minute or two."

"Right you are, love," the driver said with a laugh. "You having a bad day, are ya?"

Acid sniffed and gazed out the window. "You know what," she told him. "You don't know the half of it."

Chapter Forty-One

In the end Acid opted for a poky bed and breakfast place in Abbey Wood. It was a run-down affair, lacking in amenities and freezing cold. But that was one reason she'd chosen it. Penance. Self-flagellation. An attempt to shear off the wretched humanity she'd allowed to develop these last few weeks.

Her room was on the second floor, a long and thin space with a double bed pushed against one wall and a slim, veneered drawer unit opposite. On the wall facing the door a window looked out onto an overgrown yard littered with old furniture. To the left of the window, another door opened into a small bathroom comprising of a beige toilet and sink unit. It also had beige carpets and beige walls. Everything beige.

Another reason Acid had chosen the hotel was the 24-hour internet café and late-night off licence she'd spotted around the corner. After checking in and paying in advance for seven nights, she dumped her bag and headed straight out. First to the off licence, thankfully still open at 3 a.m.

She bought cheap scotch and a bottle of red wine, a 2015 Argentinian Malbec. She also bought note pads, a box of Sharpies and some drawing pins. Then she headed for the internet café.

The pasty-faced man on the counter wore an LA Raiders baseball cap and didn't look up from his PlayStation as Acid lay down five pound-coins for an hour online plus ten printing credits. The man typed something into a computer and shoved a slip of paper at her with a short passcode written on it. He still didn't look up.

"Much obliged." Acid picked up the paper and scanned the room, assessing which computer unit would provide maximum privacy. Only two other people occupied the café, not surprising at this time of night. They both looked to be Chinese, playing some online game. Acid made her way between the two banks of yellowing computers and chose a unit in the far corner. Here she had a wall behind her plus a clear view of the entrance. The printer was a few steps away.

She typed in the code and, while the computer loaded up, cracked open the bottle of scotch and took a long drink. It wasn't the nicest thing she'd ever put in her mouth, some weird brand she'd never heard of, but it was welcome.

Once the old PC had settled down, she opened a new browser window and signed into a secure email account. As always there was only one email in the inbox. A saved message from herself that contained a single link. Acid clicked on it and held her breath as the Annihilation Pest Control Portal appeared on screen. She typed in her login details and took another long drink as the egg timer icon appeared and the computer's fan went into overdrive.

"Come on, let's have you," she whispered at the screen. "Please."

Thirty seconds later the recognisable home screen dashboard flashed up, and she relaxed. Her login was still active.

Working fast, Acid pulled off as many details as she could find – last known whereabouts of each operative, lists of aliases, current GPS co-ordinates. She printed them all off, along with any recent photos she could find. There were eight active operatives, not including herself, and from what she could see they were scattered all over the world. Even Caesar himself was in Thailand. It appeared his new goal, to create a global nomadic assassin network, was being realised.

Bastard.

This would be harder than she'd first thought. Doubly so with this heavy despair pressing down on her soul. But she had to press on. Her thirst for revenge was all she had. She gathered together the print-outs and stuffed them into her jacket. Then she logged-off, took another long swig of the scotch and went back to the hotel.

Chapter Forty-Two

After leaving Acid at Charing Cross station, Spook had wandered the wet streets that ran down the side of the Strand for hours. She was lost, cold, miserable. She cursed Acid Vanilla and Sinclair Whitman, and this Caesar person she'd never even met – but most of all she cursed herself, for ever taking that stupid job with Cerberix Inc.

Eventually though she'd had the same idea as Acid, and got herself a room for the night in a small hotel over the river in Elephant and Castle. First chance tomorrow she'd buy a plane ticket. Canada, perhaps. Spook had always fancied going to Vancouver and, despite the precariousness of her situation, she felt excited at the prospect. She'd get settled somewhere safe, outside the city, like Acid had suggested. Then she'd set up bulletproof cloaking software and email the recording to as many people as she could. The CIA, FBI, the Cerberix board. A part of her still didn't believe she could do it. But being with Acid Vanilla these past few days she'd learnt that actions were all that mattered. Fear was something she had to make peace with.

She woke early the next morning and opened her trusty laptop, ready to move forward with the next stage of her life. So when she logged on to the exasperatingly slow broadband the hotel provided and saw an email from Rory Roberts, she was somewhat troubled.

Rory had been a classmate of Spook's at the MIT and she'd had a small crush on him – but the fact he was emailing her wasn't what made her sit up and pay attention. It was what was written in the subject line:

WTF! Seen the news on Goldballs? Poor guy (LOL)

Without taking a breath Spook clicked open the email, seeing a single link in the body, along with a sad-face emoji. Followed by two crying-laughing-face emoji. She clicked on the link. It was a news article from *TechWorld News*. The headline:

Silicon Valley Golden Boy Dead After Overdose.

At the top of the page was a photo of the titular Golden Boy. He was posing with a colourful cocktail on a white sandy beach, looking incredibly smug and self-important. He was also instantly recognisable as Eugene Goldman.

Spook took a moment to compose herself, then carried on reading. Eugene's body had been discovered by his housemaid when she arrived for work. He was in bed. With a bottle of pills in his hand. An apparent suicide. The article said he'd been rushed to hospital but was pronounced dead on arrival. The piece then asked a simple question, *Why? Why would a man with so much going for him, at the start of an illustrious career, take his own life?* Then it went off into conjecture and spin, talking about the pressures of the tech world. Spook read all the way to the end, but she'd stopped taking it in. Her mind was racing.

She'd been watching Eugene that night. The night of the murder. If they'd flagged her watching Whitman, there was no reason they wouldn't have checked who else she'd been watching. Or communicating with.

"Oh, shit. No."

Her stomach did cartwheels as she logged onto her Facebook page and scanned her feed. Nothing. Adverts mainly. A few friends sharing motivational quotes, some Star Wars memes. She let out a sigh. It was fine. Her imagination running away with her. But then she clicked over to Kelvin's page and saw all the messages of condolence, and it felt like her head would pop.

"Fuck," she whispered to herself, stretching out the word as far as it would go.

Her eyes darted around the screen, searching for answers. From what she could tell, Kelvin had been killed at his home. The victim of a robbery gone wrong. They'd taken his laptop, all his tech equipment, then staved his head in with a barbell. Wrong place, wrong time, was the consensus. But Spook knew different. Kelvin and Eugene had been murdered by Annihilation Pest Control. Their deaths paid for by Cerberix Inc.

Spook slammed her laptop down and punched the wall. Which she immediately regretted. A sharp pain shot into her hand, making her want to punch the wall again. Instead she stood and walked to the window. Outside, the sky was grey, murky. A dense mist hung in the air like a bad odour. Spook leaned against the glass. She had to do something.

She went back to her laptop and opened the IDE document she'd been working on the last few months, her facial recognition software. It was buggy as hell and she still had to assimilate it with local CCTV footage, but it was possible. She settled down on the bed and crossed her legs in front of the laptop. Spook had impetus now. A reason to make this work. No one else was going to die because of her.

Chapter Forty-Three

Acid Vanilla hadn't left her room for two days. Maybe longer. She remembered venturing out to buy more drink at one point, plus the chicken burger that sat uneaten on the windowsill. But that was it. She'd spent the rest of the time planning her revenge, drinking, and stripping and cleaning the various firearms she'd brought with her. But mainly drinking.

Now she sat on the side of the bed with a bottle of something opaque and Polish between her legs and stared at the wall opposite. At the eight photos she'd stuck there. Her ex-colleagues and her mentor all stared back. Her new kill list.

"Where the hell are you?" she sneered, swaying as she did – the effects of the half-bottle she'd downed since breakfast.

She shuffled over to the photo of Beowulf Caesar. Even this grainy, black-and-white photo stirred a rage inside her. She took another gulp from the bottle. Looked into his eyes. The problem was, if it had been pure rage she could deal with it. But she had crushing regret in there too. Sorrow. That's what bothered her the most. She felt let down. The man she'd believed in all these years, and he'd done this.

Acid moved back to the bed and laid her head on the thin pillow. Her body felt heavy. Her face sagged with the weight of absolutely everything. What else could possibly happen to her? It was as if the whole world was turning against—

There was a knock on the door.

Shit.

Acid froze, hoping whoever it was would get the message. She knew it wasn't the cleaning staff as she'd paid off the woman on reception, told her not to send anyone in until she'd vacated the room.

Another knock.

Acid raised her chin at Caesar's mug shot. "You?"

She reached under the bed and grabbed one of the guns she'd gaffer-taped underneath. A Beretta. She checked the clip and put one in the chamber before gliding over to the door. There was no spyhole.

She froze.

Listening.

The knocking went again. Louder now. More urgent. Acid held the gun aloft, her finger tense on the trigger.

"Who is it?"

"It's me," a voice whispered. "It's Spook."

Acid let the gun drop to her side. "Oh piss off," she rasped.

"Please, I need to speak with you."

"We've got nothing to say to each other," Acid replied. "You should be long gone by now."

"I can't. Not now. I need your help." She went quiet for

a moment, then added, "Can I please come in? So we can talk properly."

Acid sighed loudly, making sure Spook could hear it through the door. "Fine. But be quick, I'm working."

She unlocked the door and eased it open a touch, poking the gun through the crack and peering out over the barrel.

"Hey, I told you, it's me," Spook cried, stepping back and throwing her arms in the air.

Acid snapped her head back. "Inside. Quick. You've got one minute, then you're gone. Or I swear to god, I will shoot you." She opened the door wide and Spook slunk inside.

Chapter Forty-Four

Once in the room, Spook couldn't help but pull a face. "This place freaking stinks." She pulled her jumper over her nose and squinted at the photos on the wall. Then she walked over to the long row of empty bottles on the chest of drawers. "Been having a party, I see."

Acid went to the window and cracked it open. Her movements seemed deliberate, over-thought. It was clear she'd been drinking heavily and consistently since Spook last saw her over two days ago. She wore a pair of threadbare black leggings and an old Johnny Thunders shirt with the sleeves cut off.

"Tell me, what have I done to deserve this delightful visit?"

There was something different about her. Her hair was wild and greasy, her make-up smeared and worn. But it wasn't just her appearance that was off.

Spook was about to answer, when Acid snapped her head up. A wave of confusion cracked her supercilious expression. "How did you find me?"

Spook swallowed. "That's what I want to talk to you about. That and the fact your boss has killed two of my friends this week. Did you know about that?"

Acid didn't look at her. "I'd say him killing my mum still wins out."

"It's not a competition."

"No. It certainly is not."

Spook sighed. "Whatever. They need to be stopped. All of them."

Acid cast a hand over the wall of photos. "I know," she said. "That is what I'm working on."

"But Whitman too," Spook said. "And Clarkson. This is on them as well. They can't get away with it."

"Jesus, kid. Change the record."

"Wow. Ironic much? Don't you get bored with being so cynical?"

"Beats the alternative," Acid mumbled. "Least this way there're no surprises."

Spook folded her arms. "You keep telling yourself that."

"Piss off. You've no clue what you're talking about."

"Do you?"

Acid leapt to her feet and grabbed Spook by the arm. "Get out. I'm sick of the bloody sight of you." She dragged her over to the door, ready to throw her out. "I should have killed you when I had the chance."

She went for the door but Spook stopped her. "Wait, listen. I can help, okay? If you're hell-bent on getting Caesar and his crew, I can help you find them."

Acid halted. Her fingers gripped the door handle. "How?"

Spook shook free of her grasp and moved back into the room. She gave it a beat before speaking.

"The same way I found you. The facial recognition software I've been developing. I got it working, connected it to a spider program that scans CCTV footage from all over the world. It's extensive as hell. My best work." She beamed. "I found you in a second: coming out of a shop with a bag full of booze. Unsurprisingly. After that I made a list of the hotels in the area and did the rounds – complete with photo and sob story about you being my long-lost sister. Wasn't hard."

Acid laughed, but Spook could tell she was thinking about it. "I take it the catch is I have to help you take down Cerberix?"

Spook adjusted her glasses. "We can do this."

Acid leaned forward, resting her elbows on her knees, and at that moment Spook realised what was different about her. All the vitality had drained away. It was like she was a husk. A cheap photocopy of the person she'd been even a few days ago. Grief. It could break anyone. Even someone like Acid Vanilla. It was horrible to see.

"I'm not sure I can," Acid whispered into the floor. "Look at me. Full of bluster and fury, but what am I actually doing? Drinking myself into a stupor while I rant at photographs. I'm finished. Caesar's won. Like he always does."

Spook sat on the bed next to her.

"You don't mean that," she said. "I get it. You're sad, drunk, not thinking straight. But a good night's sleep. Some rest. We've got time. Acid, I need you. Maybe I sound like a broken record, but it's because it's true. We can't let them get away with this."

Acid wasn't listening. She was mumbling into the bottle. Talking about bad karma, about her mum and Caesar and disappearing forever. Like it was that easy. Spook clenched her teeth. This wasn't the Acid Vanilla she'd met. The one she knew. The one who – yes, it was true – she cared for. She had to help her see this was worth fighting for. Snap her out of this funk. But Acid was still muttering.

"I have a condition," she whispered, to the floor. "It's like bipolar. Though less up and down. More manageable. Usually. It can actually be helpful in this line of work. I take big risks and they pay off. I don't need sleep. I can even think more clearly. More ingeniously. I wouldn't change it. But now and again, the bats, the mania, it takes over. Sends me too far the other way. I make mistakes, lose control. You get me? I drink too much, sleep with the wrong people, think I'm invincible when I'm not." She sighed and picked at a callus on her palm.

Spook gave it a beat. "I did kind of wonder," she said. "It makes sense. I read an article once on what you're talking about: The Secret Sauce of Silicon Valley – something like that. A lot of the world's top entrepreneurs have the same condition. It's a kind of hypomania, right? Keeps you inspired, spontaneous, machinelike. Helps you hit goals whilst staying connected to reality."

Acid listened without reaction. "Well, yeah," she muttered. "But that's the problem. Staying connected to reality. I haven't been these last few weeks. Months, if I think about it." She got off the bed and moved over to the photos, speaking to the wall. "You know, I keep saying Caesar made me who I am. And he did, in a way. But the rest of it – that I couldn't leave – it's bullshit. I could have stopped. Could have disappeared. A new identity, in a new country. It would have been hard but not impossible. But I didn't want to. I was number one, and I liked that…" She trailed off.

Spook shifted on the bed as Acid dropped back down

beside her. "Well, I'd say you've stopped now, right? That's good."

"Changes nothing. Louisa's dead because of me. Those bastards are all still breathing. I still want to die."

"What the hell good would that do? For anyone," Spook said. "Yeah, you've made some bad choices over the years, but you were young. Sounds to me like you were groomed by this creep." She risked a glance at Acid, but she didn't look up. "You can't change the past, Acid. But you can change what happens next."

Acid placed her hands in her lap. "If only I'd said no to that last job... taken that holiday."

"Ah come on, you said it, enough with the bullshit. You know damn well a holiday wouldn't have solved anything." Spook hesitated, expecting a suitably terse response, but it never came. She tried again, softer now. "What I mean is, you don't have to be the person you think you are."

Acid looked up. "You know you sound like every bloody therapist I've ever had."

Spook held up one finger. "Stay focused, please. Talk to me."

"What do you want me to say, Spook? All I want to do is burn the entire universe to the fucking ground." She finished whatever she was drinking and chucked the empty bottle on the bed. "Listen, don't think I haven't thought about this. Because I have. It's all I have thought about. I'm driving myself crazy. Crazier, I mean." She got off the bed and paced. Speaking fast. With energy. "You know, maybe Banjo was right. Maybe deep down I have been searching for redemption. A way to make amends for everything I've done. But do you realise how lame that sounds? And so what? How do I even start?"

Spook got to her feet. "You know how. You help me take down those pricks."

The comment received a huff and trademark eye-roll from Acid. She made for the bathroom but Spook got in her way. She'd seen an opening. A chink in Acid Vanilla's impenetrable demeanour. She wasn't going to waste it.

"Why won't you admit it? You want to do good. You want to get justice for Paula Silva. Otherwise why would you have even helped me? You saved my life. Three times."

Acid held her hand up. "Four, actually. If you count disobeying my own orders."

"Exactly! You risked everything you had. Your career. Your life. And why? Because you couldn't bring yourself to go through with it once you heard the truth. But it's hard for you, I know, because to admit that means opening yourself up. It means admitting you have a conscience and that you care about something other than yourself. You never needed a damn holiday. You just needed to let yourself feel something again."

Spook slumped onto the bed. Her cheeks were burning and her legs shook but she'd said her piece. She put her hands on her knees and braced herself for the fallout.

But Acid said nothing. Not for a long time. She stood in the centre of the small room, still except for the rise and fall of her chest. All at once she seemed delicate. Vulnerable. When she spoke her voice had no hint of sarcasm.

"You think I can change?"

Spook smiled. "I think you already have."

Acid moved over and sat next to her. "You know, you're good. I underestimated you."

"People usually do."

She took a deep breath. "All right," she said, her voice bolder again. "Let's say we do this. You got a plan?"

"I've got a plan."

Acid considered it. "And you'll help me find Caesar?"

"It's in my best interests, right?" Spook said. "Don't worry. We'll get them. All of them. We're a good team."

"Steady on. Let's not get ahead of ourselves."

"But you're in?"

Acid sighed. "Yes. I'm in." She stood and stretched. "You are wrong about one thing though."

"Oh? What's that?"

"I do need a bloody holiday."

Chapter Forty-Five

Raaz Terabyte chewed her bottom lip as the words appeared on her monitor screen. *Line 1: Beowulf Caesar.* The robotic pulse of the web-phone reverberated around the walls.

"Bollocks."

Raaz had been hoping her first day in the new place might have been a peaceful one. Time to settle in, get to grips with the new systems. But as always, this was wishful thinking.

She wondered for a second if she might get away with ignoring the call. Tell the boss she was dealing with something in the next room – where Annihilation Pest Control's huge bank of servers were stored. But she quickly dismissed that idea. It was unprofessional. Plus the mood Caesar was in, it was likely to get her eradicated.

She sat back in her large, black leather chair and opened the connection.

"There you bloody well are, I was beginning to think

you were ignoring me." Caesar's face filled the screen. "You got everything set up?"

His movements were jumpy, the image pixilated. But that was expected. Despite having set up the main control room earlier today, Raaz was yet to install every program and server unit.

"Yes. All good here." Raaz shifted on the squeaky leather chair. "There's been a few small issues in masking our IPs. But it won't take me long to sort out."

"How are you finding the new place?"

"It's great. Thank you." Raaz looked around the room. No one would be facetious enough to call it an office, but even workspace was pushing it. The walls were bare and made of thick concrete. Apart from the blue glow from Raaz's three monitors, the only other light was a dim emergency bulb that shone down from the ceiling. Being so far underground it was also freezing cold, even with the Fireball 230V propane heater burning away in the corner like a jet engine. But it was secure and it was undetectable. That was what mattered.

Caesar had christened this new place The Bunker, but it was actually a series of six rooms, built in the sixties at the height of the Cold War and meant as a survival unit for government officials, for when the bomb dropped. Being off-grid and away from any major city, it was the perfect location for Annihilation Pest Control's new Global Communication Hub.

"Well then?" Caesar growled. "You know why I'm calling."

Raaz did. She paused. "I can't confirm for definite. Not yet. But it's likely."

"Excuse me? Likely means fuck all. Give me details."

"Sorry, boss." Raaz picked at the skin on the side of her

thumb. "I've managed to get dental records of every person pulled from the wreckage. But no concrete match. That's not to say they weren't blown to pieces if they were next to the device…"

"No. She's alive, I can feel it. Bollocks." Caesar slammed his fist on the desk, making the screen jump. Making Raaz jump as well. Beowulf Caesar was a scary individual. Even with five thousand miles between them.

"If she is alive, I'll find her," Raaz told him. "The second I have a positive ID I'll organise a strike team to take her out."

Caesar stroked his chin. "Maybe we should open up the contract. Let the world's finest have a go at her."

"Not yet, sir," Raaz replied. "Let's keep this in-house. I can find her, I'm certain."

"Fine. Make sure you do. We can't have her running around like some loose cannon. She's a bleeding pest."

Raaz was emphatic. "Don't worry, Caesar. There's only one of her. She's no match for the might of your organisation."

Caesar steepled his fingers in front of him. "Your confidence impresses me, Raaz. Okay, let everyone know. A hundred grand to the operative who takes her out. Two hundred if they do it today." He looked away from the screen, and Raaz wondered if that was remorse twitching at the corner of his eyes. But it only lasted a second. Then he was back, staring down the lens with a dark malevolence clouding his features. "The message is: eradicate as soon as possible. Show no mercy."

"Yes, boss," Raaz replied, allowing a smile to spread. "I'll put out the call the second we're finished here."

"Good." Caesar sat back from the screen. "Now, next problem. Have you heard from Cerberix?"

Raaz sighed. "Only saying the same as before. They want proof the mark is dead before they'll release the final part of the fee. Said they were extremely disappointed in how we handled the job."

"Pernickety pricks," Caesar shouted. "They've got the blasted recording. That's what they were worried about. *Extremely disappointed*, for Pete's sake. Do you know what? They can keep the pissing fee. Who gives a shit? But this makes us look bad."

Raaz had once assumed companies as big as Cerberix Inc. would be cagey about their links to organisations such as theirs. But she'd learnt over the years this was far from the case. The bigger and more powerful an organisation grew, the more cocky and wilfully illicit they became. These days a large proportion of Annihilation's top-level work came from governments, big-name companies, even royalty. What's more, most of the big-ticket jobs came from referrals, word of mouth. Caesar's concerns about Cerberix were justified.

On screen the boss pinched the bridge of his nose between thumb and forefinger. "Do we have a location on Davros Ratpack?"

"Sure," Raaz lied, but she could find him soon enough.

"Have him call me. As soon as possible," Caesar growled. "In fact, get locations on the whole team and have them call me. Direct." He grinned, exposing two gold-capped canines. "I have an idea."

Chapter Forty-Six

Acid's voice carried through from the bedroom. "You sure you got everything you need, Spook?"

It was Friday morning, three days later, and the two women were now staying in the executive suite of the Canary Riverside Plaza. It was, without doubt, the grandest place Spook had ever stayed, and a far cry from the dank hovel where she'd found Acid Vanilla a few days earlier. The suite was huge, with high ceilings and an exterior wall made of glass. A fitted kitchen ran down one side of the room and a luxurious lounge area stepped down onto a large balcony that jutted out over the river. The atmosphere was calm, relaxed, and the whole place smelt of roses and good coffee. Much more conducive for rest and recuperation.

Acid shouted through again. "And you know what you have to do?"

Spook sat back on the plush velvet couch. "For the tenth time, yes. I'm ready. Are you?"

Acid hadn't wanted to leave her sordid hotel room initially, maintaining to Spook over the course of many hours how she had to harden herself both mentally and physically for what came next. The hotel may have been cold and cramped and depressing but it represented her atonement, she'd said, it was her time in the wilderness. But then she'd sobered up and, with some coaxing from Spook, had accepted she needed proper rest. In a decent bed. The promise of Mulberry silk bed linen and Egyptian cotton sheets had helped.

"One second," Acid yelled. "Just putting the final touches to my new look."

Spook had also managed to convince Acid a few days off the liquor would be a good idea. Though what she hadn't counted on was her passing out the second they'd entered the new suite and not leaving her bedroom for the best part of thirty-six hours. She had appeared briefly, but only to shuffle to the bathroom or make herself a pot of camomile tea before returning to the bedroom and shutting the door pointedly behind her. For Spook that smarted, but Acid had made it clear, their time together in Paris was a one-off. This was how it was now, and she had to accept that.

"Have you got the video somewhere safe?" Acid called through.

"Geez. Yes, Mom," Spook replied. "Of course I have it." She checked her jacket pocket all the same, taking the new, pink thumb-drive out and holding it to the light. It looked so innocuous, so everyday. Yet contained within was a weaponised, two-minute video with the potential to destroy a multi-billion-dollar organisation.

The suite had only one bedroom, so Spook had slept on the couch the last three nights. She'd sat there for most of the past three days too, while she worked on the video. Indeed, the only time she'd got up – apart from trips to the bathroom or to make a drink – was yesterday afternoon, when Acid had appeared from the bedroom and shoved a piece of paper in her face. A shopping list of items they'd need for the plan. Clothes, mainly. Disguises.

But the downtime had done wonders for Acid's mood. Spook had been woken at 5 a.m. by the sound of her shadow boxing in the bathroom. Then had watched, bleary-eyed, as she grunted her way through an insane number of sit-ups and push-ups.

"Here we go," Acid announced, entering the front room. "What do you think?"

She was dressed in black skinny jeans, which wasn't remarkable – nor was the black vest top, despite it showing a fair amount of cleavage. But the royal blue Jimmy Choos and white Alexander McQueen lace-trimmed blazer were categorically not Acid Vanilla's usual attire. She'd also scraped her hair into a high ponytail and was wearing a pair of huge, red, plastic glasses.

"Very cool," Spook cooed. "Oh, your eyes look different. Is it the glasses?"

Acid leaned forward and opened her eyes wide. "No. See?"

"Ah, you've got two brown eyes."

Acid walked over to the mirror by the door and checked herself. "Saved me a fortune in disguises over the years. Only ever need one contact lens at a time. You look good, by the way."

Spook's own outfit, along with a stonewashed Levi jacket, comprised a black polo neck and a pair of Christian Dior wide-legged trousers in dark mustard. Not as jarring as Acid's current look but different enough, especially with her bangs gelled into a high quiff.

She watched Acid as she flitted around the room,

stuffing various items into a red Elvis & Kresse shoulder bag. She was like a coiled spring. A lethal nail bomb, ready to explode at any moment. It was kind of exciting to experience her like this. Exciting and scary. She was full of the same intense energy as before, but now it was under control. Her rage was honed, aimed in the right direction. Away from herself.

"You're sure you want to do this?" Acid asked. "It could get messy." Her eyes drifted to the red marks on Spook's hand where she'd been scratching herself. Spook shoved them in her pockets.

"I'll be fine. Honest."

"Just focus on what you have to do," Acid told her. "In high-pressure situations like this, the trick is not to overthink it. Trust yourself. You'll know what you have to do when the time comes." Spook didn't look convinced. Acid moved around the low coffee table and took a seat next to her. "Listen, kid. I'll admit when we met I thought you were a total nerd. Certainly not the devious blackmailer Caesar had led me to believe."

Spook closed one eye. "Is this supposed to be a pep talk? Because I think it might need a rewrite."

"Well, that worked in your favour," Acid told her. "But I was wrong. Not many people would have the balls to meet with the person sent to kill them. And all that information you found on me… I mean, it was rather disconcerting, but it worked. You ask me, you underestimate Spook Horowitz at your peril." She placed her hand on Spook's leg and gave it a squeeze. "If we get those bastards today it's because of you. So take a deep breath, get your shit together and let's finish what you started. Let's get justice for Paula."

"Thanks." Spook got to her feet. "Then we get justice

for you, and your mom. Like a couple of avenging angels. You like that? I've been thinking about it and we could—"

"One step at a time, doll," Acid said. "But we're ready, yeah?"

Spook slung her rucksack over her shoulder. "Ready. People see this video and those rotten pricks are finished. No question."

"All right. Super. Take this." Acid pulled a gun from her jacket pocket and held it out. "Don't fret, you won't have to use it."

Spook stared at the weapon. "Is that a real gun? It's tiny."

"It's a Beretta Pico, designed to be small – and of course it's real, so be careful. Here, put it in your belt." She shoved it at Spook, who tentatively accepted. "You've only got six rounds. But don't worry, you won't need them."

"Okay, thanks." Spook held the pistol two-handed, practising her stance. "Is the safety on?"

Acid took the gun and shoved it in Spook's belt. "There is no manual safety, but it'll be fine. Just know it's there. Like I say, if all goes to plan you won't need to use it." A strange silence fell between them. It was the realisation of what they were about to do. The weight of their mission. "So, are we good?" Acid asked.

Spook jutted her chin and puffed out her chest. Showing Acid all she was made of. "We're good," she said. "Let's finish this."

Chapter Forty-Seven

"The Cerberix Inc. Expo begins at 2 p.m. this afternoon and for the first time will go out on live-stream all around the world. This is the first time Cerberix's enigmatic CEO, Ethan Clarkson, will deliver his famous keynote in Europe rather than in the US – and it signifies a definite move onto the global stage for the soon-to-be tech giants."

The newsreader's clipped accent sounded at odds with the modern jargon. Acid turned back to the bar and swilled around the last half-centimetre of Chivas Regal. It was her first drink in three days and she was only having the one. But it sure was going down well. She leaned over to Spook who was still engrossed in the TV above the bar that was now showing a VT of Clarkson at last year's keynote smiling angelically at his audience like he was the saviour of humanity. "So, kid. You ready to rock?"

"Can you wait five?" Spook asked. "I need to go the bathroom."

"Seriously? You've been twice already."

"Yeah, well I need to go again."

"Fine. Make it quick." Acid finished her drink and watched Spook as she bobbled on down the length of the bar.

"All right, babe? Buy you another?"

Acid turned to see a red-faced man leaning on the bar beside her. He wore a bright pink Ralph Lauren polo shirt with the collar up and had an almost perfectly spherical head.

"Hey there, you," Acid replied, hitting him with a perfect Texan drawl. "How are ya?"

"Oh, you're American. Nice." He leaned in and pointed to the empty glass. "That dead, is it?"

"Dead is it?"

"Sorry, love. It means, *Is it finished with?* In English. I mean, *English*-English. Do you want another?"

"Oh. No thanks. We're about to leave." She gave him a big American smile, all teeth and sparkling personality.

The man returned a toothy grin. "You going to this computer thingy across the way?"

"That's right," Acid replied. "I'm a YouTuber. Doing a piece on the expo."

"Is that so?"

"Sure is," Acid told him, relaxing into her borrowed persona. Earlier that morning Spook had hacked into the exhibition centre's server and got the list of journalists and bloggers that still had to collect passes on the door. The *Girls Do Tech* duo seemed like a perfect fit. "The name's Felicity Bloom – Flick, to my besties – pleased to meet ya!" She offered her hand and a cornucopia of brightly coloured bangles clunked together.

"And you, darling. I'm Barry." He shook her hand,

holding on too long. "I knew it, though. I said to myself, I bet that pretty girl over there is heading for the exhibition centre. Never been in myself. Big old building."

"Sure is, Barry. It sure as hell is! Though we got them bigger back home in the States!'

"Yeah, I bet you bloody do," Barry said, both of them laughing now.

"Everything okay?" It was Spook, returning from the bathroom.

"Sure is, sweetie pie." Acid didn't miss a beat, leaning over and putting her arm around Spook. "Barry, I'd like you to meet little Annie Sugar. My co-presenter on the channel – and also my life partner."

Spook baulked. Barry's eyes almost popped out of his head. "Oh? Partner. I see."

"Not a problem, is there?" Acid asked. She picked up the rucksack and handed it to Spook.

"No problem at all, ladies. I'll leave you to it, I suppose. You have fun now, won't you?"

"You know what Barry?" Acid shoved her glasses up her nose with one finger. "I think we damn well will have fun. You have a swell day too." With that, she swivelled on her heels and marched over to the door, calling back, "Come along now, sweet pea, we don't want to miss the keynote."

Acid was already at the roadside as Spook scurried out the pub. "Partner, hey?" she said. "And I thought you just used me for sex."

Acid gave her a look. "That's enough." She pulled the white blazer closed around her. They were near the Dock-lands, the Isle of Dogs only a few hundred meters away. It was always cooler by the river.

They crossed over the road and fell in with a group of people making their way to the exhibition centre. Acid checked her watch: five minutes past one in the afternoon. That gave them less than an hour. They were cutting it fine.

"Let me do the talking," Acid whispered, as they got to the main door and the group shuffled into single file.

Two large security guards stood either side of the doorway, watching people as they entered. Acid clocked the noticeable bulges under their left arms – not your typical event security. Most likely they were a private firm. Ex-military. Acid kept her head down as they got to the front of the line, sensing the men checking her out. She closed her eyes, put on a smile.

"Keep moving, please." The gruff security man waved them through without question, and they hurried along a short glass walkway as quickly as possible.

The walkway opened out into an entrance hall that was grand, but generic. Like a chain-hotel's foyer on a massive scale.

"Over there," Spook whispered, nudging Acid in the ribs. "It says, *Check-in and Passes.*"

"Great, let's hope we've arrived before the real ones." She strutted over to the desk, swinging her hips as she went. "Hey there, y'all," she trilled, slipping back into the Texan drawl. "How's it going today?"

The two young men behind the desk stared open-mouthed at Acid as she stood in front of them with her hand on her hip. "Are you here for the Cerberix conference?" one of them asked.

"Sure are," Acid replied, flicking her ponytail about and looking for Spook. She held her arm out for her. "Myself and Annie Sugar here. We'll be down under Girls Do Tech, I would expect. See, there we are." She leaned over the table and pointed to the names on the man's list, shoving her breasts in his face. "See, Annie Sugar and Felicity Bloom. That's me."

The man busied himself, flicking through a large box of passes. He located the correct ones and looked at Acid. "Do you have some form of ID?"

Spook stiffened beside her.

Play it cool, chick. Play it cool.

"Sure thing, sweetie. Let me see." She swung the large Elvis & Kresse bag from her shoulder and placed it down on the desk. Then she unzipped it and rooted around inside. "It's in here some place. Give me a second." In a flurry of activity she began pulling out the contents: two tech magazines – bought at the Tube station on their way here – a make-up bag, three packs of cigarettes, a bottle of water, a handful of tampons, a few sanitary pads. "I'm sure it's in here some place. Got to be." The man stared at the growing pile of lady products as Acid kept going, pulling out a bottle of perfume, some roll-on deodorant, a handful of condoms. XX-large…

That did it.

"You know what, it's fine," the man squeaked. He gestured at the queue forming behind the two women. "We've got to get moving. I trust you. Here you are." He pulled out the passes and handed them to Acid.

"Thanks, sweetie. You're a diamond." She said it in her own voice, forgetting herself for a second. Then, giving it some cockney knees-up. "Apples and pears. When in Rome, and all that." She handed the passes to Spook and gave the man a wink as she stuffed the props back in her bag. Then, back to Texan, "You are a shining star, you know that? As welcome as a summer's day. Now come on, Annie Sugar, we've got an expo to cover."

Dropping the act, Acid made her way over to the far

side of the entrance space with Spook scuttling along close behind her. They stood and watched for a few moments as excited Cerberix fans funnelled through into the main auditorium. More security here. Two heavies at each door, checking bags, patting people down. It would be tricky to get anywhere near the stage today, but luckily for them that wasn't part of the plan.

Without saying a word, or even exchanging a look, the two women made their way through an innocuous wooden door in the corner of the room. Spook had downloaded the venue's schematics yesterday, and this entry point – primarily used by cleaning staff – provided access to all six floors. Moving quickly now, they made their way to the first floor, then to the second. At the top of the third flight of stairs Acid held her arm out, halting Spook, before peering around the corner.

"Okay, clear," she whispered. "Let's go." They moved like ghosts along the landing and down the short, windowless corridor that led off from it. Acid came to a stop outside a mahogany door with the words, *Capital Suite Room One*, on a brass plaque, top centre. "This is it. So far so good."

She twisted the handle and eased open the door. The room was empty, as she'd expected. Cerberix had hired the whole venue for the conference but had no cause for these small meeting rooms. Acid stepped inside and scanned the room. There were no windows but one wall was taken up by a large video screen, and on the wall opposite was a whiteboard. A pine-effect table covered most of the floor space, surrounded by ten chairs. Once they were inside Acid locked the door and tested it for strength.

"We're safe here. How long do you need?" She turned to see her accomplice was already sat at the far end of the table with her laptop open.

"Two minutes, maybe less," Spook told her. "Can you plug this in, please?" She handed Acid a cable and pointed to a plug socket on the wall. "Should be straightforward once I get through the backdoor." She began tapping away at the keyboard.

Acid checked her watch. "We've got twenty minutes until show time. Then the fun starts."

"Ah crap. Maybe not. You sneaky douche bags."

"What is it?" Acid moved over and narrowed her eyes at the screen. Not that she could decipher anything untoward in the digits and symbols causing Spook such consternation. "Spook? Talk to me."

The kid's face was gripped in a tight grimace, half-way between anger and frustration. "We're screwed. Whoever's handling the feed has got a shit-hot firewall. Better than I've ever seen. I'm not sure I can hack into it so easily."

"O-kay," Acid replied. "Do we have options?"

"Maybe," Spook said, opening Google.

"Seriously? You're Googling it?"

Spook didn't look up. "This is how it works. It's not like in the movies – seeing how fast you can type. Google is the coder's friend. When you don't know how to do something, which happens about a million times a day, you Google it." She skim-read the results and clicked on a few sites, scanning the information. Then she grabbed another thumb-drive from her bag and jammed it into the side of her laptop. Acid watched as she copy-pasted some code from one of the websites into a Terminal portal and changed some variables. "That should do it," she said. "I just need to run it through my compiler, should take a few minutes."

They waited in silence, watching a progress bar slowly fill to a hundred percent, telling them the program was complete. Then Spook dragged the file onto the thumb-drive icon and ejected it from the system. "Done."

"Good work. We're good?"

"Yes and no," Spook told her. "The only way I can get onto the system now is if we run this override program on the computer the feed is originating from."

"Meaning?"

"Meaning one of us has to get into Cerberix's control room and install it. Without being seen."

Acid took the thumb-drive from Spook. "Or without being caught?" She looked at her watch. "Fifteen minutes. All right, I can do this."

"You need to plug it into the same computer they're feeding from. I imagine they'll be running off multiple monitors, but there'll be only one console running both the feed and the presentation. You need to find that. It should be a large box and—"

"Yes, thanks," Acid cut her off. "I know I'm better at the old stabby-shooty stuff, sweetie, but I do know what a hard drive looks like."

"All you need to do is connect the thumb-drive, open it and click on the program inside – I called it *Takeover* – that'll do the rest."

"Oh, that's all I need to do, is it?" Acid shoved the thumb-drive into her pocket and checked her gun, loading one into the chamber. Then she was at the door. "Lock this behind me and do not open it to anyone until I get back. You still got your piece?"

Spook looked confused.

"The gun, Spook. Do you still have the gun?"

"Oh, yeah, sure. I'll be fine. But, Acid, please don't do any of your stabby-shooty stuff with the tech people. It's not their fault."

Acid leaned back. "Whatever do you take me for? I'm all about the good karma now, remember?" Then serious: "No killing. I promise. You wait here for me. As soon as the video is in play, I'll come get you."

"Thanks. And be careful."

Acid peered out into the hallway, then turned back to Spook. "Me?" she said, with a wink. "I'm always careful."

Chapter Forty-Eight

"Five minutes until we go live, Mr Clarkson." The owner of the voice on the other side of the door followed up with three anaemic knocks. No doubt some intern sent by Marcy, to make sure all was well.

"Yes, I do know," Ethan called back, easing himself down into the last of his push-ups. "Please, leave me to prepare."

This was the third time someone had bothered him in the last twenty minutes. Why were these imbeciles unable to read the sign he'd pinned up?

Do not disturb under any circumstances.

He'd even underlined the word, *any*. Twice. Now he cursed himself for not putting it in capital letters.

"Do you need me to bring you anything, before you go on?"

Jesus.

They were still out there.

"I'm fine," Ethan yelled, flipping onto his feet. He yanked open the door to reveal a young girl with blonde frizzy hair and huge blue eyes. "Now fuck off," Ethan said, before slamming the door in her face. "Idiot."

He drew back a deep breath – in through the nose, out through the mouth. Then he took a seat in front of the large mirror that ran along the side wall and closed his eyes. He did five more deep meditative breaths whilst reciting the Kundalini mantra he'd paid ten thousand dollars for at an exclusive retreat a few years ago.

Kirim, Kirim, Kirim, Ethan old boy.

You can do this.

He reached for a bottle of rehydrating eye drops and pulled down his bottom lid, reminding himself once again that he had nothing more to worry about. Beowulf Caesar had been adamant – the pest was dead, and Ethan had the only recording. Yet as he blinked out the excess saline solution, a niggling thought bothered him. That he wasn't being told the full story.

He stood and made final adjustments to his hair, spraying a mist of hairspray to fix it in place. Marcy had wanted to hire professional hair and make-up people, but he'd told her no. Ethan had always gotten himself ready and that wasn't going to change because they were going global. The last thing he needed was some limp-wristed moron shoving blusher in his face while he psyched himself up for what would be – by anyone's terms – a career-defining speech.

Besides, with other people around he couldn't complete the final stage of his pre-game ritual. Chiefly, a half gram of the finest cocaine that he now hoovered up his left nostril, assisted by good old Benjamin Franklin.

"Now we're talking." He sat back and sniffed violently, ensuring not one grain was lost. Pinching both nostrils, he grinned manically at his reflection. Then he stood and placed his headset mic over his ear. Now he was ready. "Apple-fucking-who? Micro-fucking-what? Come on, Ethany-boy! Let's do this."

He could already hear the excited crowd echoing through the backstage area as he left the dressing room behind and made his way down the corridor that led to the auditorium. Three large men met him at the far end – his armed security detail. He nodded sagely at them as he walked past, and they did the same. They hadn't been cheap, but he felt safer with them here.

As he turned down the final corridor that led to the stage, he halted, listening to the noise of the crowd as they chanted.

Ethan-Ethan-Ethan.

Chanting his name. Real fans. Waiting for him. Waiting to hear him announce the final stage of Cerberix's master plan – a free laptop in every home, followed by total monopoly on the app market once in place. Ethan snuffled back the last dregs of finest Colombian, tasting the reassuring bitterness in his throat.

Showtime.

"There you are," Sinclair Whitman bellowed, as Ethan appeared by his side. "You all set?"

Ethan patted his old friend on the shoulder and took the bottle of mineral water offered. "All set."

Then he was onstage, the bright lights hot on his face as he peered through the glare at the vast room full to bursting with ecstatic fans and eager journalists.

"Greetings, friends," he intoned, raising his arms in a not-unselfconscious Christ-pose. "Welcome – to the new world…"

The crowd calmed as Ethan settled into his well-rehearsed speech. Telling those watching – here in the venue, and the millions on live-stream – that today they were witness to the birth of something truly remarkable. A day they would tell their grandchildren about. But more than that, Ethan assured them, they were a part of this just as much as he was. This was about them, he said, "…about all of us."

He detailed his mission of free laptops for all. And not just any laptops – the brand-new Cerberix Gen-Z system with the soon-to-be released Hadez 3.0 installed as standard.

When they heard this, the crowd went wild, and the cheers sent intense rushes of elation surging through Ethan's veins. It wasn't just the cocaine. His mind raced with what this next phase would mean. Total control of the market, sure, but more than that. Once the AI was fully implemented and at work, they'd know exactly what people wanted, when they wanted it. They'd know everything about everyone. If knowledge was power, which it most certainly was, Cerberix would soon be the most powerful company on the globe.

Welcome to the new world, indeed.

Ethan looked over at Whitman, still in the wings, and gestured for him to join him onstage. "Let's get him up here," Ethan yelled. "Can you please give a warm welcome to our eminent CFO, and co-founder of Cerberix Inc. My friend and mentor, Mr Sinclair Whitman."

It was a carefully rehearsed moment, done to appear off-the-cuff, but it worked. The crowds lapped it up as Sinclair joined Ethan in the centre of the vast stage – empty except for a small black table. There were no airs or graces or obvious affectations for the Cerberix team. This said: *We are you. You are us. We are the same.* Though, as they'd laughed about when coming up with the idea, basing themselves in plain black t-shirts and jeans when the rest of the time it was Armani suits was maybe the biggest affectation of them all.

"Bunch of suckers," Sinclair whispered in Ethan's ear. "They'd buy anything we told them at this point."

Ethan ignored him and continued his speech, giving the rapturous audience the story of Cerberix Inc.'s journey to date. How it all began in a San Fran coffee shop fifteen years ago with a chance encounter. Then how the two mavericks risked everything, giving up their jobs and living on baked beans for a year, before launching Cerberix from a small office above Ethan's brother's garage. It was a story most Cerberix fans already knew by heart, but they sure did love hearing it again.

It was all bullshit, of course. Most of it, anyway. Spin and hyperbole to give the myth some spice. The truth was Whitman had bankrolled Ethan's vision from the off. But having an endless list of eager backers – whilst situated in a state-of-the-art office space – didn't fit the legend. *We are you. You are us. We are the same.*

"So now I want to stop talking for a while," Ethan told the audience. "I know, I know, it's hard to imagine. But seriously, we've got a special VT I want to run for you that explains our plan for what we're calling: Community Connectivity Through Cerberix."

"Great work, Ethan," Sinclair whispered as the lights went down.

The two men turned to watch the large cinema screen behind them as the Cerberix Inc. logo flashed in the middle of the screen and Wagner's *Ride of the Valkyries* boomed out over the sound system. The logo – a lion's head, with snakes for a mane and the mouth open in a roar, forming the *C* of

Cerberix – changed from white to red to turquoise in time with the music.

"Love it," Sinclair whispered. "Nothing can stop us now, son. You hear me?"

Then as the music faded a voice-over commenced, announcing the new era of technology in a voice you'd be forgiven for thinking was the rumbling baritone of Sir Ian McKellen. It was actually a much lesser known and cheaper actor named Nathaniel Baker. A sound-a-like. They could have got Sir Ian, of course. Ethan had wanted to – and they could easily have afforded him – but Whitman had put his foot down. Why hire some foppish prima donna, he'd said, when you can get someone who sounds exactly the same for a lot less? As he put it, no one would ever know.

No one would ever know.

Those words had been Whitman's response to most issues these last few months. But they were about to trip him up. With a flash, and a crackle of electricity, the high-definition image of Cerberix's genre-defining laptop disappeared from the screen. The audience gasped as the auditorium was plunged into darkness, before something new appeared on the video wall. A still photograph of a young woman.

"Sinclair, what's going on?" Ethan asked, looking around.

Sinclair didn't answer. He was too busy staring at the screen. A name appeared at the bottom – *Paula Silva* – followed by, *Single mother. Sex-worker. Murdered in Sinclair Whitman's London apartment.*

The two men watched on, impotently, as the words and images continued. Next came news footage. Whitman's private chef being led out of the building in handcuffs, his head pushed down into a waiting police car. More words flashed across the screen. *Wrongly Accused! Framed!*

Then the footage wiped to black. Silence fell over the auditorium once more, before more footage appeared. This time a video.

Ethan looked up through the glare of the stage-lights to the control room and made a violent cutting gesture across his throat. "Switch this off! Now!" Behind him, on the screen, Sinclair Whitman was viciously beating and strangling Paula Silva. "Kill the VT, for fuck's sake!" Ethan could only see a dark silhouette in the booth, and the video kept rolling. The audience were becoming more agitated as they collectively realised this wasn't a joke. Far from it. Some looked away in disgust, some in horror, but most kept watching. Many had taken out their phones and were recording the screen.

Ethan's next thought was to get the hell away from Sinclair. He could spin this. Explain how he was unaware of his CFO's misdemeanours. He looked around as new images flashed onto the screen. More photos. A leering, red-faced Sinclair in his Paris apartment with a young naked boy on each knee.

"What're we going to do?" Sinclair growled.

The two men backed into the wings as the audience became more vocal in their disgust.

"We can get ahead of this," Ethan replied. "We'll say it's doctored footage. Fake news. A rival trying to fuck with us."

Yet as he was speaking more photos were appearing on screen. Whitman with young girls, younger boys – all in various stages of undress. Doing unspeakable acts.

Ethan racked his brain for options. The old man was finished, but that didn't mean *he* was. It didn't mean his dreams for Cerberix were. He'd hire the best spin doctors. Distort the narrative. Paint himself as another unwitting victim of Whitman's duplicitous evil.

He might have pulled it off, but then the photos faded into a screen grab – an email from Ethan's personal account. Him arranging for a Cerberix employee to be killed. It could have been doctored, but it wasn't. There were bank transfers, money trails, the lot.

Then it appeared.

The photo Ethan prayed he'd never see again.

The one Sinclair had hung over his head these last ten years.

It was a colour Polaroid, showing a young man of around twenty-five reclining on a bed. His cheeks were flushed and he was grinning lasciviously into the camera. The bed was in Sinclair Whitman's Paris apartment. The young man was Ethan Clarkson. He was naked. As were the two thirteen-year-old girls lying on either side of him. Their identities had been pixilated, as had their nudity – but this did nothing to dampen the shocked and disgusted noises coming from the sell-out crowd.

"Ah bullshit," Ethan groaned, as his cool demeanour slipped away. Any semblance of character or composition he'd once held had been shattered into a million tiny shards of guilt and shame. He was done.

And now he had to get out of there. Fast.

Chapter Forty-Nine

Spook squirmed excitedly on her chair as she watched the confusion unfold on stage. The video had worked exactly as she'd hoped, and that final photo (stolen from Clement's private collection) was the icing on the cake. She clicked off the main Cerberix feed and checked the venue's security footage. A total of eight cameras covered the auditorium and each one showed irate audience members, all of them booing and jeering at the now empty stage. It was the same story in the foyer. People stormed out in disgust, flinging down their souvenir programs and laminated passes. It was working. Spook logged onto Twitter. The hashtag, *Cerberix-Murder*, was already trending all over the world. They'd done it. Clarkson and Whitman were finished.

Spook carried on flicking through the venue's numerous feeds. Her instructions were to stay put until Acid came for her, but that didn't mean she couldn't enjoy the chaos while she waited. Except then she opened the camera feed for the third floor.

"Oh no," Spook whispered at her laptop. "No, please."

On the screen, armed security guards stormed across the third-floor landing on the main side of the building. "Shit, shit, shit."

In a second Spook had stuffed the laptop in her rucksack and was at the door. She had the tiny gun on her, but she didn't fancy its chances against the scary-ass machine guns the men were carrying. She had to get to Acid. She eased open the door and looked both ways before tiptoeing around the corner then running down the next corridor as fast as she could.

She got to the main control room in under a minute and burst through the doors. "We need to move. Now."

Acid spun around, gun in hand. "I thought I told you to wait."

"Yes, but there are men coming. They've got guns."

Acid turned back to the two young techies sat quietly with their hands zip-tied behind their backs. "Well, it's been a blast working with you both," she purred. "Now remember what I told you, Jeanette? Toby? You tell anyone I was here, and I will find you and I will hurt you. Understood?"

Jeanette and Toby nodded in unison. "Don't worry," Jeanette added. "We won't tell a soul. You ask me, those two deserve everything they get."

Acid patted her on the shoulder. "Good girl. But I'm still going to leave you tied up. Looks better for you that way."

"Acid, please," Spook cried. "We need to get out of here."

In the auditorium below, the house lights had gone up. Whitman and Clarkson were nowhere to be seen. If Spook's calculations were correct, they'd already be on their way to the basement-level car park.

The two women left the control room and edged their

way towards the service elevator. Spook had jammed the main elevator's controls, meaning the Cerberix duo's only access to the basement was down the fire escape. Four flights of stairs. The plan was, Acid and Spook would get down first. Head them off.

"You get eyes on the car park?" Acid whispered, as they got to the end of the corridor.

"Yeah, there's a black Hummer waiting for them," Spook replied. "Plus, I found Clarkson's private jet – parked at a place called Biggin Hill. Probably where they're heading."

"Yes. I know it." Acid peered around the corner and beckoned Spook to follow her. "If they get to that plane they could be in South America in a day."

They walked fast, breaking into a sprint as they reached the service elevator and Acid jabbed at the button. They waited, bouncing from foot to foot as the numbers lit up, showing the elevator's ascent – Ground... One... Two...

"Stop right there. Put your hands in the air." They were too late. The security guards appeared from around the corner and stopped a few feet away, raising their guns at Acid and Spook. "Identify yourselves."

Spook stuck her hands in the air. "We're YouTubers," she yelped. "We took a wrong turn and we didn't— Shit!"

She jumped as a loud noise sent her head rattling. In front of her the three security guards' heads exploded in quick succession. She looked over to see Acid affectedly blowing on the end of her gun.

"Who says I've lost it?" She slid the gun in the back of her jeans. "Come on." The elevator doors slid open and Acid dragged Spook inside, hitting B for the basement. "Listen to me," she said, leaning in. "It's not the time to get cocky. Those security guys are tasty. So keep your wits about you."

An icy blast of dead air hit them in the face when the lift doors opened to reveal the underground car park.

"There, look." Spook pointed over to where Clarkson and Whitman were clambering in the back of a blacked-out Hummer. There were two men with them, both with shaved heads, both shouldering machine guns. They spotted the women and opened fire.

"Stay down," Acid yelled, bundling her and Spook behind a concrete pillar as a hail of bullets peppered the metal doors of the elevator. She waited a beat, then fired off a few rounds in retaliation as the men climbed into the front seats.

"They're getting away," Spook yelled.

"Yes, I can see that." Acid moved into the open, shooting as she went. The bullets pinged off the toughened bodywork of the Hummer as it screeched its tyres and disappeared up the ramp to street level.

"What now?" Spook asked. But Acid was already running over to a large black motorcycle parked in the far corner. "Ah, shit."

"Come on," Acid yelled back at her. "We can still catch them."

Acid got to the bike and removed her blazer, followed by the hipster glasses. She tossed them to the ground as Spook got to her and gasped, "Wait, I don't see any helmets."

"No. Me neither." Acid traced her fingers down the bike's handlebar shaft and located a small red box with two wires sticking out the side. "Don't worry, it'll be fine." She yanked a second set of wires from under the engine and twisted them around the ones coming from the box. Lights flashed on the dashboard.

"Maybe you should go on alone?" Spook offered, as Acid swung her leg over the bike and switched on the ignition. "I don't want to slow you down or anything."

"Get on the damn bike," Acid told her. "You haven't come this far to chicken out now." She glared at Spook as she revved the engine. "They're getting away, kid. We haven't got time for this."

"Fine. But be careful," Spook said, climbing on behind Acid.

"Lean into me and hold on," Acid yelled over the engine, as they set off up the ramp and out into daylight. Not that Spook could tell it was daylight. Not with her eyes shut tight and her face pressed into Acid's back. "Up ahead," Acid cried as they sped along at a terrifying speed. "We've got the bastards."

Spook's plan had been to keep her eyes shut for the duration of this hellish journey, but she dropped that plan soon enough as loud gunshots shook her alert. She opened her eyes to see Acid riding one-handed and firing at the Hummer's tyres. They were on a strip of tarmac by the side of the river – the sort of road used largely by freight trucks and port vehicles. In front of them the Hummer swerved wildly to avoid the shots, but didn't slow down.

"We're losing them," Spook cried, getting into the spirit, as the Hummer took a hard right down the side of an old warehouse.

Acid made to follow but at the last second steered straight past the warehouse. She took a right down the next side road, firing off another flurry of shots, this time pummelling the broad side of the Hummer as it sped by. Taking a sharp corner at the far end, she followed the Cerberix two down the side of the next building. They were closing in on them.

Spook gripped her arms tight around Acid's waist as she leaned forward on the handlebars. They were almost alongside the Hummer now and Acid raised her gun, readying herself for a decent shot at the tyres. But before she had a chance, the Hummer hit the brakes. It veered into them and clipped the bike's front tyre.

"Oh my god, help," Spook screamed in Acid's ear, as the bike buckled and shook beneath them. A memory flashed across her mind. That awful party back in college. Eugene and his cronies cajoling Spook into riding a stupid mechanical bull. She'd hated every second of the experience and hadn't stayed on too long.

She prayed this would be different.

"Hold on," Acid yelled, as she slammed on the brakes and steered out the way of a large metal skip.

Spook burrowed her head in the space between Acid's shoulder blades as the bike swayed some more. But Acid managed to regain balance and straighten them. Back in control. Except they were running out of time.

The Hummer had put good distance between them, and as Spook squinted through the sting of the wind-speed it drove under a raised barrier then disappeared behind a long building made of corrugated iron. Six large windows looked out onto the road, and above – in white lettering splattered with pigeon shit – were the words: *London Eagle Heliport*.

They were going to lose them.

Chapter Fifty

Acid leaned into the handlebars as they followed the Hummer down the sloping driveway. "Keep your head down," she yelled, as she pulled the bike to one side and they skidded under the descending arm of the barrier.

Once clear, Acid pulled the bike upright and eased off the revs, crawling the last few metres. At the end of the building, the driveway opened out onto a large concrete space with a helipad in the centre. Beyond this was a smaller landing pad jutting out onto the Thames and, across the river, the crane-studded skyline of Deptford and Rotherhithe.

The Hummer was already parked on the far side of the helipad, the security goons already on the tarmac. Acid brought the bike to a stop beside two large industrial refuse bins, and the two women dived for cover as the men released a torrent of bullets their way. Acid leaned around the side of the bin and returned fire, taking one of them out – a head shot, right between the eyes. She took cover and removed a new clip from her pocket, replacing the spent one.

"You good?" she asked Spook. "Hurt?" Spook shook her head.

Acid pushed past and moved to the other side of the refuse unit. She peered around it, but the remaining gunman had taken cover behind the Hummer. Whitman and Clarkson were still shielding themselves in the backseat. Acid made to move but froze, her attention drawn to a loud stuttering noise from above – a chopper coming into land. It hovered a hundred metres or so above the neighbouring buildings. A minute away. If that.

Acid leaned on Spook, her eyes wide. "Listen. In a second I'm going to make a run for it around the back of the vehicle. Give me a beat, then shoot off a few rounds. Aim for the bonnet – the hood – okay?" Spook stared at her. She'd gone white. "You'll be fine," Acid told her. "Keep your head down and the gun raised, you're not trying to hit anyone. I need a distraction. Point and squeeze." She looked at the chopper steadying itself for landing. "It's now or never."

With that she was off, moving swiftly around the back of the Hummer in a wide arc. She kept low, two hands on the gun. Over her right shoulder she heard gunshots, Spook doing her job, drawing the goon's fire. A second later and Acid was at the Hummer. She crouched down against the rear bumper as the chopper made its final descent.

Spook continued to draw the gunman's fire as Whitman and Clarkson leapt out the back door and ran over to the landing pad. They didn't see Acid and she had a clear shot, could take them both out. She held up the Glock and aimed it at Whitman's temple as he crouched under the helicopter's blades. She was using soft points.

From this distance she'd blow out most of his prefrontal cortex – and all the badness. Her finger quivered on the trigger. It would be so easy. Would feel so good. But she lowered her arm. It wasn't the way. Wasn't the plan. Not this time.

She glanced over at Spook. She was shooting out over the Thames. Nowhere near the gunman. Any moment now he'd realise Acid had moved position. Any moment now those bastards would be on the chopper.

Acid got to her feet and scrambled onto the roof of the Hummer. The gunman was crouched by the front wheel arch, taking pot shots at Spook. He heard Acid's footsteps on the roof and pointed his gun but he was too late. The back of his head exploded as one of her soft points bloomed out into his cranium.

Two down. Two to go.

Acid slid down onto the bonnet and jumped the last part. She was over by Whitman and Sinclair in a few strides. Just as the chopper's landing skids grazed the tarmac.

"Stop, or I'll shoot you both."

She fired a round into the air and Whitman and Clarkson spun around a few metres from the chopper door.

"I bloody well mean it." She fired another shot, aiming at their feet. A warning. The next one wouldn't miss.

"Stop shooting," Clarkson yelled over the whir of the blades. He turned to face Acid, his hands raised weakly by his head. He was crying. "You don't have to do this. We can sort something out."

Acid kept the gun trained on the men, moving it from Whitman to Clarkson and back. She glanced at the pilot. "You. Fly away."

"Don't you fucking dare." Whitman pointed a bony finger at the pilot who glanced from Acid to the men with a panicked expression. "I'm serious, son. You stay put. We're paying you a lot of money for this."

Acid kept the gun on Clarkson, toying with the trigger. "I will shoot you," she told him. "I mean it. I'd like nothing more than to put a bullet through your miserable brain." She looked over at Whitman. "Yours too, slick. Don't think I won't."

"Then why haven't you?"

The bats screeched at her.

Finish them, they said.

Finish them both.

"Because I'm better than that," she whispered, through gritted teeth. "And you'll get what's coming to you. Spook?"

"Yes?" She was a few metres behind.

Acid didn't turn around. "Put your gun on the pilot. Let him know if he doesn't fly off in the next ten seconds, you'll shoot him."

"What?"

"Spook. Do it."

"Okay." Spook raised her gun at the pilot.

"Ten," Acid began. Her eyes flicked from the pilot, to Whitman, to Clarkson, back to the pilot. Her jaw was rigid. Her muscles taut. But she was on fire. She was in control. "Nine." Spook spread her legs and adjusted her grip on the weapon. That two-handed stance again. Acid couldn't help but smile. "Eight... Seven... Six..."

That was enough for the pilot. No amount of money was worth dying for.

"Wait," Whitman screamed, as the chopper lifted from the platform. "Come back."

It hovered over the scene a few seconds, before rising further into the sky and banking left over the river. Then it disappeared behind a large office block.

"Fuck!" Clarkson screamed. He stared after it a few seconds, then turned back to Acid. "You'll pay for this."

"Keep your hands up," Acid told him. She pulled a burner phone from her pocket and offered it to Spook. "Call the police, will you, sweetie? Tell them the Cerberix two are tied up at the London Eagle Heliport."

"Sure," Spook replied. She flipped open the phone, ready to dial.

"You stupid bitches," Whitman said. "You pathetic couple of bit—"

He never finished his sentence.

The bats screamed across every neuron Acid possessed as Whitman's head jerked to one side and his brains burst out of a hole next to his ear. A second later the same happened with Clarkson. Only this time the bullet went in through his top lip – straight into the brainstem. Cleaner. No less deadly.

Spook screamed and Acid spun around to see Banjo Shawshank over the far side of the helipad. He sat astride a vintage Harley Davidson. They hadn't heard him over the noise of the chopper. He held a large gun in one hand – from the looks of it, a .44 Magnum Smith & Wesson.

He climbed off the bike and spread his arms out wide. "Have you missed me?"

"Run," Acid yelled. She grabbed Spook and dragged her over to the back of the Hummer, firing at Banjo as he took cover around the side of the building.

"How the hell is he still walking?" Spook asked, as they knelt next to each other. "And why did he kill them?"

A bullet whistled past, a few inches from Acid's head. She got to her feet, positioning herself to return fire.

"I've no idea how he's still in one piece," she replied. "But I'm not surprised Caesar wanted those two dead.

303

Annihilation messed up. Bad for business if they tell anyone."

"They wouldn't have, surely?"

Acid held up the Glock, checked the clip. Last one. "He can't take the chance of them getting arrested and trying for a deal – naming names. A rather private person is my old boss. Been in the business over twenty-five years and the authorities still have nothing on him. Not even his real name."

The two of them flinched as a bullet thudded into the thick plastic of the bumper.

"Banjo's impulsive. But he's ambitious too," Acid rasped. "Wants to be the one to take me out. You too. Sorry."

"What do we do?" Spook cried, gripping hold of Acid's arm as another bullet whizzed past on her side.

"Well, first, we try and stay calm." She brushed Spook off. She had enough to worry about keeping the bats in her corner. She risked a quick glance around the side of the car. The position of the Hummer meant Banjo had a clear shot at both doors. This would be tight. "You reckon you can make it into the passenger seat if I distract him?"

Spook looked at Acid in that now familiar way – an expression half-way between vacant and wise. "I reckon I can," she said.

"Good enough. When I give the word, I'll move around the front of the car to the driver's side, shooting as I go. That'll draw Banjo's fire. You open the passenger door and climb in. I'll be seconds behind you, then we get the hell out of here."

Spook's eyes grew. "You'll be exposed. He'll shoot you."

Acid took a breath. The bats said different.

They said, she could do this.

They said, she had to.

"I'll be fine," she told Spook. "But if anything does happen, you drive away, fast as you can. The car's bullet-proof, we know that. So put your foot down and don't stop until you know it's safe. Then get on the first plane anywhere. Chances are they'll give up searching for you once everything calms down. It's me they want."

Spook fiddled with a scuffed hole in the knee of her trousers. "Don't get killed though. Please."

"I don't plan on it. Now chin up. I need you focused." Acid gripped the Glock, poised for action. "On three. The second I start shooting, move. All right?"

Acid counted three and set off down the side of the Hummer, firing shot after shot in the direction of Banjo as he shielded himself down the wall of the building. With the gun aimed in front of her, she cautiously moved around the passenger door and out in front of the vehicle. From here she could see the curve of Banjo's left shoulder. Could see the Magnum in his hand. He was tense. Readying himself. Acid was almost at the driver's door when Banjo stepped out from his cover and retaliated. The bullets chased her path, thumping into the reinforced bodywork of the Hummer. She skidded on the loose gravel but evaded the shots, ducking and spinning like a ballet dancer. She was at the driver's door. All she had to do was pull the handle and she'd be safe. But then she saw Spook's terrified face through the glass. She was still on the other side. Couldn't get her door open.

"Hurry, Spook."

The young American stepped back and jerked at the door. Thankfully this time it opened. Acid fired off more rounds at Banjo, holding him back. They were almost there. Spook made to climb inside, one more second and she'd be safe. But then Acid went to shoot and all she heard was the ineffective click of the hammer.

"Bollocks."

She was out of bullets. Banjo knew it too. He stepped out from around the side of the building and with a toothy grin raised the Magnum in front of him and fired.

"No!"

The shot echoed around the helipad and Acid watched, helplessly, as the bullet hit Spook in the back. The force thrust her against the side of the Hummer. She cried out as her head smashed into the car window. Then she slumped, lifelessly, onto the tarmac.

Chapter Fifty-One

"You rotten bastard." Acid's scream pierced the late afternoon air as she sprinted towards Banjo. She had no bullets and no weapon, but no care either. She was a Berserker warrior speeding into battle. A ball of white-hot rage on a Kamikaze mission.

"Stop right there," Banjo said. He aimed the gun at Acid's head. But if he wanted her to stop, he'd have to kill her. A few more steps and she'd be on him. She raised her fist, wondering why she was still alive. Then she saw it. The large black BMW crawling around the side of the building.

Acid stopped in her tracks.

"Well, look who it is," Banjo chirped. He lowered the gun. "Somebody wants a word with you."

Acid panted for air as the back door of the car swung open and a large familiar form stepped out onto the tarmac. Caesar. He was wearing a charcoal-grey suit with a bright neon-pink shirt and matching pocket-square. A white tie finished the ensemble. He squinted into the bleak sky and pulled out a pair of white-framed sunglasses from his jacket pocket. Slowly, methodically, he placed them on and cracked his knuckles. Then he sauntered over to Acid, shaking his head and tutting as he went, as though disappointed with a naughty child.

"What a bleeding palaver," he growled, as he got close. "I've lost about a stone these last two weeks because of you, missy."

Acid didn't answer. Her heart felt like it was about to burst out of her chest. Caesar gestured over at the Hummer.

"The girl dead?"

"Yes."

"About bloody time." He raised his arms, as if thanking the heavens. "Jesus Christ. You'd think we were a bunch of bleeding amateurs." He looked down at Acid. "The absolute state of you. Fuck me. What happened?"

"I'm going to kill you," Acid whispered.

"Now, now, my dear," Caesar crooned. "That's no way to talk to your old friend and mentor. I'd say if anyone has a right to be annoyed, it's yours truly. You embarrassed me, girly. Risked the integrity of my whole organisation. I mean, I should have seen the signs. The sloppiness. Wanting holidays. If you wanted out, why didn't you say something, we might have come to some arrangement? Jesus Christ. After everything I did for you."

Acid bowed her head. "You used me. Groomed me."

Caesar snorted. "Sounds to me like you're projecting, poppet. I saved your life. Gave you the world. I don't remember you ever needing much persuading to do what you did. You enjoy killing people, Acid. Always have done. You like the money even more."

"I was young. Frightened. I didn't know any better."

"Oh yeah?" Caesar looked her up and down. "What's your excuse these days?"

Acid shut up. He was toying with her. Anything she said was fuel to the fire.

"Two of my best men. Dead. Plus you almost killed Banjo here. Did you honestly think you could do that without consequences?"

"My mother. Spook. The people in that home. They were all innocent."

"No one is innocent! You fucked up – they paid. And don't get me started on all the upset you've caused helping a mark to escape. I'm still reeling from that." He waved his hand over at the lifeless bodies of Whitman and Clarkson. "Good job Banjo here had the idea to silence them. Sterling job, my boy. You might make my number one yet."

Banjo smirked at Acid. As if to say, *I told you so.*

Acid sneered back. "Number one by default isn't the same, babe."

"Enough," Caesar growled, holding his arms out. "We've been through a lot together, you and I, Acid Vanilla. I'm sorry it had to come to this. But you can't live after what you did."

Acid was still breathless. "I'll kill you. Every last one of you," she rasped. "I swear on my mother's life."

Caesar and Banjo both burst out laughing. Deep belly laughs of pure cruelty. Banjo aimed his gun at Acid's head.

"No, my dear. You won't," Caesar told her.

The distant wail of police sirens reached them on the breeze. Spook hadn't had time to call them, but an apartment block stood a hundred metres down the road, close enough to hear the gunfire.

"You get off, boss," Banjo told Caesar. "They'll be here any minute and you need to be far away from this. I'll finish up here. I've got the Harley. Easy getaway."

Caesar kept his eyes on Acid. His face was stern. He removed his sunglasses and stepped closer. His eyes were watery, full of emotion. Then he smiled. "So long, Acid. Been nice working with you." He turned around and walked back to the BMW, stopping briefly to give Banjo a firm nod.

"Don't you worry, boss," Banjo said. "I won't let you down."

Without looking back, Caesar climbed into the back of the Beamer and shut the door. Acid took a breath, watching as it drove around the Hummer and slowed right down next to Spook's body. Then it picked up speed and disappeared in the same direction it had come from.

The sirens were getting louder.

"Banj, you don't have to do this..." Acid started. But she trailed off. It was pointless.

"No more talk," Banjo said. "Get on your knees."

"Oh, come on. Seriously?"

He stepped closer, his gun arm shaking. "Get on your fucking knees."

Acid did as instructed. Her heart wasn't in it anymore, so maybe this was for the best. She was nothing. Had nothing to live for.

Banjo raised the Magnum and Acid closed her eyes. Waiting. She heard him cock the hammer. One second and it would all be over. Nothing would matter. One second. The bats knew. They were ready.

A gun fired.

Acid's stomach turned over...

She'd heard the shot. But she was still alive. She opened

her eyes to see Banjo staggering backwards, holding his face. He had a small hole in his right cheek and the larger exit wound had taken out his left eye.

Acid looked over to where Spook stood with her legs spread wide and both hands on the Beretta Pico still aimed at Banjo, and she froze. Everything was happening at once and she couldn't think straight. The fangs were out. The bats calling for her.

Her name was Chaos, they said.

Her name was Justice.

Her name was Acid Vanilla.

And it was time to finish this.

She leapt to her feet. Banjo raised his gun and fired but his vision was compromised. The bullet went wide as Acid launched herself at him. They both went down. Banjo hit the ground with a dull thud and Acid rolled on top of him. She slammed the heel of her palm into his nose, shattering the cartilage. Back on her feet she grabbed for the Magnum and pointed it at him.

"Go on, finish it," he told her.

He was a mess all right. He had a gaping hole where his left eye had been, and his bloody nose was mashed to a pulp. Acid grunted. She'd be doing him a favour. Her hand trembled.

"Come on, you weak cow," Banjo snarled. "What are you waiting for?"

"It was you, wasn't it?" she asked him.

"Huh?"

"I saw your face when I let it slip in the hotel, about me visiting my mum. You twigged she was alive and you told Caesar."

"Oops. Was I not supposed to?" Banjo whispered. "Another thing you should know. It was me who slit the old

311

bird's throat. A lovely job, I thought. Like a hot knife through—"

Acid pulled the trigger and blew his head clean off. The recoil on the .44 nearly knocked her off her feet. "Well, what do you know?" she purred. "That *is* a powerful handgun."

"Acid." Spook ran over to her. "Are you okay?"

Acid chucked the gun on Banjo's prone torso. "I am thanks to you. I thought you were dead."

"Me too. For a second. But he shot my poor laptop. Straight through my rucksack." She wrinkled her nose. "I guess my laptop got me into this mess, but then it saved my life."

Acid opened her mouth to respond but changed her mind. She had a strange feeling in her chest. It felt a lot like relief. And like she might burst into tears any second. Which was why she hurried back over to the Hummer.

The sirens were even closer.

"That was so scary and amazing and crazy all at once." Spook caught up with her as she opened the driver's door and climbed in. "I thought we were screwed a few times back then."

Acid didn't look at her. "How the hell did you learn to shoot like that?"

Spook clicked on her seat belt. "Call of Duty. I don't like to brag but I'm a Command Sergeant-Major. Rank fifty."

Acid turned the key still in the ignition. "Well, once again I underestimated you, Spook. Thank you." She shoved the stick into first. "Now let's get the hell out of here."

She pulled the Hummer down the side of the hangar, then took a sharp left, flooring it until she came to a set of lights at the end of the next road. She indicated right and watched in the rear-view mirror as two police cars appeared in the distance.

But they were too late.

It was over.

Chapter Fifty-Two

"What's the plan now?" Spook asked, once they'd driven far enough away and the danger had passed.

"Simple," Acid told her. "I carry on executing every single one of those bastards. Like I told you I would."

Spook watched Canary Wharf pass by the window as they headed away from the city. "Do you still want my help?" she asked.

Acid kept her eyes on the road. "You sure you want to help? I won't hold you to it. It'll mean you giving up a lot. Your life. Your career. Like I said, I doubt they'll bother you again. As far as Caesar's concerned there's a line under the Cerberix job. You're free."

The words landed heavy on Spook's lap and she turned to the window. A frisson in her chest put a stop to the conversation. She had lots to say, but it could wait.

Ten minutes later, Acid pulled up in a side street opposite the Riverside Plaza and turned off the engine. Then she flipped down the sun visor and adjusted her hair in the mirror.

"I do want to help you," Spook whispered.

Acid licked the end of her finger and rubbed at a smear of eyeliner. Then she sat back in her seat and sighed. "Why do I feel like there's a *but* coming?"

Spook fiddled with the strap on her rucksack. "It's just, I've been thinking these last few days. How we've been a good team, me and you. And I was thinking, what if we helped people?"

Acid scoffed. "Help people? Which people?"

"People who can't get help the regular way, for whatever reason," Spook replied. "We could be like vigilantes for justice. Avenging Angels. Or whatever. What do you think?"

"I think it sounds like the bloody A-team. Which one am I?"

Spook laughed. "All of them. Rolled into one."

Acid flipped up the visor. "Yes, you're probably right. But I don't know, kid. I'm not sure I can even think about that right now."

"We could do both," Spook went on. "I'd help you find Caesar and the rest. Plus we set up some sort of agency. To help those the authorities can't. We can even charge people – those who can afford to pay, at least. We're going to need money, aren't we?"

Acid laughed. "Jesus. I don't think I'm ever going to get rid of you, am I?"

Spook leaned on her. "You love me really. I could be a big help to you, Acid Vanilla."

Acid squinted out the window. "I guess I will need another set of hands. Your computer skills too."

"You're in? The Avenging Angels?"

"Calm it down there, Murdock. I'll think about it. I do get what you're saying, we will need funds. But if I agree to this, it's on my terms. And you'd better not make me regret it."

Spook bounced on her seat. "Come on, partner. When have I made you regret anything?"

Acid blew out her cheeks. "Let's put a pin in it for now. The next step is finding a new forger. Then I do need to get away for a while. A month. Maybe longer. Get my head together properly." She clicked off her seat belt and opened the car door.

"Then what?" Spook asked.

"Then the killing starts." She shut the door and knocked on the window at Spook. "I'll wait for you by the lift."

Spook gave her the thumbs up then sat back in her seat. The car was still and her mind calm. For now, at least. She looked out the window as a light rain made its presence known on the windshield. What a crazy few weeks she'd had. She'd witnessed a murder and been on the hit list of the world's top assassin – not to mention being shot at and strangled on more than one occasion. But more than all that, she'd got justice for Paula Silva. She'd taken down Cerberix Inc. Not bad going, she decided, for an unassuming tech-nerd with dubious social skills.

Spook now understood what Acid had meant when she said she didn't know the person she once was. This experience, it had changed Spook. But it was for the better, she was certain of that. She was tougher. Braver. She felt alive. Like she could do anything. She glanced at her reflection in the rear-view mirror and laughed. It felt good. It had been a long time coming.

Chapter Fifty-Three

"Another cocktail, Miss Taylor?" Andreas asked, his Adonis-like frame silhouetted against the hot Mauritius sun.

Acid lowered her sunglasses. "*Mais oui*," she purred, letting out a deep sigh. "Another Green Isaac, please. Heavier on the gin this time."

The sun was high overhead, the only object in a vast expanse of blue. Acid Vanilla lowered her head back onto the plush cushion of her sun lounger and sighed. A deep sigh. Content for once. She watched as a young couple ran down the white sands before diving headfirst into the aquamarine foam and disappearing from view.

It was now over a month since the Cerberix case – since Acid had unceremoniously left Annihilation Pest Control – and she'd got her holiday at last. Two weeks in the sun. Time to recharge. To patch her head and heart back together.

For what came next.

The handsome waiter picked up her spent glass and

placed it on his silver tray. His eyes scanned Acid's reclining figure and he leaned forward, whispering gruffly, "Perhaps later, I come to your room again? For your private... massage?"

"Yes, Andreas, I think that would be most welcome." She pushed her sunglasses back up her nose, watching as he walked away. Twenty-five. So full of energy at that age. So eager to please. Even if the pillow talk left a lot to be desired. She watched as he strutted over to the small beach bar, then lay back and closed her eyes.

A lot had happened over the last six weeks. Cerberix had seen its shares crumble the second Spook's video went viral, but when the news broke Whitman and Clarkson were dead the entire company sank into the sea. It was a shame for the thousands of employees and shareholders, but there was always collateral damage.

Thoughts of Louisa hovered on the cusp of Acid's consciousness. Snapshots of her room that day. The blood. Her empty eyes.

Acid shook it off and looked out to sea. At the endless azure of the Indian Ocean. So still. So tranquil. So at odds with what now bubbled inside of her. At first she dismissed it as plain old anger. But as the weeks had ticked on it had morphed into something much more affirming. It was yearning for justice. For vengeance. For bloody retribution.

And she was going to get it.

She got to her feet, ready to take a dip in the sea, when she heard Andreas calling her. Or rather, calling Miss Tanika Taylor – the most recent alias purchased a few weeks earlier from her new forger, Ari Gold. It was Spook who had found him, using some dark web connections. Acid had to admit, the kid was already proving herself to be a worthy ally.

"What is it, sweets?" Acid called back, pulling her sunglasses from her eyes to better see.

The waiter pointed to the hut and gave the universal hand gesture for telephone. Acid slipped her sunglasses back on and made her way over to the small wooden hut. She'd been waiting on this call.

"Telephone for you, Miss Taylor." Andreas presented her with an old-fashioned handset on his silver tray. "The lady says it is urgent."

"Thanks, doll." Acid took the phone and turned away, leaning against the bar and holding the receiver to her ear. "Hello, this is Tanika Taylor."

"I can't believe you went with that name," Spook said, on the other end. "How's the holiday?"

"Wonderful. I've freed up some headspace. Got my focus back." She watched as Andreas bent over and lifted a crate of tonic water. "And the views here are magnificent."

"Awesome."

"Do you have news for me?" Acid asked.

"Sure do. I've had a sighting. Beowulf Caesar is in Berlin."

Acid paused. "You sure it's him?"

"Eighty percent. I'm downloading all the nearby CCTV footage I can get hold of."

Acid raised her head, looking out to sea. "Great work, Spook. You did good."

"Thanks. So I'll see you in a week?"

Acid looked at Andreas. "No. Book me on the next flight out of here. Time to go to work. Partner."

She could almost hear the kid beaming down the line. "Cool. I'll see you soon. *Partner.*"

Acid handed the phone back to Andreas. "Thanks a lot. But I'm afraid I must take a rain check on that massage."

He looked dismayed. "I see. Maybe before you go?"

But Acid had already set off back to the hotel. "Can't, sorry. I've got to get back to England, and then it seems I'm going to Germany for a few days." She turned and smiled. "You know what they say, sweetie. No rest for the wicked."

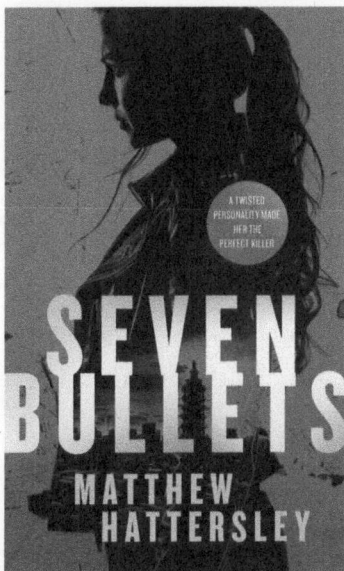

Seven Bullets Preview

Chapter 1

A house, somewhere in North London. A rental property furnished only with basic fixtures and fittings. The furniture is the cheapest money can buy and each item is at least ten years old. There is a single couch in the front room, two single beds in the rooms upstairs. The house isn't the nicest place you could ever wish to live, but it's out of the way and unremarkable. For its current inhabitants, that's what matters.

They're not planning on staying here long.

Through the front door and straight up the stairs you can hear the faint grunts of concentration. Past the cramped bathroom and into the larger of the two bedrooms, a woman hunches over a large desk. On one side sits a battered cardboard box, half-full of ammo - 115gr FMJ 9mm rounds, made by Sellier & Bellot. Next to the box is a small stereo system - what people once called a 'ghetto blaster.' The woman leans over and twists the volume up a few notches to better hear the song – the Ramones, doing Today Your Love, Tomorrow The World *– before selecting a single round from the box of ammo. She holds it up* *in a beam of sunlight that slices through the gap in the threadbare curtains and smiles to herself. The cold metal is pleasing to touch. She rolls the cartridge between an expertly manicured thumb and forefinger.*

Last one.

A large industrial vice is fastened to the length of the table in front of her. She winds the handle anti-clockwise a few turns and places the 9mm round into the steel jaws of the vice. Then she tightens it and picks up the Dremel industrial engraver she bought from Amazon a month earlier. As she flicks the switch it whirrs into life, reminiscent of a dentist's drill. She goes to work on the bullet casing, scratching out letters. The metal is polished and smooth, a tough surface to work with, and the drill is not top of the line, but she has the hang of it now. Slowly, methodically, she scratches a name into the brass casing, tracing the pencil markings she made earlier and blowing off the residue of metal filings.

It doesn't take her long to finish. She loosens the vice and removes the bullet from its clutches. Done. She examines her handiwork and smiles once more. This entire process is crazy, she knows that. Yet creating these bullets – these symbols of revenge – has also quietened something inside of her. She now has a visual aid. A reminder of what she must do. But more so, with each bullet created, she exorcises some of the pent-up rage she has carried around for too long.

Acid Vanilla carries the last bullet over to the tall wardrobe in the corner of the room. The door hinges creak and groan as she opens it to reveal a space empty of clothes. There is, however, a wooden shelf half-way up. On the shelf stand six bullets, spaced out, upright in a row. Six bullets, each with a name etched down the side - Raaz Terabyte, Spitfire Creosote, Magpie Stiletto, Ethel Sinister, Doris Sinister, Davros Ratpack. *And now the last one. Bullet number seven.*

Beowulf Caesar.

Acid places the final bullet at the end of the row and steps back.

Seven bullets on a shelf. Seven names. Seven people who took everything from her. And who will pay with their lives.
Her new kill list.

vinci-books.com/sevenbullets

Get your FREE ebook

We'll send you a free Acid Vanilla prequel.

Discover how Acid Vanilla transformed from a London teenager into the world's deadliest female assassin.

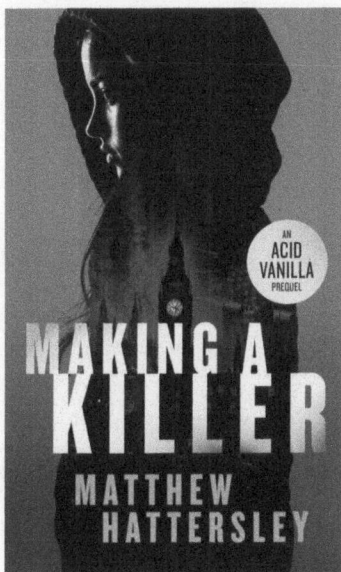

vinci-books.com/making-a-killer

About the Author

Over the last twenty years Matthew Hattersley has toured Europe in rock n roll bands, trained as a professional actor and founded a theatre and media company. He's also had a lot of dead end jobs...

Now he writes Neo-Noir Thrillers and Crime Fiction. He has also had his writing featured in The New York Observer & Huffington Post.

He lives with his wife and young daughter in Manchester, UK.